My Turkish Fling

Love Istanbul ✳ Book 2

Enni Amanda

1st edition, 2024

Lumi Publishing

ISBN 978-1-0670235-0-8 (paperback)

ISBN 978-1-0670235-1-5 (hardcover)

ISBN 978-1-99-116509-1 (ebook)

Designed by Yummy Book Covers
Edited by Roxana Coumans
Typeset in PT Serif, 10pt

To my seven readers

The Glossary

This book features some Turkish words. The meaning of each should be clear enough from the context, but in case you're a fellow language geek, here's a quick glossary:

Türk dizileri (dizi) - Turkish TV series. Longer format than your usual Netflix shows, often highly emotional, romantic, and more chaste than the Hollywood variety.

Allah, Allah! - My goodness!

Lokum – Turkish delight

Hoşgeldiniz - Welcome

Tamam - Okay

Menemen – Traditional Turkish breakfast dish with scrambled eggs cooked with diced tomatoes (see recipe at the end)

Evet - Yes

Safsata - Nonsense

Prounciation Guide

Turkish names can be difficult to pronounce. Here's a quick guide to the main characters:

Emir: Pronounced like "eh-meer" with the stress on the first syllable. The "e" sound is pronounced like the "e" in the word "pet," and the "i" sound is pronounced like the "ee" in the word "see."

Cem: Pronounced like "jem" with a soft "j" sound, similar to the "s" sound in the word "measure."

Burcu: Pronounced like "boor-joo" with the stress on the second syllable. The "u" sound is pronounced like the "oo" in the word "boot," and the "c" is pronounced like the "j" sound in "jeans."

My Turkish Fling

Emir

Two people so over-the-top in love should have come with a warning label, flashing lights and sirens. Then maybe I could have avoided the sickening displays of affection. Except I was at a family dinner, and there was no escape.

I buttered a dry piece of breadstick, trying my best not to look at my brother Cem and his fiancée Aria. Despite my carefully selective focal points of a half-eaten lamb carcass, brass candle sticks and my own plate, I'd already witnessed five achingly long looks, two lingering kisses and was certain Cem's left hand was doing something inappropriate under the table.

"Could you at least try to look like you're not here to murder everyone?" Cem hissed in Turkish.

"Could you stop the public foreplay?" I hissed back.

Mom gave me a warning look, then turned her sharp eyes at Cem. "*Allah, Allah!* Behave, both of you."

Aria threw us a cautious look, nudging a little further from Cem. She couldn't understand Turkish but must have picked up on the vibe. I tried to relax my face, counting minutes. How long would this dinner last?

"Did anyone want seconds?" Aria's mother Lyn pushed the silver tray of roasted vegetables towards my parents. Mom smiled and refilled their plates.

"How are you supporting yourself, Cem?" Aria's father, Greg, asked, leaning forward. "Apart from this... acting?"

Okay, now we were getting somewhere, I thought. I much preferred straight talk to this simmering tension in the air.

"I am an actor," Cem confirmed with a wide smile. "I've mostly worked in Turkey, but I'm hoping to get English-speaking roles here in New Zealand."

I was still angry with Cem for throwing away the biggest opportunity of his career on a whim. First, he'd mooned the paparazzi and ended up with scandalous photos all over the internet. Then, just as I'd found a solution by staging photos with a Kiwi actress who resembled his co-star, he'd fallen in love with the stand-in and followed her to New Zealand, ruining our million-dollar deal with Epic Studios.

I had to admit one thing, though: I'd never seen Cem this happy. Stupidly happy. Forget Epic Studios. He could have starred on Sesame Street without a hint of irony.

"Actor, huh? It's a hard slog," Greg's mostly bald head bobbed, bushy eyebrows drawing together. "Good to have a fallback career, maybe?"

"Definitely!" Aria's mother, Lyn, echoed. "Our Aria did the smart thing, moving back here and taking a job at the film office."

Aria's eyes flashed with alarm. "I'm thinking of quitting," She nibbled at her thumbnail. "I want to try acting one more time. See how this film does."

She'd recently starred in an American feature film with Cem. The film would premiere next weekend, and a week before their engagement party—the reason I'd suffered the endless flights to this far-flung corner of the earth, with my parents.

"Besides, Cem's very successful in Turkey," Aria added. "He's making way more money with his endorsement deals than I ever did at the film office."

Aria's parents gazed at their future son-in-law, surprised. Did they not know the extent of my brother's fame and fortune?

After the dessert, we moved to the worn leather couches in the living room.

Cem stopped me at the doorway. "Are you coming with us to check the farm?"

"What farm?"

"Aria's boss's place. She said we can use it for the engagement party."

I shrugged, torn between the thankless jobs of babysitting my parents and third-wheeling the nauseatingly-in-love couple.

"You don't want me there," I said.

"True. But you don't want to stay here." Cem nodded at Lyn, who'd already placed two, thick photo albums on the coffee table, saying something about Aria being such a cute, fat baby. Mom attacked the first one like it was a new romance novel.

I turned to Cem, pain throbbing in my forehead. "I'll come with you."

Three months after our first visit, the air felt different. Warm and humid, like in a greenhouse. Early autumn heat wave, I was told. The nights were a little cooler though, which I appreciated.

We piled into Aria's tiny hybrid car and drove through endless greenery dotted with sheep and cows. The emptiness soothed my nerves. I much preferred animals to people.

No longer Cem's manager, I'd been at a loose end, feeling increasingly anxious. For years, his drama-filled life had distracted me from my own. Or the lack thereof. With Cem happy and settled with no crisis looming in the horizon, I'd have to turn my attention to the struggling antique store. Or even worse, myself. What was I doing with my life?

Growing up, I'd been good at many things. I'd studied business, but I'd never built one for myself. I knew I'd one day inherit my father's antique store.

The opportunity to become Cem's manager had come at the perfect time—the perfect distraction from the life I didn't want and a woman I was trying to forget. I'd poured my energy into turning my brother into a star, and succeeded, beyond our wildest dreams. And now he didn't want to be one.

We drove through endless greenery, and the emptiness of it

soothed my nerves. No people, only sheep and cows.

"We shouldn't have left our parents together like that," Aria's voice wobbled with concern, hands tight around the steering wheel. "What if they fight and cancel the engagement?"

Cem shot her a sharp glance. "They can't cancel anything. It's our wedding."

"Engagement," she corrected.

"Why are there so many steps?" Cem moaned, adjusting his chair until it hit my knees. "Can't we skip the rehearsal and get married? We got the marriage license and everything."

"That was to check how it works. Because of the immigration and—"

"But we have it! Why can't we just—"

Aria's voice brimmed with frustration. "Because the health sector is in crisis, and we can't have four ambulances on stand-by for all the heart attacks. We have to ease them into it. If they survive the engagement, they might survive the wedding."

"I think she's right," I told my brother.

I'd walked in on Mom crying more than once. She was losing her baby to a stranger on the other side of the world. My family had already thought Cem was back together with his old co-star Burcu and nobody was more invested in that outcome than our mother.

With Cem away in New Zealand, I'd broken the news to them and spent a long time explaining the events that sounded eerily similar to plot lines of Mom's favorite *dizis* (Turkish soap operas). Yes, my brother had fallen in love with a New Zealand woman who was the spitting image of Burcu, and no, she didn't speak Turkish or come from a Turkish family. She wasn't even Catholic. When the reality finally sank in, I'd dealt with the backlash—tears upon tears, elaborate prayers and long phone calls with trusted friends and relatives.

I didn't mind. Over the years, I'd become accustomed to being hated. Water off a duck's back, I told myself.

"Besides, we couldn't ask Janie to host our wedding," Aria added, turning onto a small, tree-lined driveway. "Even the engagement party is a big ask. She's been through a divorce and running the place by herself."

"We'll take care of everything," I said. "We can check her into a hotel—"

"No." Aria threw me a warning look over her shoulder. "Janie would never go for that! She's already planning the party. She's... involved."

Oh, great. One of those. This Janie sounded a lot like every one of my aunties.

"Okay, fine. But we will cover the cost and hire her some help." I was representing my parents. I could almost hear their voices in my head, behind the words that came out of my mouth. Regardless of how they felt about the union, they were proud Turks and would insist on helping and showering the couple with gifts.

"She'll appreciate that," Aria said diplomatically. "But don't suggest she leaves her house. She'd never."

Aria parked on the side of a large turning bay, and I took in Janie's house. That's when I understood. I wouldn't have wanted to leave this place, either. A sprawling timber building nestled on the side of a hill, bathing in the sun. The flowering trees created an atmosphere someone else might have described as romantic.

I catalogued the photo opportunities, raising my trusted Sony camera. I hung back as Cem kissed Aria, whispering something in her ear. The evening light made everything glow golden. I raised my trusted Sony and snapped a couple of pictures of them.

When the kissing turned French, I directed my lens at the house, framing the entrance between tall bird of paradise bushes. The spiky, orange flowers hung over the stone steps leading to the blue door.

A familiar rush traveled through me, almost overtaking the headache. I enjoyed photography: The journey of looking for the perfect angle, perfect lighting and that perfect moment, capturing it and later, teasing out my vision in Photoshop.

I checked the focus and pressed my finger on the shutter. And that's when the front door opened. My finger kept rapid firing on autopilot as a willowy blonde hopped over two steps and strode down the path towards us. Her tiny shorts showed off long, tanned legs, which disappeared inside heavy-duty rubber boots. Her hair fell over her shoulders in golden waves, and she smiled so brightly I almost reached for my sunglasses.

"Welcome!" She offered her hand to Cem and Aria, then turned to me.

"Hello! I'm Janie. You must be…"

I lowered my camera. "Emir Erkam, Cem's brother."

I held her hand and gaze a moment too long, unable to look away.

"Yes, of course you are." Janie's eyes sparkled with curiosity. "Like two peas in a pod."

I furrowed my brow. "We look alike?"

"Yes, we do!" Cem confirmed, assuming a comically deep frown.

I shook my head, chest tight. I wasn't used to anyone noticing me, especially next to my magnetic brother. I much preferred being invisible behind the camera.

"Emir is in charge of the photos," Cem told Janie. "That way nobody is frowning in them."

Janie laughed, playfully slapping my arm. My spine tingled at her sudden touch. "I'm sure he's not that much of a grump. Wait, are you?"

I turned to look at the house. "So, this is your place? It's beautiful."

Janie stepped back, spreading her arms. "Yes! I'm freshly divorced, so I'm still considering titles. I like the sound of countess."

I tried to detect sadness in her bubbly voice. No one should look and sound that happy right after a divorce. She must have been an actress. I remembered Aria mentioning a TV career. Was she one of those who faked so expertly they ended up believing their own lies? I knew the type.

"I'm sorry to hear about the divorce," I said.

She met my gaze and her laughter fizzled out. "Don't be sorry. I got to keep this house. I love it here." The little wobble in her voice relaxed me. Maybe she wasn't a complete phony.

I lifted my camera, pointing it away from the house. Rolling hills stretched out to the horizon, dotted by occasional houses, too far to even count the windows. Absolute privacy, far away from civilization. A paragon of peace.

"I'd give you a tour, but I'm on my way to give a horse eyedrops," Janie flashed us an apologetic smile and pulled a small bottle out of her pocket. "But if you want to have a wee look around, I'll catch you later?"

"Yeah, sure," Aria agreed, taking Cem's hand. "I want to show you the deck. It might be big enough for everyone so we could eat outdoors."

"Please ignore the broken trellis and ceramic planters. I know it's weeks since the storm, but I've been so busy." Janie looked away, her cheeks rosy.

"Don't worry! We have great imagination," Aria smiled.

As soon as Janie turned around, strolling down the driveway, Cem pulled Aria into his arms, his hands shamelessly roaming down her backside.

"You go ahead. I'll take a look at the... garden," I gestured in the opposite direction where there may or may not have been a garden. If my brother and his fiancée were off to dry hump on the verandah, I'd investigate anything else. A compost. A scum pond.

"Catch you later!" Cem pulled Aria with him, disappearing around the corner. They couldn't get away from me fast enough.

I saw Janie's slight frame advancing down the tree-lined dirt road, her hair and shirt flapping in the breeze. Something was pulling me towards the stables. It was the horse, I told myself. I wanted to see the horse.

CHAPTER 2

Janie

I opened the door to the stables, bracing myself for how much Molly's eye might have deteriorated since the morning. So far, I hadn't managed to get even a tiny drop of the medicine in it, and couldn't afford to call the vet back in. I had to do this, or my beloved, moody mare might lose her sight.

Hearing my footsteps, Molly neighed in her corner. I changed her hay and let her out of the stall to take a little walk. She'd be more agreeable this way, I told myself. Not that it seemed to make a difference. What I'd learned about horses so far was that if they didn't want to do something, they didn't do it. You couldn't force them or sway them. Especially if you were 5 foot 3 inches tall with limited equestrian skills.

I'd chosen this life. Maybe I hadn't expected to run it alone, too broke to hire help, but I was dealing with the consequences of my actions, so self-pity was not allowed. Things had to be done, and there was nobody else here to do them.

I kept the eyedrops hidden inside the loose sleeve of my linen top and used my other hand to pick up a brush. I patted and brushed Molly, trying to act as usual. As I got closer, I saw the puss draining from the corner of her eye and my chest squeezed. What if she did lose her eyesight? It wasn't right for her to pay the price for my divorce.

I took a deep breath and swung my arm to her eye level, trying to spray directly into the infected eye. But Molly must have sensed my ruse and reared on her hind legs. The sudden move threw me off balance. I felt eyedrops sprinkling on my face before I stumbled and fell on my bottom.

"Are you okay?"

I heard the Turkish accent over the sound of clanking hooves and before I could answer, Emir appeared, reaching for me with both hands. He helped me up, just in time before my panicked horse trampled us both.

Disoriented and with my ass aching, I tried to grab Molly's reins to stop her thrashing around, but Emir was faster. I watched, stunned, as he took hold of her, soothing her so quickly I instinctively checked his hands for a needle. Molly didn't calm down like that, not with me or the vet. Not without a tranquilizer.

She wasn't the easiest horse, which no one had warned me about. I'd been duped more than once when buying the farm and its animals. In my experience, the country folk absolutely loved to fleece naïve city people who took up farming in their 40s. Being a well-known TV presenter, swindling me probably earned them a special mention. Maybe there was a hall of fame at the local pub. I'd been too scared to visit.

"How did you do that?" I whispered, trying to breathe soundlessly so I wouldn't disturb the magical scene.

Emir kept his gaze on Molly. There was a strange connection there, a mutual understanding. "She's in pain."

"Yeah, I know. I'm trying to give her the medicine, but she freaks out every time I go anywhere near her eye."

"Do you want me to try?"

My hand shaking, I handed him the eye drop bottle, my muscles tensing as I retreated towards the door. Molly would hate this. She would bolt.

Maintaining eye contact while stroking the horse's mane, Emir slowly raised his other hand above her head and squeezed the bottle empty, moving his hand so that the medicine fell over her swollen eye like raindrops. Molly shook her head and her hooves clanked against the concrete floor, but she didn't even rear.

I stared at Emir, stunned silent. He was a foot taller than me, which gave him an advantage, but I could have sworn Molly responded to something about him. A presence. I'd struggled with the temperamental mare for months but in that moment, I understood her. There was something about Emir. Quiet, reserved, dark... even angry, but also earnest. Direct. Something that forced you to pay attention and submit.

I released a pent-up sigh. I wanted to possess that power. I wanted to find out what his secret was and steal it.

"Do you have another one? She'll need more later if that doesn't clear up." Emir handled back the nearly empty bottle.

"I'll get more. It's a lot cheaper than calling the vet."

"Should we let her out for a walk?" Emir glanced at the door.

"Yeah, sure. She's usually happy out there, even overnight. I only brought her in so I could try the eye drops again. I already failed once this morning."

Emir patted Molly and led her through the double doors. I followed at their heels, watching the way he stroked the horse's mane, my belly wobbling from jealousy. There was so much care and tenderness, and I hadn't been touched for quite a while. As much as I told myself I was fine, as much as I focused on the positive, I couldn't help the pang of longing. The sensation zapped through me like a hit from an electric fence, only a little lower. Dang.

He was a treat for the eyes, this dark Turk. Especially from behind, when I couldn't see that unnerving frown, only the blue dress shirt hugging his broad shoulders, tapering down to a narrow waist. He'd tucked the shirt into a pair of grey dress pants, far too formal for any farm, and way too warm for the weather. But I couldn't deny how well they accentuated his rear end.

I hurried ahead of them, to stop myself from leering over his form. I'd gone soft in the head, living here all by myself. Had I known I'd one day find myself single out here, I would have never taken the leap. But there was no point in second guessing. I'd made every decision leading up to this moment, and I'd own each one of them. Janie Andrews wasn't a quitter.

Emir turned to me. "Do you need to close any gates?"

"No, it's all fenced. Although the fence is falling apart in a couple of places but Molly's good. She won't escape."

He let go of the horse, but Molly didn't leave. Not until Emir patted her again, as if giving permission.

As the horse finally launched into a lazy gallop towards the green hill, I edged closer to Emir. "How did you gain her trust like that? I think she's still wary of me, after eight months."

He lifted an eyebrow. "Maybe you smile too much."

I nearly protested, until I detected the slightest hint of amusement behind his eyes.

"I'll try to frown more. Molly seems to love that." I folded my arms to stop myself from playfully slapping his arm.

I touched people all the time without even noticing. I walked up to my sons and hugged them from behind. I rubbed Aria's shoulders as I passed her in the office and hugged fans who came to talk to me. But with Emir, I obviously needed to reel in my usual impulses. When I'd rested my hand on his olive skin, brushing the rolled-up shirt sleeve he'd shot me a stomach-turning glare. A warning.

"Do you really live here by yourself?" he asked.

"Yeah. That was not the plan, but it worked out that way. My ex organized the boys into a top school in Auckland. They are in their teens, and I understand their choice."

His shoulders dropped as he let out a deep exhale, looking out to the hills. "It's perfect."

"What's perfect?"

"No people, only animals. A beautiful place." His expression softened. "You're very lucky."

My chest welled. "It's beautiful and I love it. But it gets lonely. I wasn't supposed to live here by myself. The change of scenery was supposed to fix my marriage and bring the family closer together. It... didn't." I swallowed. Why was I pouring out the sad details of my life to this man?

He turned slowly to peer at me and caught the side of my mouth twitching downwards. "You're not smiling anymore."

I gave him a defiant look. "No. Happy now?"

"I'm sorry. It's not what I wanted. You should smile if you can. If you're not faking it."

His accent gave the words an odd rhythm that gave me pause. I was used to the chitchat that followed its own meaningless flow, the words almost secondary to the agreed progression of question and answers that built and then fizzled in a predictable pattern. Nothing seemed to follow a pattern with this man. I didn't know the steps to this dance. I'd interviewed the most awkward, hostile individuals and I always got something out of them. I could anticipate their moves and approach the topic from different angles. I got what I wanted. But now I didn't even know what I wanted.

Except for one thing.

"Are you available tomorrow to give Molly her drops? I'll get a new bottle."

Emir stared out into the field where the horse had now disappeared. "I can do that."

"And the day after," I added, casting a quick glance at his pensive face.

"Okay."

"And—"

"How many days?" He shot me a look, eyebrows elevated.

"Seven." I bit my lip.

"Why don't you ask for seven days?"

I smiled, my face warm. "I thought I should... ease you in."

His brow furrowed. "What is this easing-in business? Is it a New Zealand thing? Ask for what you want. That's the only way to get it."

If only it was that easy. I cleared my throat. "Would you be available to give Molly her drops for seven days in a row?" My voice nearly broke at the end. It was a lot to ask, and I wasn't one who asked for help. I paid people. The fact that I couldn't hire someone to deal with this made me nauseous.

"I'll do it for the horse. I like her."

Was he saying he didn't like me? "Thank you."

He studied my face for an unnervingly long time. "But there's something else I want to do for you, and I was warned that you might not accept help."

For some dirty, inexcusable reason, my heart jumped into my throat, and I only managed to nod.

Emir took a step closer, so close I could smell his spicy aftershave. It's a cultural thing, I reminded myself. It doesn't mean anything. I'd travelled in the Middle East where people constantly invaded your personal space, which for us Kiwis was a mile wide.

"My parents are worried that hosting the party will inconvenience you. It's usually paid for by the bride's parents but in this case, the bride's parents are not wealthy. And you're not even family. It's not fair for you to spend on this. My parents are more than happy to cover the costs."

"What are you talking about? There're no costs to cover! It's my place and I'm happy to offer it to Aria and Cem. We're not that strict about protocol down here."

He stared at me like I'd suggested the earth is flat. "Of course, there are costs. Even the time you put in is quantifiable."

I met his sharp stare and marveled at the deep brown of his eyes. They were far too beautiful a window to such a cold, calculating mind. "Stop quantifying. I can do what I want with my own time and property."

"But you worry about money." He crossed his arms, gazing out to the fields.

"No! I'm fine."

He turned to me with a look that beckoned me to give it up. "You'd rather ask me to treat your horse for a week than call the vet."

I huffed. "Maybe I like your company."

The way he scoffed made me sad. Was that so far-fetched? He wasn't the most cheerful sort, but he might be able to save my horse and if I was honest, Emir fascinated me. I couldn't see any of his buttons, but I itched to find them. Push them.

"Why not?" I insisted, winking at him. "You're very handsome."

"If you like looking at Turkish men, look at Cem. He's always smiling."

"But he's not as handsome." The simple truth of it slipped from my mouth before I could fully process the implications.

Was I trying to flirt with this guy? To what end? I hugged myself, noting the evening chill. The sun was already low, casting long shadows across the green grass. Should I leave Molly out for the night, or get her back inside? I still googled half the decisions I had to make on the farm. The more I learned, the more I realized how little I knew about looking after animals or growing anything.

Not waiting for his response, I wandered after my horse, to check that she was still within the boundary. If she seemed happy, I'd let her stay out. It didn't look like the weather was about to turn. I was surprised when I heard Emir's footsteps behind me. When I reached a higher point on the hill and climbed on a flat rock, he stopped next to me. Even standing on the rock, I only reached his eye level.

"Do you mean it?" he asked.

"What?" I blinked, pretending like I had no idea what he was talking about. To make him squirm.

"Do you honestly prefer my looks to Cem's or are you making fun of me?" I could see the faint glow of embarrassment behind his eyes, but he held my gaze without flinching.

Was he insecure about his looks? This tall, dark, menacing man? His hair was shorter than Cem's and he only had a slight shadow of a stubble. I could certainly appreciate Cem's movie star looks, but there was something about Emir that captivated me.

Emir kept looking at me, expectantly, until I could only give him the truth. I could feel the fight seep out of me, all the flirty fun I'd planned to have on his expense, or with him, or to amuse myself. Everything vaporized and I found my jaw wobbling a little when I replied. "Yes, I think you're more handsome. That's my personal preference. Is that important to you?"

The question threw him a little, and I congratulated myself for that tiny hit. I couldn't allow him to dominate our conversation with that dark stare.

Emir folded his arms, giving me an unobstructed view of forearm muscle. Well played, sir. I spotted Molly in the distance, grazing by the large hazelnut tree. At least she was still on the property.

I hopped off the rock and headed back towards the house. He reached me at the door. "To answer your question, I think it is important. Not because I care about being handsome but... other reasons." His enigmatic eyes flicked past my shoulder and the expression on his face darkened. "So, thank you. For saying that."

My cheeks pulsed with warmth. If only he knew how attractive I found him, especially in that moment of sincerity. I had to wedge my hands into my pockets to keep from placing them on his chest and gasping like some sort of Regency lady overcome by emotion. I'd picked up a couple of old romance books from the library, to ease my loneliness and probably inflate my expectations. I hadn't read them yet, but the covers had already given me ideas. "No problem. I mean it."

The corner of his mouth lifted a fraction, and I felt a sharp, unexpected tug deep in my belly. So, it was true. His smile was magic. Those facial muscles were connected to my insides by an invisible string. "You almost smiled!" My voice crept up and my hands flew to my mouth.

He cocked his head and huffed a sad, short laugh. "What is it with New Zealanders and smiling?"

"I don't think it's a cultural thing." I edged closer to the door and opened it, despite having to step so close that my arm brushed his stomach. A shiver ran through me, and I slipped inside the cool foyer, leaving the door open in case he wanted to follow. My Boston Terrier greeted us with excited jumping. I'd been too nervous to take him with me to see Molly, worried he'd get trampled.

Emir bent down to pet him. "What's his name?"

"Gru." I bit my lip. "My younger son named him five years ago, when he was eight."

He nodded. "Nice to meet you, Gru."

When I reached the kitchen, Emir stopped at the doorway. "What is it if not cultural? Everyone here smiles all the time, and you seem intent on making me smile." His eyebrows drew together as he observed me.

I turned on the kettle and set down two teacups. I'd learned from Aria that Turkish men liked their tea strong and sweet, with no milk. That was as close to Turkish as I could make it, and I wanted to try.

He'd followed me all the way from the stables, and now stood in my kitchen. I had to assume Cem and Aria were somewhere outside, but he didn't seem concerned about their whereabouts, his eyes trained at me. Frowning or not, I had this man's attention. I decided to use it.

I couldn't say what gave me the courage. Maybe it was the loneliness carving me hollow, blurring boundaries, as I crossed the floor and placed my thumb on that deep crease between his brows, pressing hard enough to smooth it a little as I massaged my thumb up his forehead. "This here. It must be giving you a headache."

To my surprise, he didn't step back from my touch, but allowed me to stroke my thumb across his forehead. I rose to my toes to get closer to his eye level, but still had to hold my arm up in an awkward angle.

Emir closed his eyes, and a deep, weary sigh escaped his lips. "I do have a headache," he confessed. "Lately, it's been constant."

My heart went out to him. Without thinking, I took him by the arm and led him to the dining room, guiding him onto one of the chairs. Never breaking the connection, I placed my fingers on his forehead and massaged along his scalp.

"What are you doing?" he asked but didn't pull away.

Gru followed us, settling at his feet.

"Indian head massage," I said. "Do you want me to stop?"

"No," he groaned. The sound came from somewhere deep and shot right through me. Oh, the fire. How I'd missed the fire! The feeling of someone's presence taking over my personal space, forcing me out of my head and into my body. Challenging my self-control.

I liked being in control. I was capable and didn't need saving. I didn't need a man. But as the heat pulsed through me, I momentarily wanted to forget every enlightened diary entry I'd written in the dead of night. Every interview I'd given to an enthusiastically nodding journalist. For a moment, I wanted to cancel every word.

I'd been so determined to rise from the ashes of my widely publicized divorce that I'd increased my public appearances. I knew how it worked. If you didn't tell your own story, they told it for you. If I didn't sell them on my newfound independence and tranquility of country life, I became a sad little anecdote on every story they wrote about Shaun and his new girlfriend. Even when my name wasn't mentioned, I was there. When they said, 'Shaun's new life after divorce', I was the divorce. And I refused to be that. So, I'd taken on a new identity like a quick outfit change and become an icon of self-reliant divorced women. The last part wasn't intentional, but the messages of support that poured in had reaffirmed my conviction.

It hurt. Sometimes even smiling hurt. But it also helped to keep me sane, and over the last few months I'd noticed the smiles coming more easily. I wasn't faking it. I truly loved my new life, lonely as it was. I didn't need that fire pulsing in me, not like this. But I could enjoy it all the same.

My fingers worked on Emir's scalp, diving into his thick hair like I was looking for diamonds in a sheepskin rug. The massage technique I'd learned a long time ago must have been a muscle memory as I didn't have to think about it. My hands knew what to do, guided by the gruff sounds rising from his throat. This man was in pain. I could feel it now. That frown on his face was starting to make more sense.

After a few minutes, I moved down to his neck. His muscles felt like concrete under my fingertips. "I think you should see a professional. You feel really... wound up."

"No." His tone was clipped but he didn't move.

"But you're so... stiff." I gently tapped on the bulging, rock solid trapezius muscle with my thumb, wincing at my choice of words.

Emir grunted. "I don't like to be touched by strangers."

I lifted my hands off his skin, my fingertips prickling. "Am I not a stranger?"

He held still for so long I almost filled the silence with another comment out of sheer awkwardness.

Finally, he spoke. "For some reason, your touch doesn't bother me. It helps."

I placed my hands back on his neck, a sudden warmth gushing through me like I'd swallowed hot tea. The warmth spread beyond my stomach, compelling me to continue. If I could help this dark, mysterious creature... My fingers kept working, driven by curiosity. What made him so tightly wound? And how had I slipped past his defenses, getting this close?

I needed answers.

CHAPTER 3

Emir

I should have stopped her the moment those long, agile fingers landed on my forehead, but the sweet absence of pain radiated through my body, making it hard to think clearly. I hadn't felt this good in months. Her touch was pure sorcery.

I'd let Mom loosen the knots in my neck and shoulders a couple of times, but the idea of letting a massage therapist into my personal space, kneading me like dough abhorred me. Janie was right, though. She was a stranger, and my willingness to accept her fingers against my skin made no sense. She'd crossed the line, and I'd let her. I didn't enjoy other people, women in particular. Not anymore. I had needs, but looking after myself was a lot easier than risking a relationship.

"Let's make a deal then," she said. "I need your help with Molly. And in return, I'll massage you. For seven days. Unless you have other plans?"

Her dog reared on his hind legs, pawing my seat, and I scratched him around the ears. Gru. What a name. Maybe Janie had a thing for frowning villain types? It was her child's idea, but she would have agreed to it.

"For seven days." My voice came out gruff. Did I have other plans? It was hard to engage that part of my brain, with her fingers still turning soft circles on my scalp, running down my neck like rivulets of water.

"It's two weeks until the engagement party, if you want to extend it until then. When do you fly back?"

"The day after the party."

There it was. Our deadline. I had to be careful not to get used to this incredible feeling.

"Your horse only needs seven days of eyedrops, so that wouldn't be fair. I'd have to pay you."

Her fingers lifted off my skin. "Definitely not."

I sensed my bargaining position. "Then let me help with the property. I'll fix the storm damage."

"You haven't even seen it yet." Her nails gently tapped my hair, as if she was resting her hands over me, on pause. I shivered.

"Well, you have me by the scalp. Use it to your advantage."

Her bubbly laugh filled the room, and those fingers dove back into my hair, like liquid being poured down, washing away tension and pain, replacing it with a delicious vibration that made me almost drowsy. If she'd suggested a trading deal involving stocks and diamonds, I would have humored her, to keep it going. This was so much better than painkillers.

"I also know some good Pilates moves that might help."

"Pilates?"

"Yes, it's a kind of floor exercise—"

"I know what it is. I'm just..." I blew a breath, trying to think of a way to politely decline. Me, in tights, trying to twist myself into a pretzel. "I'm not very flexible."

"No shit." She giggled, gently drumming the sides of her palms against my shoulder. It felt amazing. "You're well on your way to becoming a statue. Where do you envision the final work of art? In the town square? In a gallery?"

"Very funny." She'd earned a laugh, but I couldn't do it naturally. I couldn't remember the last time I'd laughed. My body must have moved that reflex into long-term storage.

"I'm not joking, though. Pilates is great for improving your mobility. Could save you from surgery later."

"Surgery? What surgery?"

"When you're this tight it's only a matter of time before you pull or dislocate something. I've seen it. My ex-husband..." Her voice became strained and petered off.

"I've been under a lot of stress lately," I inserted quickly, to change the topic. "It didn't use to be this bad. I know I need to do something, but when there are more pressing things with the business and the family—"

"You neglect yourself," she finished for me. "I know what it's like. But it's a mistake. Never again."

"Never again," I repeated, with less conviction. I liked how she put it though, so simply. With no anger or resentment. She was on this new path, but I saw no path ahead of me.

"Do you like this?" She tightened her fist in my hair, giving it a gentle tug. "It's something they taught me when I did the head massage course."

Her voice sounded a little breathless, with a hint of embarrassment.

"It's... nice," I managed.

It was only a massage technique, I argued, but my body had other ideas. The way she tugged my hair, with both hands now, tilting my head back, felt too intimate. I imagined returning the favor—sinking my fingers into that long, blond hair and tugging. Her eyes rolling back and lips parting.

"It's supposed to increase blood flow," she explained.

"Sure," I agreed, because blood was now rushing towards my groin, the image of her face overcome by pleasure lingering behind my eyes. What would she look like or sound like? I groaned, almost involuntarily.

"That's right," she encouraged me. "Just relax."

Her voice was bright and professional, as if to convince us nothing inappropriate was going on. But life has a way of revealing your lies.

Gru barked and the front door clicked, announcing Cem and Aria. I stood up, nearly knocking over my chair. Our gazes locked, I saw a smile spread across Janie's face. Her cheeks looked pink. I coughed, trying to gather my thoughts. Why was I this embarrassed? What was the big deal with someone massaging you? It wasn't, obviously. Yet, I didn't want my brother to find out.

Janie's mouth twitched and my stomach tightened. Was she going to tell them?

CHAPTER 4

Janie

I'd never seen anyone rise from a chair that fast. Emir straightened like a string on a bow, released by the archer. I almost corrected my assessment on his mobility, until I saw him wince from pain.

As he turned to his smiling brother, the frown on his face deepened, signaling tightness that ran deeper than muscles and tendons. Something ran under the surface that no amount of massage could loosen.

"The verandah is perfect!" Aria exclaimed, crouching down to pet Gru. "We figured out the set up." Her cheeks glowed pink as she picked a loose leaf out of her hair.

I smiled at the embarrassed glance they shared, fighting a bout of jealousy. They'd found each other and used every available moment to enjoy that connection. I could barely remember... had I ever been that in love?

"I hope you behave yourselves at the actual party," Emir grunted, pointedly picking a dry leaf off Cem's T-shirt sleeve.

"I'll keep my pants on." He winked, not the least bit offended.

I stared at the brothers, one beaming, one frowning, trying to figure out what I was missing. I would have been livid at a comment like that. What did Emir have against happy couples, anyway? I didn't care if they both orgasmed out in the garden, and it was my house.

I turned to Aria. "I have some champagne glasses and other things you can use if you want. That way the caterer doesn't have to bring them."

She lifted her eyes from her phone screen. "Yes, please! That sounds great."

"Are you coming back before the party?" I asked. "With the movie premiere and everything."

"We'll be back a week from now, next Sunday. We can come over to do the decorations then, right?" She raised her eyes at Cem, who nodded.

"And Emir can probably plan the photos now." Aria glanced out the window and frowned. "Although the party will be a lot earlier in the day so the light will be different. Does that matter?"

Emir shot me a quick look under his brow. "I... I'll be back here tomorrow. Janie needs help with the horse."

"How're you going to get here?" Cem asked.

He shrugged. "I'll take the bus."

Oh no. Why hadn't I thought about the logistics?

"The busses don't come very close… or very often," I said. "But I can pick you up from town. Where are you staying?"

"In a hotel."

"About that." Aria raised her phone-holding hand. "Mom called before and she said that they've invited Cem's parents and Emir to stay with them. Apparently, the hotel rates are daylight robbery."

"It's fine," Cem insisted. "I'll pay."

She shot him a reproaching look. "There's no point wasting money. That's why we're staying in my tiny rental, remember? So that we can afford other stuff, like Kerim's catering."

"Sure. Our parents will appreciate the authentic Turkish food," Cem deadpanned.

Aria glared at him. "Are you being sarcastic? You know I love Turkish food and Kerim's half the reason we're together!"

I chuckled, remembering what Aria had told me about their first date in Napier. The owners of Aria's favorite Turkish restaurant had immediately recognized both Cem the movie star and Aria, their local client, becoming accomplices in their fake dating ploy.

Cem raised his hands, his face the picture of innocence. "No! I mean it. Dad thinks Turkish cuisine, cooked by a Turk is superior to any other food in the world. He's not here to broaden his horizons. He will stop at every kebab shop around the country to judge the offerings."

"Well, at least Kerim's will pass the test," Aria concluded, relaxing a little. "I can't say the same about my mom's cooking, but maybe they can order takeaways…"

I noticed Emir's rod-straight frame tensing even more. "Our parents would never accept. They couldn't possibly inconvenience—"

"They said yes." Aria stared back at him with an unsure smile. "Hopefully it's not that bad. They've turned my old room into a guest room and there's another bed in my dad's little office. It's not full-length, though." She threw Emir an apologetic glance, then turned to Cem. "Mom says they got it for grandchildren."

Cem stared back in confusion. "But they don't have grandchildren."

"Exactly." Aria's gaze was heavy with meaning.

Cem's confusion morphed into understanding, then slight shock.

I gave Emir a visual scan, confirming what I already knew. "You'll need a full-length bed."

"Maybe I can put the mattress on the floor." He stared at his leather shoes, looking like he was mentally preparing for a prison stay. "It would make sense to save money on accommodation."

Words rushed out of my mouth. "I have a guest suite! Come, I'll show you!" I led them to the little used end of my house, my mind reeling with possible repercussions of what I was about to suggest. Gru zoomed ahead of us, scanning every corner.

I'd spent so much money on the guest quarters, thinking I'd have regular visitors from Auckland. But we'd been friends with other couples, as a couple, and after the divorce, I hadn't heard from any of them. Being out of town and single, I'd been wiped off everyone's address book.

I opened the door to the large bedroom with an extra-wide king bed, decorated in soft shades of walnut, sage and cream, in perfect harmony with the garden view behind the large ranch sliders. A spacious ensuite bathroom and a private deck with a sun sail completed the oasis. "I mean, you can invite your parents to stay here if you want. I can put you in one of my sons' bedrooms." I stepped backwards and glimpsed at the absolute teenage chaos in Josh's room. Okay, not that one. On the other side of the hallway, Alex's room seemed in a slightly better order.

Emir joined me at the door. "Thank you, that's very kind. I will let my parents know."

But Aria was already on it. "Hi, Mom! We're still here at Janie's." She lifted her phone, capturing all of us with her camera. I caught her brightly smiling mother on the screen. "Janie showed us around her house, and she has this amazing guest suite. This would be perfect for Cem's parents!" She pointed her phone at the guest room.

"We checked them out of the hotel and got back home. They're getting settled." I detected a hint of defensiveness in her mother's voice. "I think they want to stay close to Cem and you, not out in the middle of nowhere. Serkan is keen on the earthquake museum. We've been talking about what's happened in Turkey and Syria. It's so sad."

"Okay," Aria conceded. "Let's talk about it later. We'll drive back soon."

She ended the call. "Sounds like they're getting along."

Cem raised an eyebrow. "Bonding over earthquakes."

I looked at Emir, my stomach wobbling. "You could still stay here if you wanted. So, it's not too crowded in their house." As soon as I said it, I cringed. What if he accepted? "But I understand it's not that convenient if you don't have a car. We're a bit out of the way here."

"That's a great idea!" Cem grinned. "Far away from other humans is Emir's happy place."

"I don't mind the location," Emir confirmed, looking out the hallway window. The floor-to-ceiling glass framed a picture of my empty front yard. The lack of curtains had bothered me at first, but I'd gradually gotten used. With no one around, the concept of privacy took on a new meaning.

"If you can tolerate his face, Emir's good at fixing things," Cem pressed on. "He could help you prepare for the party, do some maintenance. So, you get something out of this deal."

I swallowed, afraid to look Emir in the eye. I could feel his presence from several feet away, and it told me one thing. My body wanted something out of this deal. Something it couldn't have. I couldn't afford wild affairs with Turkish strangers. I had to start dating. I had to find someone local, respectable, solid... I needed a serious, long-term relationship—more serious than what Shaun had with that actress. That would help me feel grounded, I decided. Like I belonged here.

Emir cleared his throat. "I would love to be useful if I can. I'm quite handy with tools."

I gave Emir a curt nod, trying to not imagine him in a tool belt. After a fifteen-year marriage to a man who paid for someone else to shave him, I had a certain weakness for the DIY types.

"I do have some fencing that needs repairs. And other bits and pieces. But I don't feel right about—"

"Okay, it's decided," Emir cut me off, addressing Aria. "I'll come with you to town and gather my things. It sounds like everything is now in your parents' house. Then I'll order a taxi back here."

"No! I'll drive you." My heart pounded in my chest, but I tried to smile. "If you're going to work on my property, that's the least I can do."

I had a feeling Emir didn't want me to mention our massaging deal.

"How about go straight away? It's already seven-thirty." Emir glanced at his watch. "I'm still quite jet-lagged. You know we only arrived yesterday."

I felt a flash of guilt. "Of course! Sorry. I'll hop in my car and follow you."

I grabbed my car keys on the way out and followed them outside, getting my Lexus out of the garage. It was an ostentatious car, chosen by Shaun. Switching to something small and practical was on my to-do list, but I didn't feel particularly confident about car shopping. It was one of those annoying tasks I'd had a man for. And now I didn't. I wondered if Emir knew anything about cars.

Based on the look on his face, he at least appreciated the price tag of the golden vehicle.

Emir opened the rear door of Aria's little hybrid, but Cem grabbed his shoulder. "Why don't you ride with Janie, so she doesn't have to drive by herself?"

"And if she gets lost, you can direct her to my parents' house," Aria added, excitement lighting up her face. "She's never been there."

Emir looked confused. "I've been there once."

I smiled. The love birds clearly wanted privacy. Emir shrugged and walked over to my car. We both entered at the same time, somehow bumping elbows. My car had never felt smaller.

"Apologies," Emir muttered. "It seems they don't want me as a third wheel."

"It's pretty obvious." I grinned.

As I started the car and followed Aria's Toyota down the driveway, I felt Emir's probing eyes on me. "Do you think they're good together? You smile like you're happy for them."

"I am! Ninety-nine percent happy, maybe one percent jealous."

"You don't think it's a little... impractical? To marry someone from the other side of the world? I mean, it's exactly the kind of thing my brother would do, but he doesn't consider the long-term implications of anything."

I took a deep breath, considering this. "I take it you're not a romantic?"

He coughed up something that almost sounded like a laugh. "No, I'm not."

"Well, maybe it wouldn't work for you. But if they believe in it, they will make it work. Besides, being born in the same country doesn't guarantee a lasting relationship, either."

From the corner of my eye, I saw his face fall. "No, it doesn't."

"So, you'd never even consider it? Even if you fell in love, and..."

Where was I going with this?

"I don't fall in love."

"You've never been in love?"

"Never again."

The pain in his voice told me I wouldn't get more out of him, so we drove in silence. Someone had hurt him. Who, and how? It was none of my business, I reminded myself. This was not the time to turn into a borderline creepy investigative journalist. I didn't need to know. Yet, I couldn't stop thinking about it.

CHAPTER 5

Emir

Janie's fingers tightened around the steering wheel and her jaw twitched, but she said nothing. I knew I sounded like an uncommunicative jerk, but I sounded like that most of the time. She'd get used to it.

Janie kept her gaze on the road, giving me an opportunity to study her. Her expressive blue-grey eyes and high cheekbones caught the evening light like she was posing for a portrait. Her blond hair curled slightly around the temples. She was exquisite, there was no denying that. I wanted to photograph her, from every angle. I wanted her fingers on my neck, stroking and kneading away the pain, even if only for a moment. But I wouldn't let myself get carried away. I wasn't Cem. I had some self-control.

Janie followed Aria's car, weaving through the green hills and occasional ferns which gradually turned into a quiet suburbia. I was prepared to give her instructions—I'd memorized the route—but we were never in any danger of losing sight of Aria.

"It's the white house on the left," I told her, unnecessarily, as Aria turned on the driveway.

I was used to being in charge, or at least feeling like I had a purpose, and this trip was making me increasingly uncomfortable. I couldn't wait to get back to Janie's house. The fewer people I had around me, the better.

Janie double parked behind Aria. "We're leaving soon, right?"

"I'm happy to."

She gave me a long, probing look. "You really are, aren't you?" She cocked her head, mouth tugging. "You don't look particularly happy, but you're not frowning. And your voice... It had a softness to it. Did you notice?"

"No," I harrumphed, my chest feeling strangely warm.

Her smile turned giddy. "That's right. You're not that hard to read, mister. I'll figure it out."

I unfastened my seatbelt, trying to ignore the odd sensation those words had inserted inside my ribcage. I wasn't the one women wanted. She was only teasing me, waiting to hear me giggle or something. She'd be waiting a long time.

"I like your horse," I blurted. "So, I'm happy to go back."

"You like my horse," she repeated, her smile now so wide it must have been hurting her face. "And you enjoy my unprofessional massages."

I gripped the car door handle, fear tightening my throat. "Can we... um... keep that between us?"

Janie's spine straightened. "Is it... culturally not okay? I mean, would your parents be horrified to find out you're getting massaged by an old, divorced lady?"

I shook my head, a bit amused. "No. And you're not old. But I don't want anyone to make a big deal out of it. They keep saying I should see a professional, and I know I should. I will. But in the meantime..."

"Yeah, okay. I get it."

We got out of the car and joined Aria, Cem and the two sets of parents on the deck. They'd formed a semi-circle around an outdoor table loaded with various Turkish delights and nuts my parents had dragged across the world. They were the reason we'd wasted an extra hour in customs, declaring every nut, seed and sugary roll hiding in our luggage.

"Come join us for some exotic snacks," Aria's mother called us as we stood awkwardly on the other side of the table.

Aria got up. "Everyone! This is Janie! She's my boss and a wonderful friend who's letting us use her house for the engagement party."

Janie went around the table, shaking hands with Lyn and Greg. When she moved onto my mother, she leaned in and kissed her hand, bringing it to her forehead like she'd done it a thousand times. Mom didn't even blink, smiling her usual smile. Dad eyed her with suspicion but accepted the traditional greeting in his turn.

How did she know?

I edged closer to the table and snuck a handful of almonds, glancing at Janie. "I bet we didn't need to bring these all the way from Turkey, right?"

She laughed like I'd cracked a particularly funny joke. "No, but these are definitely worth braving the biosecurity." She pointed at the tray of *lokum,* chose a piece of a pomegranate-coated one and bit into it, closing her eyes. "Ah! This brings back memories."

"Memories?"

I waited for her answer, staring at her so intently I didn't notice Mom talking to me until she yanked at my sleeve. "I said, are you really going to stay at another house?"

I glanced at the crowded kitchen showing through the open doorway. "This place is too small for all of us. I know Aria's parents are very generous to offer, but two weeks is a long time."

"But we're leaving for South Island in a couple of days. We won't be here long."

I took a deep breath. I'd been biding my time, waiting for the right moment to tell them I wasn't coming. I'd never even booked a seat for myself. I couldn't stomach the idea of third-wheeling them around the country, and I knew, once they got over their fear of traveling without me, they'd appreciate the privacy.

"You go! It's all arranged, and I've emailed you both the itinerary and all the details. I managed to cancel my seat and got a full refund."

"Full refund?" Mom narrowed her eyes, playing with the bangles on her wrist.

"Yes. We had flexi tickets. It's fine. Meanwhile, I'll help on Janie's farm to get it ready for the party."

Mom gave me a slow nod, her eyes lighting with understanding. "Tamam! You do that. Work hard. If she won't let us pay for the party, we make sure we leave the place in a better shape. How is it looking?"

I took the camera off my shoulder and showed her some of the pictures.

"Those flowering trees are so beautiful!" She tried to take the camera off me, but I grabbed it back and switched it off. She didn't need to see pictures of Janie walking out of her house.

"There's a verandah with more flowering trees around it. It needs some work, but it'll look great in the pictures. I'll plan the photos when I'm there."

Dad tuned into our conversation, frowning. "You're not coming to South Island with us? What if we get lost? I don't understand these people. Every word sounds the same. Are they talking through their noses?"

Mom patted my arm. "We'll be fine. I have a translator app. It'll be an adventure! Like when we were young." She winked at him, and I saw a flash of interest behind Dad's eyes.

Looking after Janie's horse was sounding better and better by the minute. I didn't even care how much she teased me about it. I wanted to get back to the farm, with no people in sight.

After an appropriate duration of snacking and chitchatting, I fetched my suitcase from the house and farewelled the Dunnes, as well as my parents. Mom slipped a wad of cash into my pocket.

"Don't be a burden. I don't want that woman to cook for you all day long. Buy some yogurt. It'll keep you healthy."

I nodded, feeling heavy. It was Cem's money that we passed around, not mine. I wasn't his manager anymore, and I hated these handouts. But what could I do? Mom was right. I couldn't let Janie cook for me. Letting me stay in her house was more than enough. I'd find a way to be useful. Not just with the horse, but with everything. Whatever she needed.

CHAPTER 1

Janie

"Are you sure? I have a lot of food. I buy bulk. I grow food."

"Yes," Emir insisted. "I will buy some groceries for us. Anything you need."

I sighed, turning into the grocery store carpark. "I told you I don't need anything."

Emir didn't budge. "Can we take turns cooking?"

"Do you enjoy cooking?"

"I know some recipes."

"Turkish ones?" My voice rose in excitement.

"*Tamam*. I'll buy some ingredients. Do you want to wait here?" Emir opened the car door, nodding at the entrance.

I froze, my hand on the seatbelt fastener. I had no reason to follow him, yet I wanted to. An emotionally unavailable, grumpy foreigner who possibly found me repulsive? I'd developed some questionable catnip.

"I'll pick up something for breakfast," I finally decided, releasing my seatbelt.

"I thought you didn't need anything?"

I smiled sweetly. "No, but I want something."

He shrugged and fell into step with me, entering the cool atmosphere of the store. Picking up a basket, he looked up something on his phone and headed to the fresh produce aisle. I hung back, watching him examine tomatoes, the frown on his face deepening.

"I grow tomatoes," I informed him, stepping a bit closer. "Should use them before buying more." Mine existed as a tangled heap I hadn't managed to support with proper stakes, but they were sweet and ripe. Probably overripe.

He looked up from the pale piece of fruit. "Okay. Good. I'll get some eggs and spices."

"I have chickens," I reminded him, feeling my face warming.

Was I trying to impress him with my hobby farm? Only half of my chooks produced any eggs, and half of those they hid around the coop so well I'd probably never find them—and didn't even try too hard now that I was mostly a one-person household.

"Do you grow spices? Paprika? Chili pepper?"

"No. But I do have a pretty good selection at home, which you're welcome to use."

He took a deep breath, his expression wary. "Okay. What can

I contribute?"

I could tell that he had to. If I dwarfed his every attempt, this man would overheat and burn a circuit board.

"Bread," I said decisively, taking his arm and leading him to the bakery aisle.

Tingly warmth shot through me, and I questioned my own bravery. But I was also determined to establish a level of familiarity. Touching was my love language, and I couldn't let his odd, standoffish attitude take that away from me. If he pulled away, I'd step back. But Emir let me keep my fingers on his forearm.

The scent of fresh bread filled my nostrils and his muscles twitched under the shirt fabric, sending a tingle up my arm. I closed my eyes for a second and inhaled, hoping that nobody I knew happened to be around. I didn't want to explain my relationship to this man. I only wanted to keep touching him.

We stood by the baguettes and loaves for a moment before I finally let go of him, scanning our surroundings. Only a group of kids milled about the iced doughnuts.

"I don't have fresh bread and don't feel like baking," I said. "You choose whatever you think will work with... whatever you're cooking."

Emir reached for some flat bread. "So, you've been to Turkey?"

"Yes! I travelled around Europe when I worked in London for a while. I've only been to Antalya, which is obviously very touristy, but I had a Turkish colleague who taught me a few things, what to try in restaurants and so on."

He looked at me for a long moment, head tilted. "How did you find it?"

I felt my cheeks warming. "I loved it. The food. The language. Everything. But I was younger, and single. I got a lot of attention. People were so friendly. Men…" I paused, looking for the right word.

Emir held up his hand. "You don't have to say it. Turkish men can be very forward. Persistent." Pain registered behind his eyes, as if he was apologizing for something he couldn't change about his culture, or himself.

"It's okay." I smiled, remembering the Turkish man who'd joined my dinner table, harassing the waiters to refill my tea glass. "It was mostly very sweet."

"Sweet?" His eyes narrowed.

"For sure! Everyone was looking after me, asking questions, feeding me… One guy asked me to marry him after a five-minute conversation." I'd meant it as a quick joke, even if it was true, but Emir's dark gaze sucked the fun out of my words. A hot, burgeoning blush crept up my cheeks, which at my age felt more like an alarming medical event than anything cute. "I mean, at least it feels that way now," I rambled on. "Fond memories. I guess when you go years without it, you realize how special that attention is." I'd entered a full body blush, my words coming out fast and frantic.

Something about his open gaze had loosened my tongue to the point that I felt slightly drunk. There was nothing flirty or playful about Emir. He was 6 feet and five inches of breathtaking intensity, like standing in front of an arcangel who towered over me, staring straight into my soul, cataloguing everything inside me. There was nowhere to hide.

"If you were harassed, say so. I can take it."

I shook my head. "No, I wasn't. And it's not your job to apologize for it anyway. You don't seem like those guys."

"I used to be," he said quietly, dropping the bread into his basket. "But I don't want to cross any boundaries. So, please tell me if you ever feel that way."

I nodded; my mouth dry as I imagined myself crossing societal boundaries with him. I could feel my own pulse between my legs. The man was clearly so restrained he'd never even look at me funny. The sensations awakening in my body were as useless as they were delicious, but I wasn't that young anymore. I knew how quickly romance dried up and life turned into a race for money and comfort, a slow decline towards the grave. I knew how lucky I was to feel anything at all.

I'd have to do my best not to cross his boundaries.

We made it out of the shop with the bread and some Turkish delight I couldn't resist, despite Emir's eye-rolling. The chocolate covered kind they sold in New Zealand wasn't the real thing, but I wanted something Turkish in my mouth and the sweet treat would have to do.

CHAPTER 7

Emir

Janie showed me to the guest bedroom, quickly clearing two bags from the wardrobe to create space for my luggage. The room was tastefully designed, with soft carpets and soothing tones. Back when I'd been managing Cem, traveling around Europe and staying in hotels, I would have felt like I belonged. I might have even felt like a man worthy of Janie's time. But I'd lost my way. I didn't have a real job. I was across the world, performing menial tasks for my brother, no longer calling the shots.

Janie held at the doorway, her face frozen into a half smile, her eyes cast down to my feet. She'd seemed a bit flustered since our shopping trip. "Is there anything else you need?"

"No, thank you."

"I'll make some tea if you want to join me. If you're not too tired?"

She looked up at me with such open interest I couldn't deny that part of me wanted to explore it. What would it feel like to be chosen?

"Tea sounds great."

I'd been by myself for so long I didn't even know how to allow someone closer. Was there any way to do that without entering a world of hurt? Probably not, if history was any indication. I couldn't do fun and casual. I was neither of those things. I'd fallen in love once and it had destroyed me. I knew the power of it, and I knew better than to go near that fire.

I wouldn't risk it for a woman who lived a world away. A woman who had roots in this soil. A family. I shook my head at the thought. This was exactly what I'd been warning Cem about. Not that he ever listened. And now my family paid the price of their ill-considered love story. If I did the same, there'd be nobody left to look after my parents. I was a downer, but I'd always been the dependable one.

Janie flashed me a hopeful smile and disappeared, leaving the hallway darker, as if she'd been the source of light.

Fifteen minutes later, showered and changed into slacks and a T-shirt, I met her in the kitchen. She'd changed into a pair of black leggings and a pale purple shirt, and her hair swayed in a high ponytail. Her smile caught me off guard, again. "You look so much more comfortable!"

"It's not too casual?" I glanced at the outfit I never wore outside the privacy of my bedroom. But I was starting to learn how casual New Zealand was.

"No!" She handed me a cup of tea. It smelled strong and sweet and familiar. "It's not Turkish but as close I could get." She shot me an apologetic smile.

My chest tightened at the thought. "You didn't have to. I'll drink whatever you drink."

"I love Turkish tea."

I liked the way her cheeks colored, so at odds with her confidence that I almost wanted to tease her. If I'd known how to do that without offending.

I tasted the tea. "It's nice. Thank you."

"Do you want me to..." she gestured at her own neck, then at the dining table.

Against my better judgment, I sat down. Her dog appeared, tail wagging, raising its paws on my knee, as perky as its owner. "Only if you tell me all the things you need help with. I'll make a list and start first thing tomorrow morning."

The second her hands landed on my skin; my body flooded with incredible, tingly warmth. An uncontrollable sound gurgled out of my throat, and I tried to cover it with a cough.

I heard the smile in Janie's voice. "If you insist, I do have some broken fencing. And some of the trellis around the verandah was damaged by the storm."

"Did you have flooding around here?" I'd heard about the floods that hit Napier only weeks after the earthquake that devastated much of Turkey and Syria.

"No. I'm lucky my house is so elevated. I only had heavy rain and a couple of landslides. It destroyed some of my crop. Spooked Molly. But I was lucky. I didn't drown inside my own house."

Her hands trembled and the same shiver ran through me. "Was that what happened?"

"To some people. Esk Valley got hit hard. It's not in the news anymore, but I think the aftereffects will linger for years. Like in Turkey and Syria."

I sighed. "It'll take decades to rebuild. Many people will deal with PTSD for the rest of their lives. You can't even measure the cost."

"I thought everything could be calculated?"

I harrumphed. "Okay. I concede my point. Natural disasters might be too difficult in that sense."

"How is your English so good? Your accent is stronger than your brother's, but your vocabulary is… impressive."

I shivered again, and this time it had nothing to do with her fingers shaking. How could she put so much reverence into that word? "I read a lot. I study." What else could you do when you weren't invited to parties, nor wanted to attend them? Books had been my escape for two decades. And as a result, I found most people, especially those who didn't read, tedious to talk to.

"What was the last book you read?"

"It was a collection of stories by Haruki Murakami. Picked it up from the airport. Their selection wasn't great."

"Did you like it?"

"It had an arresting atmosphere."

"Just like you."

"Just like me?"

"Maybe it's the accent," she mused and chuckled. "A little bit of a culture shock, in a good way. When I'm talking to you, I feel like I'm traveling." Her voice sounded dreamy.

"I thought I was the one traveling."

"No. We both are," she insisted, sadness bleeding into her words. "I don't get to travel anymore, so this is as good as it gets. Don't take it away from me."

"*Tamam,*" I said. I could give her this. "*Sen çok çekici bir kadın.*"

She sighed and I heard the smile in her voice. "Now it feels like I'm traveling! What does it mean?"

"That you're welcome back to Turkey," I lied.

"I thought Turkey was *Türkiye?*" Her fingers stilled on my neck and a chill traveled through me. "You didn't say *Türkiye.*"

How could she pick my words apart like that? I thought about covering with another lie, but what was the point?

"Okay, you got me. I said you're very attractive."

She burst into laughter. "Now it definitely feels like I'm traveling in Turkey!" As her laughter settled, her fingers dove into my hair. "Thank you," she whispered, leaning so close I felt her warm breath on my ear.

I could usually control myself, at least in company. Pain had a way of dampening other urges, making me feel like I'd conquered what ailed most of my fellow men. But I wasn't that different. When her soft, husky voice flooded my ear, I felt like another Turkish man, ready to chase what I desired. I took a deep breath, trying to push those thoughts away. Focus on the relief her touch brought to my tight muscles.

"How about some Pilates?" she murmured, her voice all smiles. "I could show you some basic moves to help with your back. I've been doing it for years."

"I don't have any… tights." I winced. "I mean, whatever you wear to that sort of fancy exercise."

I felt her bubbly laugh in my body as if it spilled through her fingertips. "It's not that fancy. What you're wearing is fine."

"Where do you do it? Do you have a gym here, or…"

She gestured at the shaggy rug surrounded by plush couches. "You don't need any equipment. It's so easy. I'll show you."

I set down my teacup and followed her to the rug, maybe out of politeness, or because I'd become addicted to her touch. If there was a chance that she needed to physically guide me through this strange exercise, it was worth it. Embarrassment and all.

Darkness had fallen outside, and Janie pulled the heavy curtains, turning the living room into a cozy haven. The shades of cream, grey and soft green again made me think of a hotel.

I lowered myself onto the floor, wincing at the pressure in my lower back as I folded my legs to mirror hers. "We shall never speak of this."

Janie's smile sparkled. "You don't want to take photos for your family? They'd be so proud!"

She looked so comfortable sitting like a monk on the floor, her back straight, shoulders pulled back. I tried to imitate her posture, but a pain seared through my lower back. "I can't."

Her eyes flashed with concern, and she moved closer. "Okay. Sitting this way is hard on your lower back. Let's start on the floor."

I looked around me, confused. "But we are on the floor."

"I mean..." She moved closer and guided me onto my back, legs folded. "Can you lift your hips?"

My face flushed. I'd never been this uncomfortable in my life. Janie scooted backwards and lay on the rug next to me, peeling her hips off the floor. The movement made her T-shirt shift down her body, revealing a slice of tanned midriff. She was in incredible shape. I forced my eyes at the ceiling and tried to copy the move. I couldn't get my hips aligned with hers, no matter what I tried. Groaning, I lowered myself back against the floor. The soft rug hugged my sore back. She was right. I needed this.

Janie guided me through the gentle moves, curving my back to imitate cats and cows, then something she called 'rolling on the floor'. Again, she looked like an actual ball as she rocked and rolled, back rounded, arms around her folded legs. I was more like a plank falling against the floor, but after a few tries, I felt my spine curving and managed to rock back and forth a little.

"Good job!" Janie clapped her hands and grabbed my shoulder, helping me back up to sitting. "Great progress."

Her praise flooded me with warmth, and I told myself to chill. This woman was a performer. Essentially an actress. She played a part. She told you what you wanted to hear. Still, I wanted to sit next to her, basking in that light that shone from her eyes. Even if for one fake moment.

"My back feels better. Can we continue tomorrow?"

"Are you giving up already?" Her smile had a teasing edge.

"Is there more?" I stifled a yawn. The room was spinning.

"We're only getting started."

She rolled back onto the floor, this time on her side, and lifted her leg up, pointing her toe at the ceiling. I tried to copy her move but managed to only lift my leg third of the way. Was her leg even connected to her pelvis? "How are you doing that?"

She cocked her head, examining my feeble attempts, and guided me up and into a yoga move I remembered from years ago. Downward something. It hurt even more, but I persevered, and followed her example through a simple series of movements. My back stretched and ached, but I could tell it was good pain. Necessary pain. I should have tried this a long time ago. I jogged and trained at the gym, but I'd never enjoyed stretching. Pilates was strange—a workout designed to cause maximum amount of pain with minimum movement, but it obviously worked.

After twenty minutes of surprisingly challenging workout, she guided us into a 'child pose', and announced we were finished.

"Thank you," I mumbled, my cheek against the rug. "I think this helped. Even if I can no longer stand up or walk."

"You need to get some rest. Jetlag is the worst."

She straightened, placing her hand on my lower back. "But you should do this every day. It's great for your back."

"Okay," I rasped, feeling like a heavy-duty cardboard box

someone was trying to fold into a recycling bin. Yet, I wanted to keep her hand where it was. The magic hand that took the pain away.

Holding onto the couch, I made it upright and wobbled out of the living room, wishing her good night on my way out.

When I made it to my room, I closed the door and spent a long time leaning against it, my heart pounding. Something was happening to me. Something within me felt softer, and it wasn't just muscles. Staying in her house was not a safe choice. I'd been so careful, stepping only on the solid stones, navigating life like a board game that only required good strategy and stupid co-players. Nothing mushy or confusing. No chance of getting knifed in my exposed underbelly. I'd begun to feel pleased with myself, observing the mess and heartbreak of fellow humans like an alien sent to investigate human life on earth. Superior and unaffected. A smug asshole.

But now my foot had made contact with something soft, and I was sinking.

CHAPTER 8

Janie

I woke up to a heavenly smell. I rolled over in bed, disoriented, thinking I was away from home. Nobody else cooked in my house. And then I remembered Emir. He'd been with me for four days now—fixing fences, feeding animals, and administering eyedrops. He'd insisted he wanted to cook, but I'd thrown his flatbread in the freezer and told him he needed to rest and get over his jetlag. So far, I'd been up before him, making breakfast and leaving some for him before I left for work.

I'd been happy to cook for him. It was only fair since he was doing so much work around the farm. I hadn't even realized how many things needed fixing until Emir had brought them to my attention.

Every night, as per our agreement, I'd massaged his head and shoulders. Feeling his body relax, those deep sighs and groans that erupted from his throat... I couldn't stop my imagination running wild. I could tell he had incredible self-control, but as I kicked off the sheet tangled around my legs, I realized he'd been there in my dream, again. I'd dreamed of his hard body pressed against mine. I'd dreamed of him losing control.

I wrapped myself in a bathrobe and patted to the kitchen. I was expecting him, yet the sight of the dark, tall and Turkish man made my breath hitch. He stood by the stove, frowning at the frying pan, my kowhaiwhai-patterned apron protecting his white dress shirt as he pushed something red and eggy with a spatula. How it had materialized in the pan, I had no idea. The kitchen showed no signs of cooking.

"Good morning!" A wide smile rose from deep inside of me, and I waited for him to turn around.

Emir looked up. "*Günaydın!* Good morning." There was no smile, but a relaxed softness to him I hadn't seen before.

"Did you sleep okay?" I asked.

"Yes, thank you. It's a comfortable bed."

"Good." I peered into the pan. "*Menemen*?"

"Yes." He looked surprised.

"Wait. You got the tomatoes from the garden?" My stomach dropped at the thought. My garden was such a mess I'd been hoping to keep him out of it and fetch the produce myself. I glimpsed at him from behind my face palm. "I'm so sorry. I haven't had the time to... The storm flattened all the stakes and I let the tomatoes grow into that heap."

"It's okay. The best ones were hiding in the middle. I suppose the birds can't get to them." Emir ladled the red mush onto two plates and took them to the dining table where he'd already sliced the flatbread.

A pot of tea stood in the middle, steam rising from it. I fought tears. I hadn't shared breakfast with anyone, let alone a man, in more than a year. And the last time hadn't been that enjoyable. I worked hard not to revisit those memories, but standing there, staring at the perfect spread of food on my table, the thoughts bombarded me, clouding my vision.

"Is something wrong?" Emir's thick accent made me shiver.

"It's beautiful," I managed, my voice wobbly and thick. "So beautiful."

"It's a very basic breakfast." He sounded almost offended.

I took a breath and looked him in the eye. "No one has done this for me in a very long time. So, it's beautiful. No arguments."

His arms dropped to his sides. "Okay. Then I'm glad." He met my gaze with such sincerity, letting that unhurried moment of connection shift and stretch, that I didn't notice the tear until it rolled all the way to my upper lip.

He caught it with his fingertip, never breaking the eye contact. "I didn't mean to make you cry."

I turned away, wiping my eyes on my sleeve. "Sorry. I'm making you uncomfortable. I'll try to keep my issues at bay and enjoy the food." I took a deep breath and gave him a reassuring smile.

"I prefer real. I can't do the pretending very well." His eyes flashed with pain.

I blinked away the last of my stubborn tears. "I get it. But I don't want to dump my issues on you. It's not fair."

"We all have issues." He kept looking at me until I dropped the smile.

"Yeah, we do."

"If you felt comfortable sharing your issues with me, I'd be honored, Janie." He held my gaze until the words faded, and only the meaning lingered, unchanged. He wasn't being polite.

I'd interviewed politicians and celebrities. I was used to looking for the truth behind meaningless, self-absorbed babble. What was left unsaid? What was implied? With Emir, my journalist skills were useless. So much hid behind his eyes, yet his words felt true.

"Likewise," I finally responded, turning away to catch my breath. "I'd be honored, if you decided I was worth your trust."

His eyes darkened and the forehead crease deepened. "Let's eat."

He guided me to the table and pulled out a chair. I dropped onto the seat, thinking that this was the first time I'd been offered a chair in my own dining room.

I scooped a forkful of menemen and moaned from pleasure. "This is so good! I remember trying this somewhere in Antalya, but it wasn't like this."

Emir scoffed. "Antalya is a tourist trap."

"Well, this is the real deal."

"It's the best I could do with local ingredients."

"Take the compliment, Emir." I gave him a pointed look.

"Okay."

The sound of the doorbell gave me a start. Not now, I pleaded. Whoever it was, I didn't want them here. Not now.

The doorbell rang again.

I held up a finger. "Wait, I'll go check."

Approaching the door, I heard the familiar high-pitched shriek of laughter, muffled but unmistakable. Tabitha, the head of the Art Deco festival committee, with her trusted secretary, Maree. They'd begun visiting me regularly since my divorce. At first, I'd welcomed the distraction, but as my social calendar filled with pointless outings, my enthusiasm waned. They wanted to capitalize on my lingering fame to advance Tabitha's causes. Arts and culture. Historical restorations. I supported her causes, in theory, but mostly played along to avoid making enemies in my new hometown. And in some ways, loneliness was worse.

However, at that moment, Tabitha and Maree were the last people on earth I wanted to invite into my home and introduce to Emir. These ladies were influential, as well as the worst gossips in town. The stories they would tell... My mind whirled, searching for a way out.

I ran back to the dining room, gesturing wildly at the door. "Emir? Do you maybe want to hide for a bit? I'm so sorry, I'm not embarrassed by you or anything, but these ladies are so nosy. They will rip you to shreds. Figure of speech. I mean... What am I saying. I just—"

"Janie. Calm down." He stood up, silencing me with a sharp look. "You don't have to convince me to avoid people. I'll be in my room." He grabbed his plate and took his exit as I rushed back to the front door, taking a centering breath before I opened it.

"Good morning, ladies!"

Tabitha smoothed her helmet-like dark bob, one that transformed annually into a perfect 1920s hairdo for the Art Deco festival. Her pursed lips stretched into a wide smile. "Good morning, Janie! How are you holding up? We come bearing gifts."

Holding up?

Maree, the less extroverted version of her with a heavy breath that always sounded like she was asleep, held up a brown paper bag. "Croissants."

Their silky pastel blouses seemed color coordinated, as well as expensive. They were my age, stinking rich, high profile and so immaculate I always felt judged. It was a bit like receiving a delegation from the royal court. A great honor, but not one you could particularly enjoy. A sheer glimpse of Tabitha's flawless makeup flooded my body with cortisol.

I took a breath so deep my lungs ached, smoothed my hair, and offered them the fakest of smiles. "Come on in. I was having breakfast. I'm afraid I'm not quite dressed and ready yet. I like my Sunday mornings slow and lazy."

"Oh, we understand." Tabitha made a show of flicking the remote in her hand, to which her Maserati answered with a dutiful beep. "If I were you, I would have started cocktail hour."

Cocktail hour? Her choice of words, along with the theatrical looks of sympathy, were starting to build up panic in my belly. "Alcohol is not my choice of breakfast." I kept my smile in check and tightened the robe around my waist. It was a bit bulky, and I didn't want them to spread any rumors about weight gain.

I led them to the dining room, where Emir's menemen pan and a bowl of flatbread still sat on the table.

"What is this?" Maree leaned in to investigate the Turkish eggs.

"It's a Mediterranean breakfast dish. I felt like trying out something different." I bit back a wayward smile.

"Good on you! I knew our Janie could not be knocked down!" Tabitha winked, exchanging a knowing look with Maree.

The sick feeling in my stomach amped up. What an earth was going on?

"How do you make it?" Maree asked.

I glanced at my suspiciously clean kitchen. "Um… it's eggs and tomatoes and a few other ingredients."

"What other ingredients?" Maree took out her phone, ready to take notes.

She was a fan, which was in its own way more unbearable than Tabitha's veiled judgment. I knew I was social collateral to both, a name to be dropped at certain moments to raise the price of their own stock. That's how being on TV worked, and I accepted it. But right then, I swallowed a groan.

"I'll email you the recipe, okay?"

I took their coffee orders and slipped into the kitchen to make the drinks. I was hoping they'd entertain themselves, but Tabitha followed me. "I'll grab a couple of plates for the croissants."

I couldn't remember ever showing her around my kitchen, but she found the plates on first try. "I love your space," she gestured at the cabinets. "Very shabby chic."

I hid my frown. There was nothing intentionally shabby about my kitchen. It was simply fifteen years old, and I had no budget for renovations. These were things Shaun had cared about, except when it came to this house. Moving here, I thought he'd finally relaxed about appearances, but it turned out he didn't care because he never intended to live here.

"You're brave, living all alone in the middle of nowhere like this." She gazed out the window like the green hills behind my house were teeming with bears or lions.

"My sons are coming down for the holidays."

Tabitha gave a knowing nod, her eyes solemn. "Life certainly throws us curve balls, doesn't it?"

I smiled, switching on the milk steamer, happy for the loud hiss that would soon drown out her voice. "Nothing I can't handle."

She left me to it and I relished my short break, taking my time with the coffees. As much as they got on my nerves, Tabitha and Maree were part of the package. Napier was a small town, and they were involved in every committee. The film office I ran regularly needed their help. If I wanted to make this place my home, I had to stay on their good side.

We'd started off fine, with polite invitations and endless admiration for my wardrobe, skin, hair, perfume... There wasn't a part of my appearance Tabitha hadn't made a point of loudly approving of. Her comments made me feel equal parts flattered and uncomfortable. Even if I passed the assessment, I felt like I was under the microscope—much like I'd been in Auckland, on morning TV. And it was that constant scrutiny I'd chosen to leave behind me. Back then, I'd had the income to keep myself in anti-aging serums and regular treatments, and even then, felt like I was always lacking. Compared to those days, I now lived like a wild woman. By choice, I might add. Yet, I felt like Tabitha and her ladies expected me 'as seen on TV'. Which was why I suspected their gracious comments were rather embellished. They wanted a celebrity friend and knew what to say. And I was needy and lonely enough to go along with it.

But now our symbiotically dysfunctional friendship had hit the rocks. Ever since my divorce, I didn't fit their social group. Tabitha and Maree were married to high profile men—a retired investment banker and the owner of the local supermarket. I'd been introduced to them as part of a power couple including Shaun. And now I was a single woman running a farm by myself. As much as Tabitha and Maree wanted to appear supportive, my single status bothered them. It was something to fix.

I took two coffees to the dining room, setting them down next to a newspaper. Wait. A newspaper? I didn't subscribe to any papers. I'd been on a blissful media fast ever since I'd quit my job.

Tabitha cleared her throat, a sound that immediately gave me shivers.

I scanned the paper for my own name and face, like I always did, but it was something worse. Shaun. Shaun and his new girlfriend. A baby bump. My eyes landed on the rounded shape of Kelly's stomach. Woman half my age. Such a cliché. Shaun had turned my life into a cliché.

"We saw this and thought you might need some emotional support." Maree's eyes rounded in sympathy as she pulled out a chair for me.

I sat, almost against my will, my mind spinning. Was I supposed to know about this? Was I supposed to pretend like I knew about it? As much as I hated playing that part, the alternative was so much worse. I couldn't show weakness. These vultures would clamp onto me and never let go.

I smiled as brightly as I could. "Let's hope Shaun has the energy to do it all again. He's not getting any younger."

Tabitha slapped the newspaper and cackled. "That's what I said! Didn't I?" She turned to Maree, who nodded animatedly, her eyes filled with adoration. "It's great that you're taking this in your stride. You're such an inspiration."

I knew how to keep smiling. How to keep myself composed while the cameras were still rolling. It shouldn't have been this hard.

"Easy for men. They can start again. A new wife, new family. But at our age..." Tabitha shook her head, finally taking a sip of coffee.

I wanted to hold her nose and pour it all in, to keep her mouth occupied.

"Good thing I don't want to start a new family." My smile didn't waver, but my fingers curled around the edge of the table. There'd be nail marks later.

Tabitha shifted back in her chair. "Of course. I didn't mean having kids but just... starting over. With someone else. It's a bit different for women, don't you think? Not a great selection out there unless you're shopping in the junior section." Her eyes widened in horror. "I mean, we know how to keep the goods from spoiling, but the men are hardly giving us the same courtesy." She ran a finger up the edge of her jawline, demonstrating how much money she paid to keep her skin from sagging.

The image of Emir flashed behind my eyes. He was my junior. I wondered by how many years. Too many for this company.

"Double standards," Maree echoed, gathering the empty coffee cups to take to the kitchen.

"I'm only 41," I said, anger bubbling in my chest. "That's not old."

"And you look after yourself," Tabitha confirmed. "You must be happy now that you put in the effort. Some women get married and let themselves go. They think they'll never have to put themselves out there again." She straightened her spine, highlighting her firm physique. She was five years older than me, and unbelievably perky.

I got to my feet and picked up the menemen pan and carried it to the kitchen island, to create a bit of distance between us. "I'm not looking to put myself out there. I enjoy my own company."

Tabitha stood up as well and leapt to my side. "Of course. But, we all need someone. It's a lot of work to take care of a place this big. Did you get a good settlement?"

"I did okay," I muttered. To call it good would have been a blatant lie.

Tabitha sensed a sore spot and lifted her finger. I almost braced myself for a physical poke. "He shafted you, didn't he? They know how to hide the money. Needs every penny for the new family, right? Happened to my friend Mary, but she found out, took him to court."

I briefly closed my eyes, gathering my resolve. "I'm okay. I'll manage." I didn't have money for more lawyers.

Tabitha edged even closer, rubbing her ice cold hand up and down my bathrobe sleeve. Her head tilted in sympathy and voice turned into a low purr. "Are you, though? We saw the broken fences. It's been weeks since the floods."

I circled her, picked up the frying pan again and busied myself with moving the rest of the eggs into a glass container. "It's okay. I've hired some help."

Her eyes widened. "Have you? That's great! Who did you book? Harry?"

I had no idea who Harry was, but I nodded anyway. Anything to make the questions stop.

Maree entered the kitchen, giving Tabitha a nervous look. "Did you tell her about Len yet?"

"Len who?"

"Len Harding. The pastor! His wife just died." Tabitha beamed like this was the best news she'd heard all week. "Him and Adrian are golf buddies, so he gets all the goss."

"That's terrible."

"No, no. She was on life support for months. It's a relief, I'm sure. Len will be looking for a new wife. A man like that won't stay single. We've already dropped your name and he seemed to… liven up. Well, Adrian used a different phrase which I won't repeat, but anyway, let me know if you'd like me to set you two up."

"He's so dreamy," Maree smiled, eyes half-closed, her heavy breath sounding like an air-con unit. "The ladies will be lining up."

Why was I friends with these people?

I sighed, chucked the egg container in the fridge, and shifted closer to the front door, hoping the ladies got the hint. "I hope people give him time. It takes a while to get over a relationship."

"How long has it been for you now?" Tabitha asked, only moving an inch towards the door. "Eight... nine months?"

Had she marked my divorce in her personal calendar?

"Something like that." I took another step towards the door, digging my fingernails into the sleeves of my robe. "I'm not ready for anything yet. I'm focusing on work."

Tabitha's face lit up. "Work! Thank you for reminding me! That's another thing we need to discuss. We could really use your help with the Art Deco Gala. Everyone was so gutted when the festival got cancelled because of the floods and I think this gala will bridge the gap. And it's so important to fundraise right now. The next meeting is on Wednesday this coming week. It's vital that everyone is present."

My mind kicked into overdrive, searching for excuses, sorting them in order of usefulness... I needed an out. Not an engagement party I was hosting next weekend. Something long-term, time consuming and worthwhile that would save me from weeks of mind-numbing planning meetings.

The answer came to me almost at the same time I opened my mouth, the words forming on my tongue. "Unfortunately, I've taken on a big documentary project and that will eat up most of my time in the coming weeks. Apologies."

Tabitha's eyes sharpened. "Documentary? What sort?"

My mind sprinted. "About the after effect of the floods. The real stories… forgotten people who still deal with the long-term effects as the mainstream media moves on." With every word, my confidence grew, and I noticed excitement bubbling in my chest. I could do this.

Sometimes, your subconscious has all the answers, waiting to be released under extreme pressure. Thank you, Tabitha. She was pressure personified, and the answer I'd been looking for burst out of my mouth so fully cooked I could hardly believe it. I'd always been fast, thinking and speaking simultaneously. Sometimes, I heard the words as if spoken by someone else and found myself agreeing or disagreeing. My brain was wired a bit funny.

"That sounds wonderful, Janie." Maree blinked several times. "Who are you working with?"

I paused. No matter how much my brain galloped, I couldn't spin the truth any further. I had to offer some honesty. "It's very early days and it's a low budget production, so I'm still looking for crew members. Let me know if you can think of anyone."

Tabitha raised her terrifying pointer finger. "My nephew Gus is a cameraman! I'll send him over for a visit!"

My stomach tightened but I smiled as I finally grasped the front door, my savior, and cracked it open. "Wonderful. Please do."

Gus couldn't be worse than Tabitha.

When we finally got through the goodbyes and the ladies

shuffled outside, I closed the door and leaned against it, forcefully breathing in and out. My chest felt so tight I had to fight for every lungful of oxygen. I couldn't be this easily rattled, could I? I had to be stronger than this.

But the tears came anyway. The tears of loneliness and humiliation. All the things I worried and grieved about, laid out in front of me on a platter by Tabitha fucking Witts. She knew everyone. She talked to everyone. She'd report all over town about my husband's new family, my perpetually broken fence, and my low budget documentary. The last one probably didn't hurt if I wanted to get a production off the ground. Did I, really? I'd felt the excitement in the moment, but now, it was replaced by dread. Maybe I didn't have it in me.

I wiped my face on my sleeve and returned to the dining room, the newspaper article beckoning me like fly paper—sticky, deadly and irresistible. Shaun posed with his hand resting on Kelly's baby bump, looking a little sunburnt, his forehead shining like a glazed Christmas ham, a proud smile on his face. I blinked away the blurry blobs of tears, to see it clearly. I remembered his smile from years ago when he'd still had hair. But with that shiny dome? I felt like I'd never seen the combination. When had I last seen him smile? Maybe men simply didn't smile around me. That Turkish guy was so strait-laced I didn't even know if he had incisors.

I shook my head at my racing thoughts. In a way, I welcomed the thoughts of Emir and the distraction he brought. How badly out of control would I spiral if he wasn't here right now? I didn't even want to find out. Where was he anyway?

I dabbed my eyes with a tissue, trying to bring my sniffles under control. But no amount of deep breathing could stop the quiver in my chest. My gaze brushed across the close-up photo of their engagement rings, diamonds glinting in the sun, and a fresh wave of emotion washed over me. Why was I learning about this from the fucking newspaper?

I picked up my phone and checked my messages. There it was. A short, evasive email from Shaun, apologizing for the 'late notice'. I wanted to scream. My body shook from the rage, then tears burst out with full force.

I couldn't let anyone see me like this.

I balled up the newspaper, heaved it into the trash can and ran. Journal. Rubber boots. Phone. House keys. That's all I needed.

It was only when I made it to the track behind my house, weaving through the bush with dewy ferns swiping my face and arms, that I felt a little more in control. I needed a minute. A moment to sit in my secret spot and vomit every incoherent thought onto the pages of my journal. I'd pull myself together, then return to the house. I'd resume being a lovely hostess. Emir would never know.

CHAPTER 9

Emir

The bang of the front door rang through the house, and I stumbled away from the door I'd been pressing my ear against, trying to swallow the intense ball of shame. I shouldn't have been listening. This was none of my business. I'd told myself I was only looking out for Janie in case she needed help. I'd seen the panic in her eyes as she'd told me about the visitors. She didn't want to receive these people.

Yet, she'd let them into her house, served them and listened to their probing comments and questions. I couldn't tell exactly what they'd talked about, but I could detect the universal tone of curiosity. I'd been around enough gossiping neighbors and cousins to recognize the dirt-digging behavior.

I stepped into the dining room. The table had been cleaned, but I immediately spotted something sticking out of the garbage can—a crumpled newspaper.

Instinctively, I glanced out the window. No cars, apart from Janie's. The visitors had left, but so had Janie. Where had she gone?

With a strange sense of urgency, I dug up the newspaper, smoothed the pages and flipped through it to find what I was looking for. It didn't take long for my eyes to land on Janie. She looked younger and more polished, posing in a TV studio. The story was about her ex-husband and his new family. Understanding dawned as I scanned the article, focused on sugary words on her ex-husband's new engagement and their pregnancy.

Where was Janie? Last time I'd seen her, she'd been in her bathrobe. Had she left the house like that?

"Stay," I told Gru who'd followed me to the door.

Making sure I didn't lock myself out of the house, I snuck out the door and circled the building. The timing must have been God's doing, because my eyes caught a glimpse of her coral bathrobe, flashing between the lush greenery covering the hill behind her house. Where was she going? Was there a path?

I glanced at my own leather shoes. Not the best hiking gear, but I had to make sure she was okay. I had to follow her. I ran towards the thicket of ferns and eventually spotted the beginning of a narrow path. Ducking my head to avoid hitting low-hanging branches, I pushed my way in.

The bright daylight transformed into somber tones of dark

green, punctuated by the occasional sunbeam. My nostrils filled with the humid smell of earth and its creatures. The sense of wilderness sent a vibration through me. When had I last entered anywhere like this?

I picked up speed until I caught the sight of Janie again. She was taking long strides but rather slow in her heavy rubber boots. I contemplated calling out for her but held back. Was it better to make myself known, or trail her from a distance, to make sure she didn't throw herself off a cliff or something? How could I stop her, though? If I was too far away, I'd only end up witnessing her death.

My stomach twisted at the thought. But when I was about to call her name, she arrived at a small hut. It peeked through the bushes, its greenish brown color almost blending in. Moss grew up the walls and the door hung off its hinges, daylight seeping in through the cracks.

I held back, watching Janie as she slowed down and sat on the wonky-looking steps, her bathrobe flaring over them like an exotic flower. She produced a notebook I hadn't noticed and sat there, with a pen in her hand, staring into the distance.

Okay. She hadn't come here to end her life. I berated myself for even thinking that. Clearly, she needed a moment alone, writing in her diary. And I needed to leave her alone.

But it was quiet now. Too quiet. She hadn't noticed me yet, but without her footsteps obscuring the sound of mine, she would hear me if I moved. If I wasn't fast enough, she'd recognize me. My white T-shirt glowed against the dark green of the forest. She'd know I'd followed her.

Part of me wanted to make a mad dash and run back without looking over my shoulder. Deny everything. Had I been any younger, or more flexible, I could have taken a shot at that. But, as Janie had so painfully proven last night, I wasn't agile like my brother. I was a stiff rod of a man. A pathetic man currently stalking his beautiful hostess. Why was I involving myself in this woman's life? She obviously had enough to deal with.

She doesn't need you here.

I told myself this, several times to be sure, but my feet stayed glued to the ground, my eyes trained on her, watching the pen move against the paper, her gaze occasionally lifting, then dipping back on the page.

I picked up a short stick, as quietly as I could, and looked across the clearing. If I flung the stick hard enough to hit the largest tree out there, I could create sufficient distraction. She'd turn to look at the tree, giving me a moment to run off in the opposite direction. It wasn't a great plan, but I had no other ideas, and time was running out. Any second now, she'd look to her left and spot me, and I'd have to explain why I was standing in the bush, eyeballing her.

I drew in a sharp breath, trained my gaze on the tree trunk, and forced my body into action.

CHAPTER 10

Janie

I heard his footsteps behind me but didn't turn around. I didn't know why he'd followed me, but I knew it was him. It had to be him. People didn't randomly wander around the bush behind my house.

I waited for him to call my name, to force me to respond. I'd have to show my face. I imagined my swollen eyes and my blotchy, red cheeks streaked with tears.

But he didn't call for me. So, when I reached the hunting cabin, I sat down and waited. In my peripheral vision, I could see his white shirt peeking behind a silver fern. It was definitely Emir. Why was he standing there?

I took a few breaths and attempted to write something, but

no words came to mind. I doodled them along the side of the page, biding time. I still didn't feel ready. I couldn't talk to him. Yet, I felt oddly content with his presence. He cared enough, for some reason, to be here and that gave me hope. It elevated my insignificant existence.

And then something crashed.

I didn't look at the source of the sound. I'd been so focused on his presence that my entire attention zeroed in on the spot where he stood. I looked at him, and saw him hurdling an exposed root, shaking the ferns as he scrambled to get away.

"Emir!"

He froze, then slowly turned around and stepped into the clearing. "Hello."

I gestured for him to step closer, and he did, looking half spooked, half embarrassed.

I wiped my eyes. "What are you doing here?"

"I followed you. I was worried." He scratched the back of his head.

"About me?" My heart squeezed at the way he looked away, fingers still deep in his hair.

He turned to me with a frown. "Well, you ran into the forest, all by yourself. It seemed... dangerous."

A little laugh bubbled out of me like a surprise gift, lightening the load. "Dangerous?"

He walked closer until he was looming over me. "What if there's a bear? Or a snake?"

"New Zealand doesn't have bears or snakes."

He groaned, scratching his head again. "Just an example. There are always dangerous things in the wild."

I laughed, despite the pain still sitting in my chest. "The most dangerous thing in the New Zealand bush is the whitetail spider, and even that's not lethal."

"Are you serious?"

I smiled at his confusion, blinking away a fresh batch of tears. "I appreciate your concern, though."

He dipped his chin, searching for my eyes. "Even if the forest is not dangerous, you're upset. So, I'm worried."

I turned away, summoning all my willpower to regain some control. "I'll be okay. I'll meet you back at the house, okay?"

Despite my best efforts, my voice cracked, and I cursed under my breath. Fucking Shaun. I'd never been like this. I'd always been able to reel it in. I'd always been able to rise above it.

Grunting with pain, he lowered himself onto the cabin steps, right next to me. "I can't leave you here by yourself, Janie. Not like this."

"Like what?" I spat, wiping my nose on my sleeve. "Emotional? I'm not allowed to be emotional? In private?"

I risked a glance at him and met a shocked pair of brown eyes. "Of course, you're allowed to. But can you come back to the house with me and cry there? I'd feel better if I knew you were safe."

I blinked at him, trying to process the words. His face held no judgment, only concern. The longer I stared at that pair of eyes, the less shame I felt. Something about him made me feel okay to be seen, even in my current state. "You want me to be safe when

I cry?" I narrowed my eyes, too curious about him to even care about how red and puffy I looked.

He nodded.

"And you followed me because you thought New Zealand had bears and snakes? Or because I was upset?"

He huffed, a slight glow of embarrassment on his cheeks. "I did read about New Zealand flora and fauna."

"So, you followed me because I was upset? How did you know I was upset?"

"I saw the newspaper. I'm sorry. It's none of my business. But I needed to make sure you were okay."

"Emir." I smiled, a warm glow bursting in my chest. "That's sweet. Dangerously sweet."

"Dangerously?"

I sighed and nodded. He was so direct with me I had no choice. The truth beckoned forward like it had been waiting to be released. "I'm feeling very vulnerable, and you're being very sweet. Right now, you're the most dangerous thing in the New Zealand bush, for me."

He tilted his head, that frown between his eyes deepening. I couldn't resist running my thumb across it, smoothing it like before. His hand jerked towards me, but halted in the air, fingers curling into a fist. I stared at the white knuckles, my breath hot and heavy, my stomach suddenly as tight as that hand, as if he was squeezing my insides. The earthy smell of the forest intensified.

"I'd never hurt you, Janie. I don't hurt women."

"Love hurts, Emir. It hurts the most."

He flung his arms around his bent knees, blowing out a deep breath. "You're right."

He'd been hurt. I'd wondered about it, and now, I was sure. Would he one day tell me what had happened? Did I want him to?

"How old are you, Emir?" I asked.

His chin jerked up and he looked at me quizzically. "Thirty-five."

I sighed. "Baby."

"What? You can't be older than me." His gaze intensified, studying my face.

"I'm 41, Emir."

"Oh." He turned to gaze at a tall kauri tree. "Well, you don't look it."

We sat in silence for a long time, listening to the birds and the wind that rustled the leaves. I wanted to touch him again. That moment my thumb had rested on his forehead, I'd felt okay. Attached to life. And now I was drowning again. Fighting to stay afloat.

"Could you hold me?" I finally asked. "Only for a moment." I was too old for him, but he was here. Maybe I could lean on him a little, to get back on my feet.

Emir looked a little shell shocked but edged closer. Quietly grunting from pain, he draped his arm around my shoulder.

"You still sore from Pilates?"

"Injured to the point of needing a wheelchair."

I chuckled. "I'm sorry. Sounds like you need another session."

"You nearly murdered me with your weird exercise routine and now you suggest I need more of the same?"

I heard the lightness in his voice, and my heart fluttered. "Emir? Are you joking to make me feel better?"

"Sorry, it's not my domain."

"Thank you," I whispered, resting my head against his shoulder.

He squeezed me tighter. "Anything you need, Janie." His fingers stroked my shoulder, fast and restless, yet restrained.

Emotion welled in my chest, but it was quickly replaced by fluttering. Intense fluttering. I imagined what those fingers would feel like on my skin. I shoved my journal and pen into my robe pocket and took his other hand. "Anything, huh?" My laugh sounded a bit choked.

"Anything you need," he said again, and I heard it in his voice now. Those long fingers curled tighter around my shoulder.

"What if I asked you to kiss me?" My voice was barely above a whisper and a shiver ran through me. I hadn't felt like this with anyone in such a long time. My heart hammered so hard I feared it would completely lose the plot.

Emir turned to look me in the eye, capturing my face between his huge hands. "I would be torn, Janie. Because I want to, but it's not right. We're not... right for each other." His eyes held both desire and pain.

"Why?"

"I'm a guest in your house. And I'm not like my brother. I'm not a romantic. I'm not who you're looking for. You're feeling sad, but I'm only here for two weeks. It'd be foolish to get involved."

I blew a frustrated sigh, sucking in my lower lip. "Who said anything about getting involved? I only wanted a kiss. I wanted to feel… alive." I pushed his hands away and stood up. "But I guess you're right. Let's go back."

He shot up as well, wincing from pain. "I don't know what to say."

"Don't say anything." I stomped down the path, not looking over my shoulder.

He followed me in silence, and we made it back in record time. I wrestled the front door open, making sure he couldn't jump in to help, and ran into my bedroom, locking the door behind me. There, I crumbled onto the floor against it, heaving cries of shame.

He found me hideous. Or at least not good enough in some way. I was too old. Too puffy-eyed and snotty. I waited until the cries fizzled out and peeled myself off the floor. Shaun had done a number on me; I thought as I undressed and stepped into the shower. I had to get myself under control. And most importantly, I had to stop throwing myself at Turkish strangers. I must have made the poor man so uncomfortable. I shuddered, remembering the pain behind those brown eyes.

As I scrubbed myself clean, I made a promise to myself. I'd work through this pain, just like I'd worked through everything else. And I'd keep it to myself.

I'd also nip this stupid crush in the bud. I'd date someone else. Someone respectable. My body resisted the idea, but my mind was firm. I wasn't a fan of dating apps. In fact, I was terrified of them. Everyone knew my face, so it was almost impossible to tell if any interest in me was genuine or not. I'd have to find someone with a reasonably high profile, who understood what it was like. Someone local, who actually wanted to live here. Unlike Shaun. Or Emir.

I leaned my exhausted body against the ceramic tiles, letting the water run down my face. Like crying, but more efficient. And that's when the answer came to me.

As much as Tabitha turned my stomach, she was right. The recently widowed pastor, who I'd met in passing at Tabitha's son's wedding, was the perfect fit. Handsome, nice, and local. Someone at the heart of the community. Not in the public eye but known and respected in this town. And now, single. I'd barely given him a second glance at the wedding and couldn't remember anything he'd said. But he'd had a nice voice. Resonant, slightly soporific. I remembered the old ladies flocking around him, vying for attention. He must have had some charisma, even if he hadn't particularly caught my eye. But I'd been married at the time, just like him.

Okay. I closed my eyes, trying to recall Len. A good head of light brown hair, a fit body, a nice voice, taller than me. Not imposing like Emir, but tall enough. I had to stop thinking about Emir. Back to Len, I ordered myself, getting out of the shower and wrapping myself in a towel. Len was the smart, safe choice. He probably wasn't looking for a quick fling with a has-been celebrity he could boast about to his buddies. And if I got into a stable relationship and got some, I could stop humiliating myself with younger men like Emir.

Would Len even be interested in going out with me? I dressed up and, steeling my nerves, reached for my phone. Tabitha would know, and she'd be more than happy to get involved.

CHAPTER 11

Emir

I stepped into the guest room I already thought of as my bedroom, feeling surprisingly pain-free and mobile after a long run and a shower. Janie had been avoiding me for two days now, rather successfully. This morning, she'd got up so early that by the time I made it to the kitchen, I'd only found the cold remains of scrambled eggs on the counter. Later, when I went to check on Molly, I saw her coming from the pigsty, carrying an empty bucket. She'd hurried past me with a quick smile, claiming she was late for something.

I dressed up and threw myself on the bed, letting my face sink into the pillow. My neck felt stiff, as usual, but the headache was gone. I wanted to stay right here forever, holding onto that feeling. Along with the memory I'd been turning over in my mind for hours on end.

I'd held her delicate face in my hands, her lips parted, eyelids dipped. I'd seen the raw emotion on her face, the rivulets of the tears zigzagging down her cheeks. She'd looked so distraught, but it only made me want her more. Because I believed her. For the first time since I'd met her, Janie had felt unequivocally authentic. If I didn't believe the tears, I believed the way her body jerked from their force, overpowered. It held me spellbound.

I should have kissed her.

The thought wouldn't leave me alone, even if I knew my reasons. I didn't want to take advantage of her weak moment. I couldn't get involved with someone tied up to this land. What may have worked for my brother and his fiancée would never work for us. We both had too much baggage, and I didn't believe in fairy tales. I didn't even believe in casual affairs. That was for people who could take things lightly, not worrying about the future. Still, the moment she'd turned away from me and headed back to the house, I felt like I'd let go of the winning lottery ticket, watching it float down the river.

I should have kissed her.

I'd never experienced this level of regret after a well-reasoned, sensible decision, which told me something: I had to get back to dating. The way my body reacted to her was a dead giveaway that I'd been alone for too long. As soon as I got back to Istanbul, I'd force myself out there again, chatting to girls in nightclubs. The thought nearly made me dry heave, but maybe it'd be easier now, with Cem here in New Zealand. I'd represent myself, not my famous brother. With Cem engaged and our business arrangement finished, I wouldn't be seen as a gateway to a celebrity—at least I could hope so.

I filled my lungs, listening for any sounds from the kitchen. Was Janie out there? Would I run into her? No matter how awkward things had become between us, I still wanted to be near her. I wanted to make sure she was okay.

After the almost-kiss, she'd driven away and stayed out until late at night. I'd felt her absence even stronger than her presence. I'd got her phone number from Aria, through my brother, and spent all day thinking of how to approach her as I worked on her broken fencing.

At dinner time, I'd cooked some pasta and eaten it alone, thinking of her and what she was going through, and then cleaned the entire kitchen. Not that it was particularly dirty. I just wanted to do something for her.

Emir: Are you okay?

That was the only message I managed to compose and send.

Janie: Yes. Be back soon.

Okay, I didn't excel at texting, and probably deserved that response. But her 'soon' ended up being nearly an hour later, and I had to all but sit on my hands to not text her again and demand to know her location.

I brushed my teeth, changed into a fresh shirt, and padded down the corridor, announcing my arrival by clearing my throat. Janie sat at the dining table, staring at her laptop, looking polished in a mustard yellow blazer. The dining area looked the same, but one side of the living room had been cleared two armchairs pushed into the opposite corner. Had she been doing Pilates or some other exercise that needed more room?

"Hey!" She looked up and her eyes caught the sun rays streaming through the window. The dog slept on the chair right next to her, his head perched in her lap. For a second, all was well, and I braced myself for a teasing comment. In fact, I wished for it. But within a couple of seconds, her smile withered, and she returned to her screen. "There're some chicken salad and boiled eggs if you want."

I missed the teasing. I missed her smile, fake or not. I wanted to see it again. She'd been hurt by her ex-husband, and I'd somehow made things worse.

"Thank you." I snuck past her to make myself a cup of coffee. I'd spent some time yesterday figuring out how her coffee machine worked so I didn't have to bother her.

Janie turned around, meeting my eyes across the kitchen island. "I'm ordering some materials for replacing the trellis on the deck and fixing the rest of the fencing. Do you want to have a look?"

I crossed the floor to look over her shoulder, grateful for the invitation. She scrolled through her shopping cart a little too fast, so I leaned in, replacing her fingers on the touchpad with mine, scrolling again a little more slowly.

Focus on the screen, I told myself. Don't sound like an idiot.

I was no renovation expert. I'd done a bit of work on my grandfather's property, and some maintenance on my own apartment in Istanbul, but I didn't know the lingo. Whatever she gave me, I'd use. So, technically, I didn't need to finger her touchpad. Which sounded about as dirty as everything else that ran through my mind as my gaze swept across the drooping neckline of her silky top, and I caught a glimpse of a lacy bra.

"You still have a lot of nails and screws, and this looks like enough timber. Is this the same thickness you had before? Maybe you want to upgrade to something sturdier, for the next storm."

She sighed. "I wish I could, but the heavier stuff is so expensive. And I can't afford to replace everything, so it has to match."

My hand landed on her shoulder before I could assess the smartness of the move. "Don't worry. It'll be fine. I can reinforce it with some bits and pieces you have in the shed."

She shifted sideways to break contact. "I have a film crew coming in soon to do some test shots for a documentary I'm producing."

I glanced across the open space at the empty corner of the living room. Of course. "What documentary?"

"It's about the aftereffects of the floods."

"Okay." I circled the kitchen island and popped a piece of bread in the toaster. "I'll stay out of the way. I still have some work to do outside. The last stretch of the fencing up on the hill."

"That's great, thank you!" She ran her fingers through a strand of hair, avoiding my eyes. "Also, I won't be home this evening. I have a... date."

A sharp jolt travelled through me, realigning my spine. "A date? With a man?"

She finally looked at me, eyes full of defiance. "Yes. With a man."

I gave her a slow-motion nod, to buy time. "Uh-huh. I hope he's... good."

Well, that was a retarded sentence. I wasn't this unskilled at English. But her words had wiped my mind blank.

"I'm sure he's better than my ex-husband."

Desperate to close the awkward distance between us, I went back to gather my lunch and joined her at the table. I gently moved Gru one chair over and chose a seat right next to her, earning a sideways look. "I don't think you should settle for a slightly better man than your ex-husband. I read the article." I nodded at the trash can, which had since been emptied. "I think you deserve much better."

She blinked at me, her eyes wavering between emotions I couldn't quite read. "How would you know? It's one article."

I took a deep breath, silently advising myself to not get involved. To not, under any circumstances, open my mouth and share my thoughts about this woman's past relationships. But words tumbled out regardless, as if sucked out of me by the vacuum of awkward silence between us. "You're right, it's one article. And maybe it's misleading. But he did give an interview and unless they misquoted him several times, I detected, based on those quotes, that he's a pleasure-seeking, short-sighted individual who needs a lot of outside validation. Is that how you put it in English? A person who would struggle to appreciate what's right in front of them. Their eyes would always be set on something new in the horizon, anything that can fill the void. Anyone to tell them they're attractive and relevant."

She stared at me, unblinking, until I had to look away. "I apologize, Janie. I think I overstepped."

"No. You're scarily accurate." Her voice wobbled. "How do you do that? Based on one article where he's gushing about his new love and his new baby? You don't even know how our marriage ended."

The article hadn't covered the divorce in detail, yet I'd instinctively known this Shaun guy had been playing away for a long time. It was him. I could almost smell it through the cheap ink on that page.

"There were hints," I said softly. "Everything he said was about the future, what he envisioned and how excited he was about it. Nothing about the present. What he has right now doesn't excite him. The words he used, like 'surprise' and 'fate'. Like he's a mere token in a cosmic game of love. People who speak this way, they are trying to evade responsibility, to manufacture freedom for themselves... They don't have a strong sense of right and wrong. It's all relative, they say. They want to think they are helpless targets of the Cupid's arrows."

She dropped her chin to her chest, releasing a sad laugh. As her body language confirmed my words, my chest flared in anger. I wanted to hurt that guy. Badly.

I raised her chin with my fingertips, catching her eyes, making sure she was listening. "But I'm not basing this on one article. I also have solid, undeniable evidence of him being an absolute moron."

"What evidence?"

I raised an eyebrow. "Come on. He gave up on you."

Tears burst out of her eyes, and she slapped my hand away. "God dammit, Emir! Why are you doing this to me?"

I shifted backwards and turned back to my lunch. Cem was right. I should never talk to women. I'd tried to encourage her, to help her see her worth. But no. I'd made her cry.

"I'm sorry." I took a bite of my toast and tasted my lukewarm coffee. "I've been told I'm not the best at these social situations. I tend to say the wrong thing." My chest felt like it had rubber bands around it, squeezing my lungs. I listened to her gentle sobs as her face disappeared behind a wad of tissues she yanked out of a box.

"No. You say the perfect thing, and it sucks, because I can't fall for you. And I'm so vulnerable and messed up enough right now that I would do exactly that. It'd be a disaster." She sobbed harder, her voice muffled by the layers of tissue.

My heart leapt and tried to swallow the toast swarming around in my mouth. "Fall for me?" Surely, she hadn't meant to say that. "You're very upset and confused right now, Janie. But don't worry, I'm not that charming. I'm fully aware of how not charming I am. Any fleeting feelings you may have will resolve with a good night's sleep."

She looked up at me, her eyes red-rimmed and huge. "Do you not see what you are, Emir?"

"What am I?"

I hated the neediness in my voice. I'd decided long ago I was okay with being in my brother's shadow. I'd moved on. Yet, every word from her fell into a bottomless void inside of me. I was probably worse than her ex-husband, more oblivious to my own need of outside validation.

Janie shifted closer to me, running her fingers down the side of my face, her soft skin catching on my short stubble. "You're the most insightful and earnest man I've ever met. And you're way too hot not to be aware of it."

I'd heard comments about my looks, usually in comparison to Cem. If only I smiled more, I'd be so much more attractive. It made me want to smile less, to exclude myself from the pointless beauty contest I had no interest in.

"I'm sorry, Janie. I shouldn't be fishing for compliments. Or competing for your affections. You're right. Our lives are too far apart. It would never work. But I can't help feeling protective towards you. I can't help..." Pining for you? I'd run out of appropriate words. "I mean, I will keep my distance. If that's what you want."

Her eyebrows drew together. "That's what you think I want? Distance?" Her gaze flicked up at the ceiling, like casting away the stupid thought.

"Maybe it's not what either of us wants, but it's what we have to do."

She nodded, looking angry. "I know. I'm supposed to date this great guy who's local and age appropriate and a widower, for crying out loud."

"And you should! I won't stop you." I fought out the words, my throat tight.

Someone else would get to enjoy her fighting spirit. Someone else would get to touch her, and I wanted to snap their neck.

"Part of me wishes you did. Because your words are so good. They're so, so good, Emir." She looked at me, her eyes like two flames. "To be honest, I don't just want you to kiss me. I want you all over me, saying all those things. I'm sure that sounds too forward, but that's how I feel. I know you have to set boundaries, and I'll do my best to stay away from you because you're right. I feel this way because I'm lonely and sad and going through something. I tell myself I'm strong, and I am. But when you speak to me... When you... clean my kitchen!" She blinked at me, shaking her head, tears running again. "You're making me feel things I shouldn't feel."

I pulled another tissue out of the box and dried her eyes, then peeled strands of blond hair off her damp cheeks, tucking them behind her ears.

I trusted my own self-control. Maybe I could comfort her for a moment, to make sure she was okay. Still contemplating my actions, I noticed I'd already pulled her against my chest, holding her tightly against my thudding heart.

Janie. I could sense her strength, underneath the welling emotion. She was made of something durable. Something so headstrong it almost scared me. I'd never met anyone like her. A woman who allowed me to see her vulnerability, yet didn't seem to need me, or anyone, to define who she was. I inhaled her hair, a sweet smell of exotic flowers. Fresh and intoxicating. With every breath, my arm around her tightened further, my chest expanded, and the realization took hold.

I was in trouble.

CHAPTER 12

Janie

I couldn't remember feeling that good in months. Maybe years. He held me so tight my lungs flattened, but I no longer wanted to breathe. I only wanted to bathe in Emir's words and exist against his chest, breathing in the smell of his aftershave. Cinnamon, coffee, and earth.

Through the waves of endorphins coursing through me, I became aware of how I'd ended up there, like a distant, nagging sound that gradually grew louder. I'd thrown myself at him, again. I'd brought him all this hurt he hadn't caused and made it his problem.

You must be better than this, Janie.

With my every cell wailing in protest, I tore myself away and wiped my eyes. "Thank you, Emir. I needed that. I shouldn't have… but thank you."

"Anything you need, Janie." His voice was a rough whisper. "That's what I'm here for."

I didn't have time to contemplate his words because the doorbell rang, shrill like a fire alarm.

Not yet. Not yet.

I winced, drawing deep breaths to regain some control. "It's the film crew," I told Emir, and almost apologized.

He got up, stepping aside so that I could get to the door. "I'll get out of your way."

I cleared the used tissues into the trash can, straightened my blazer and approached the door.

I'm a professional. I can do this.

Gru followed me to the door, greeting everyone with far more enthusiasm than I could muster.

The two gentlemen on my doorstep smiled back, channeling a mix of nerves and cockiness. The younger and shorter one was dressed in head-to-toe army green, his vest adorned with so many pockets it must have taken him hours to find his keys. He had three giant black bags on his shoulder and huge smile on his face.

"Janie Andrews? I mean, I know it's you. I've seen you on TV. My name is Caleb Barnes, I'm the camera assistant. We're so excited to work with you!"

I shook his hand, quickly warming to his enthusiasm.

"Gus Allan. DOP." The taller and older one stuck out his hand. He had a slouchy posture, long beard and shoulder-length hair that was combed back with great care. "You're very lucky. I've just updated the gear. I told Tabitha I wasn't taking on anything new, but when she said it's for Janie Andrews, I was swayed."

"Welcome! I'm so glad you could make it."

Gru ran circles around everyone's legs. I noticed Gus's eyes flash with annoyance before he covered it with a smile, offering me a lingering handshake. "You should know that I'm bringing you the absolute best. Superior image quality. This baby can shoot 12k, raw—"

"I don't need 12k." I waved my hand, flashing him a brisk smile.

"Well, it's there if you need it. Why go for smaller if you can go big?" He widened his stance, as if to highlight his height next to his shorter assistant.

I was used to guys trying to impress me, and used to ignoring a lot of innuendo, but the way his eyes roamed my body made me nervous. If it hadn't been for Caleb, and the knowledge that Emir was around, I would have hesitated to let him in the house.

"Great! If we need to shoot a shorter piece to pull high-res screenshots, that'll come in very handy. Looks like an expensive camera." I pointed at the piece of equipment he cradled in his arms.

"You know a lot about filmmaking, don't you?" Caleb stared at me, his eyes shining.

"Very little, all in all," I assured him.

From the corner of my eye, I saw Gus's spine straighten.

"I used to be a runner, but I've been picking up some skills on the way," Caleb explained.

Gus fiddled with his camera, his jaw twitching. "You can edit 12k with proxies. And if you're worried about long takes, I have some extra memory cards that—

"Please, come in." I exchanged a quick smile with Caleb, guiding them both into the living room, quickly steering Gru out of the way. Maybe Emir could keep him company at his end of the house.

Evidently, these were the best and brightest filmmakers I could scrape together on short notice. I could only hope Gus had some skills, not just a major gear acquisition syndrome, or 'GAS' as it was more commonly called.

"You can set up here," I told them, gesturing at the cleared-up end of the living room. "I've prepared my intro which I can read to the camera once you're set up. We can use this as a test shoot. This will be part of the teaser I'm using to pitch the idea to a couple of channels."

"Setting up here?" Gus inspected the room, his eyebrows drawn.

"We'll have to work with natural light, sorry. I don't have a lot of time. I have an... appointment in town I need to get ready for."

Gus raised his hand. "No. Absolutely not. Natural light is far too unpredictable. If we need to cut it together, nothing will match. I have lights in my car. Caleb will bring them in shortly. You just go powder your nose or whatever you need to do while we set up."

Caleb heaved his bags on the floor and ran off with a giddy smile.

"Okay, fine." I grabbed my laptop and left them to it, settling into a chair in my bedroom.

So, this is what I had to work with. I could already tell Gus's interest in filmmaking was largely technical and Caleb seemed too inexperienced to be of much help. I'd have to present, direct, and figure it all out by myself.

I checked myself in the bathroom mirror and fixed my makeup. My eyes still looked slightly red, but maybe that worked for the subject matter. Over my long career, I'd heard some scathing feedback, and I knew my 'peppiness' annoyed some viewers. Well, problem solved. I didn't look peppy now. I looked like I'd been hung to dry, which seemed appropriate for a documentary on flooding.

I went over the pitch I'd written on my laptop, memorizing the lines again. If my ragtag crew managed to record both image and sound, I could make this work.

When I returned to the living room, I found the curtains drawn and a makeshift studio with a white backdrop surrounded by incredibly bright spotlights. In the middle, someone had placed one of my bar stools. The setup looked so stark and lifeless I struggled to keep the smile on my face. "Thank you, guys! This is very... professional."

Gus puffed his chest, his fingers resting on the camera he'd set up on a tripod. "We're ready for you. I have a teleprompter if you need one."

"That's okay. It's a short piece and I've memorized it. I'll do it in two parts. We'll have to get some extra footage from Esk Valley and around to use as inserts anyway."

"I have a steady cam setup that's perfect for those moving shots," Gus announced. "And a small crane and a drone in case you need them."

"No helicopter?"

"No..." He looked baffled. "But a drone is as good as—"

"Just kidding." I smiled, enjoying the way his face twitched.

Caleb laughed and Gus gave me a half-hearted chuckle in response, but his hand tightened around the grip. I shouldn't have poked back, but I couldn't help myself.

I sat on the stool, blinking at the bright spotlight. I couldn't remember the lights ever being this blinding in the TV studio. I braced myself for purple floaters and faced the camera. "Can we turn down the lighting just a bit?" I asked. "Maybe move the one that's closest to me? It's a bit distracting."

"This is classic three-point lighting." Gus grumbled, staring at his camera. "The picture looks great." He beckoned Caleb to step closer. "Once the subject is in first position, you'll want to go in manually, focus and lock it in. This way, if she moves her hand over her face to gesture or anything like that, the focus won't suddenly shift to her hand." He looked up. "Could you move your hand over your face? I'm just showing him something."

I lifted my hand, resisting the urge to flip him off as I did so. Once they finished the camera focus lecture, Gus attached a wireless microphone to the collar of my top, hovering over my neckline for needlessly long, his fingers brushing over my skin several times. I held my breath, trying not to breathe in his aftershave, which had momentarily replaced oxygen around me.

Finally, he backed away and raised his hand. "Aaand... action!"

The film set lingo felt exaggerated, given the context, but I ignored his theatrics and delivered my lines to the camera, inserting as much passion for the subject as I possibly could. I spoke about the devastation of the floods and detailed the financial losses and emotional trauma that the locals would be dealing with for a long time.

I held a subtle smile until Gus called 'cut', then got up. "Can I watch it?"

Gus pulled out a long cable and connected the camera to a large field monitor he'd set up on a side table. "Here you go."

Nothing could have prepared me for the sight. The extremely sharp footage highlighted every pore and fine line on my face. I looked old, haggard, and somehow menacing, even when I smiled. My voice sounded harsh. How long had it been since my last TV broadcast? What the hell had happened to my face?

I turned away from the screen, trying to curb my reaction. I couldn't go on camera like this. What did I need? Botox? Plastic surgery? Where could I get it on short notice, with no money?

"Is there anything we could do to make me look a bit... um... better?" I asked. "There's something wrong with this picture. It's too sharp or something. Maybe if we tried a shallower depth of field and natural light..."

"Maybe you've been looking at yourself through those TikTok filters?" Gus flashed me a condescending smile. "This is the real world. You look fine, though. Nobody's perfect." He stared at the image on the screen, his gaze pointed so low I could have sworn he was staring at my cleavage. "You can apply some filters. I have some very advanced, AI-powered ones. I'm happy to come over and help you edit."

He turned to Caleb, assuming the earlier lecturing voice. "This is what the camera does. All the insecurities come out and you'll have to soothe the star, make them feel better about themselves. Let's both tell Janie that a few wrinkles don't make her unattractive."

"You look amazing for your age, Ms. Andrews," Caleb said obligingly, smiling at me.

I could tell he was genuine, but Gus's patronizing tone had already gotten under my skin. "Okay. You can stop that. I know exactly how old I am. I don't have a problem with aging. It's society that has a problem."

Caleb nodded vigorously, his blond fringe shaking. "Exactly."

"I'll just redo my makeup and we can go again." I held my chin high, even if my voice quivered ever-so-slightly.

Maybe I was losing my looks. Maybe it was all over now. Living in the countryside, tending to plants and animals, I hadn't focused on my face. The couple of mirrors I had in the house had strategically soft lighting. I'd enjoyed the break. Between working in the garden and running the film office, I didn't have too much time for navel-gazing, the professional disease that had infected a hundred percent of my peers on TV. If that meant I now had to face the inevitable changes my face and body had undergone in the last couple of years, so be it. I'd face it. In high definition. Thousands of women would feel better about themselves when they saw me like that.

But no matter what I told myself, I couldn't shake the

desperation. Being on TV messed with your head. It made you feel like your appearance was everything. Your net worth, earning potential and job opportunities all depended on it.

I thought I could leave it behind and rid myself of those values, but it wasn't just TV. It was the world. It was my reality, even here in Napier. I'd thrown myself at Emir, a gorgeous younger man, and he'd turned me down. He'd seen what I'd seen on that screen. I was far too old for him.

Tears burning behind my eyes again, I removed the wireless mic and left the room, forcing myself to walk slowly when I felt like running for the hills.

CHAPTER 13

Emir

I shouldn't have been spying on her. Had I not learned anything from that trip to the forest? I'd just finished fixing the fence and made it back to the house, when I saw the small, blond man in some kind of G.I. Joe outfit carrying a large LED light.

My interest in photography and lighting went back years. It had been a handy skill when managing my brother. His public image depended on photos and videos, and Cem was as fragile as any actor. A bad photo attracted mean comments which in turn ruined days and weeks. It was bad business. My brother was an exceptionally handsome man, but anyone looked undesirable from an unflattering angle, or in poor lighting. So, I'd learned to do it right. I'd always made sure he looked his absolute best, even after a rough night.

I told myself it was my professional curiosity that drew me closer. Watching the blond guy enter through the front door, I circled the building, peeking in through the living room window.

"Shh," I told Gru, who'd found me in the field and kept following me around, climbing up to the windowsill to peer inside. I didn't mind the company. The dog was excitable but surprisingly smart.

I'm not getting involved, I told myself. This is none of my business.

The two guys had their backs to me, allowing me to observe how they set up the worst three-point lighting I'd ever witnessed. Cranking the huge LED screens to their highest setting, they lit poor Janie like a late-night football game, throwing dark shadows under her nose and chin. Even from a few yards away, through a windowpane, I could tell how bad the picture looked.

She was such a gorgeous woman that even the substandard lighting couldn't hide her beauty. It made me angry, though. So angry that I stayed, getting more involved by the minute.

I snuck into the house through the back door and tracked all the way to the living room doorway, giving Gru another warning to stay quiet. Not wanting to disturb them in the middle of a take, no matter how poorly lit, I waited behind the door until I heard sounds of conversation. I cracked the door, listening to assess the situation.

My heart pounded in my ribcage as I heard the stupid excuses and gaslighting from the pompous, bearded guy. How could he talk to her like that? Something about his manner made the blood chill in my veins. This guy wasn't just a terrible filmmaker. He was bad news.

As Janie left the room, her footsteps fading away, my anger grew even more palpable. Before I had time to think it through, I barged in. The two guys turned to me, startled.

"What the hell do you think you're doing with that lighting setup?" My voice was edged with barely controlled rage, my eyes locked onto the bearded guy. "Do you have any idea how unflattering that is? You're casting harsh shadows and making her look older than she is."

The bearded guy's initial surprise turned to defensiveness. "I know what I'm doing. This is classic three-point lighting, which achieves—"

"Nothing! The only thing you achieved is counting to three! The lights are too hot, too high and everything is too close together." I gestured at the screen with a terrifying freeze frame of Janie. "She looks like she's being interrogated at a police station."

The smaller guy whipped his head from side to side like he was watching a tennis game, not sure who to root for.

I moved closer to the lighting equipment, assessing it critically. "You need to lower these two and add a hair light here. Do you have anything to bounce the light off? A white board? You can't point those LED lights to her face at full volume or you'll have her squinting through the entire shoot."

The bigger guy straightened his back, which made him look a little less like a sack of potatoes. He couldn't reach my height though. I glared down at him until he finally shuffled his feet and began adjusting the lights.

"I don't usually take direction from non-professionals," he muttered.

My lips curled. "Well, it's your lucky day. I have a master's degree in photography."

I'd only minored in it, but he didn't need to know that. I watched for a moment as he haplessly moved the lights down, then up again, until I pushed him aside and did it myself. Asking the small guy to sit in Janie's spot, I adjusted the angles, added a diffuser, and tweaked the color temperature until the blond guy bathed in a warm soft glow. Taking a test shot, I asked them to view the new picture on the screen.

The blond guy stared at it in awe. "Man, you're a pro! I'm Caleb, by the way. Nice to meet you!"

He offered his hand, and I shook it, ignoring the scoff from the bearded dude.

"I've been learning from Gus," Caleb said, gesturing at him, "but I'd love to learn from you as well. Anything you could teach me."

I gave him a distracted nod. "Sure. I'll explain it later."

My mind was already on Janie. Where was she? How was she feeling? Leaving the makeshift set, I walked down the corridor towards where I thought Janie's bedroom must have been. Out of the three doors, only one was closed. I knocked on it.

"One minute," she called from inside, her voice strained.

"It's me. Emir."

After a moment, the door opened a crack and her red-rimmed eyes peered at me. "Is something wrong?"

"Yes."

The door flung open. "What? Is it Molly?"

I shook my head, my chest squeezing from frustration. "Your horse is fine. You're not."

She shook her head, her eyebrows drawn. "I'm okay. Just, regrouping for the next take. I—"

"You're working with idiots." There was no polite way to say it. And I didn't feel like being polite. I felt like punching someone. Preferably someone with a scraggly beard and a stupid sneer on their face.

Janie's eyes flicked down the hallway. "Yeah, it's hard to find talent in Napier. But at least they have a lot of gear. I'm grateful."

"I redid the lighting. They botched it up. Horrible. I haven't seen anything that bad in a long time."

Hope lit up her eyes. "Seriously? You think the lighting was bad?"

Her voice broke and something inside me snapped.

"Stay," I told Gru, leaving him in the hallway as I grabbed Janie by the shoulders and pushed us into the bedroom, closing the door behind us.

She responded to my touch like a dance partner, matching my steps, giving in just enough to keep us moving, reversing until I had her pinned against the opposite wall.

How could I make her see what I saw? One hand on her shoulder, my fingers traced her face, catching wayward tears, brushing soft, pink lips. I spoke quietly, my face a breath away from hers. "You're gorgeous, Janie. Someone like you needs to be lit like a goddess. Those morons..." My jaw tightened.

Her breath turned shallow, and she blinked at me. "Emir. Why are you so angry?"

Why, indeed?

I shook my head. "Because it's not right. Those halfwits don't deserve to be anywhere near you. I'll shoot your film, Janie. Let me do it. I can't watch that incompetence."

"You want to shoot my documentary?" She looked confused.

I couldn't blame her. Part of me was equally confused by the words pouring out of me. This wasn't what I'd come here to say, although I hadn't planned any words at all. I'd only wanted to see her, make sure she was okay.

"I'll do what I can in the time we have. I promise."

She frowned. "But we're supposed to prepare for the engagement party. There's no time. I was only planning to film the teaser so that I can pitch the project and maybe secure some funding. The filming will happen later. If it ever happens."

"Perfect! I'll shoot the teaser for you. And when you get funding, you hire a better crew, okay?"

Her palms pressed against the wall, her chest rising and falling. "Okay."

The silky fabric of her top dipped lower in the middle, offering a glimpse between her breasts. Not that I was looking. With heroic effort, I coaxed my gaze higher, admiring those cheekbones and the elegant arch of her eyebrows. She was a work of art, and I couldn't wait to film her.

The corner of her mouth tugged into a small smile. "Do you like me, Emir?"

I swallowed, lifting my hand off her shoulder and taking half a step back. "You're my hostess. I appreciate you. I—"

"Emir. I keep telling myself it's a cultural thing, that you have this protective streak and a misplaced sense of responsibility, because you're staying in my house. But I'm confused."

She was right. As much as I wanted to pretend my feelings were appropriate and my actions logical, we were currently standing in her bedroom and the pulsing in my groin told me my body had made note of the fact before my conscious brain even kicked in. I wanted her, and she deserved the truth.

"I'm sorry, Janie. I'm attracted to you, and that's obviously confusing things. But I don't want to make you uncomfortable. I only wanted to make sure you're okay."

"You're not making me uncomfortable," she said, reaching for my arm.

Her fingers grazed the hair on my arm, making it stand up. "You're making me frustrated."

"Frustrated?"

"And undesirable."

"Undesirable?" That was the last thing I wanted. "Why?"

She gave me a sad smile. "Because you don't want me." She held up her hand. "And it's okay. I respect your reasons, whatever they are. I'm just telling you how I feel. How it makes me feel."

I rubbed my forehead, trying to banish the sting of pain that had settled in again. "But you are so desirable. You should feel like... a queen."

"Then kiss me."

CHAPTER 14

Janie

I hadn't felt such a surge of nerves since my first time on live TV. My heart pounded in my ears and face burned like I was peering into a hot oven, trying to see if the scones had risen or utterly failed. The moment of truth.

His brown eyes narrowed at me, then flicked to the side as if searching for an answer and came up empty, desperate. Bested.

He lifted my chin and held my gaze for one intense moment before his mouth claimed mine. I'd never been kissed like that, plucked like a flower, admired, and then devoured. As his tongue swept in to meet mine, my knees wobbled, wet heat surged between my thighs and a multi-syllable gasp erupted from my mouth into his. This was better than anything I'd imagined. Like blowing a lid off a pressurized bottle, watching the contents spill out. I was equally scared and desperate to find out what it held inside.

Emir's hand rested on my waist, flattening me against the wall. It felt hot and hard, like every part of him. I knew he was holding back. I could see it in his eyes as he pulled away, studying my face, before he trailed his mouth across my cheek, his stubble teasing the tiny nerve endings on my skin.

"Janie." His rough whisper landed in the crook of my neck, then his mouth landed on my skin. I rested my head against the wall, offering myself to him like I was feeding a vampire. I wanted to offer him everything.

The sheer force of the kiss tensed every muscle in my body. His hands slipped on my lower back, pulling our hips together, confirming what I'd suspected. Those dress pants were hiding serious weaponry. I wanted to reach out and touch him, but I feared he would jump. So, I slid my hands down his backside, tracing his buttocks. Tight as a drum. Just like every other part of him. Hard and demanding.

With each passing second, my excitement built, yet I became more aware of the situation. This wasn't our moment. I couldn't stay here. I had a film crew in my living room and a piece to camera I had to record.

"Emir."

He pulled back, his stubble grazing the skin on my neck, and looked at me with dazed, glossy eyes. "I apologize."

"Don't you dare." I took his face in my hands and placed one more kiss on his lips. Slow, soft and savoring. "I needed that. But I have to deal with the camera guys. I have to redo my lines. I'm not done with you, though."

His brow knitted and he stepped backwards, running his hands through his hair. "I never should have…"

I gave him an apologetic smile. "I know, but the way you kiss, Emir. I'm going to need more."

He shook his head, eyes dark and troubled. "If you want to date that other guy, you need to stay away from me. I mean it." His front teeth clamped over his bottom lip, and he hissed a breath.

"Why?" I raised an eyebrow, risking a subtle smile. "You jealous?"

He launched at me, again trapping me against the wall. His mouth stopped a breath away from mine and his low growl caressed my lips. "Yes, Janie. Very jealous. I can't stand the idea. But you shouldn't let that stop you." I winced as his fingers tightened around my arms. I would never stop him. No part of me contained a shred of will to push him away. I only wanted to see how far I could take him. If I could make him give up the fight.

"Right now, I can't even remember his name." Sliding my arm between us, I brushed my thumb across the corner of his mouth, hoping he'd smile back, even a little. "I'm having an acute memory lapse. It has something to do with your mouth."

His lips tugged a little and I felt it in my belly. What was that odd connection? Why was it so satisfying to tease tiny smiles out of this man? I'd happily cancel the date and spend all evening chasing one smile, or even a smirk. But from the resolute darkness that fell over his gaze, I knew that option wasn't on the table.

He stepped back, adjusting the crotch of his pants. "I apologize. I won't touch you again. I don't want to complicate your life. If you want to date this other man, date him. Go, Janie."

What *was* the other guy's name? Lester? Link?

"I'd rather date you," I said boldly.

He looked at me with regret. "It's not a good idea."

His hands twitched, and for a moment, I thought he might touch me again, but he folded his arms tightly. Securely. Moments ago, I'd felt his desire, and I didn't doubt it. He wanted me, but his mind had overruled his body, again.

"Maybe we don't have much of a future, but we're both single, right?"

He nodded.

"And I don't know about you, but I'm lonely."

He nodded again.

"So, I don't see why we couldn't be right for each other, right now."

"I don't want you to get hurt."

"I'm already hurt."

"It'll hurt more later if we get more attached."

His logic was flawless, but the pain behind his eyes radiated across the space between us. I could almost touch it.

"Someone hurt you, didn't they? Something happened."

He looked out the window, his jaw stiff, giving me no answer. I didn't need one.

"And you're hellbent on avoiding the pain."

His eyes were hard when they returned to me. "Why manufacture more of it? There are much better options, for both of us. You can date this local man and I can find someone in Istanbul. We can both build something long-term and secure."

Long-term and secure. Like a treasury bond.

"That's logical," I conceded. "But you can't avoid pain. It's part of life. It'll find you."

He rubbed his forehead, the evidence of pain right there. I guided him to the bedroom chair and began massaging his shoulders. As I pulled his head against the back rest to work on his scalp, he closed his eyes and exhaled so heavily my chest tightened.

"I hate to see you in pain, Emir. And I admire your willpower. Thank you for kissing me. You made me feel alive. Attractive. I'm sorry if I made you uncomfortable—" I placed a finger over his lips to shush his protests— "I don't want to cause you pain, even if I feel like I could take it myself. Even if I feel like it doesn't matter, because I'm already in pain. I'm glad you have more willpower than I do. Maybe it's enough for both of us."

CHAPTER 15

Emir

I stifled a groan because my willpower was hanging by a hair. But if I admitted that to her, I'd lose my only advantage. I had to at least pretend I was under control, until I could get out of here and give my junk an ice bath or something. But I couldn't leave, not while her fingers were working their magic on my head, chasing away the pain. I needed Janie. Even if I managed to keep my hands off her, I was already in for a world of hurt. I didn't want to leave this house. I didn't want to be away from her.

"I think I have to go back," she finally said, stroking my hair to smooth the tangles she'd created. "I'm happy to massage you again later. As much as you want."

"Except when you're out with that guy." My voice took on a

dark tone that betrayed me. "But that's okay."

"Okay." Her voice sounded strained as she stepped away to check her makeup at the bathroom mirror, then left the room.

I followed a few steps behind, watching from the living room doorway as she directed the beardy and blondie and did another take. I stared in awe as she pulled back her shoulders, faced the lens and delivered her passionate, heartfelt piece to the camera. Janie was a professional. My admiration for her grew every moment I spent in her house, but it wasn't her skill and charisma that drew me closer. It was the vulnerability. Right now, she was essentially faking it for the camera, her entire being brimming with friendly confidence. But I'd seen behind the curtain, and I found the real Janie even more fascinating.

What were the chances I'd find someone like her back home? Someone so captivating, yet local and thus acceptable to my family. I'd sworn to myself I'd stay away from actresses, but how could I? There was a reason I'd been drawn to one in the first place—the deep admiration, even jealousy I felt when I watched someone like Janie. She was so connected. So attuned. She sensed my pain and immediately put her hands on it, easing the tightness that gripped my whole being.

I'd never be like that, but she'd looked at me like she was riveted by my very being. Was it real? She was experiencing major upheaval and feeling down on herself. She wanted to feel seen and loved. Didn't we all? And I was conveniently in her house and attracted to her. I couldn't hide it. But what if something deeper was growing between us? Something I couldn't control.

Taking a step back, I could usually analyze anything—reduce the reality into cause and effect, predictable chess moves. This time, I could see the unavoidable hurt down the line, but the details remained hazy. I couldn't tell how this would play out. I couldn't even tell how I was going to behave. Would my willpower hold?

Janie ran her lines one more time, and we all watched the playback of the final take. I edged closer, pulled in by the radiant image on the screen. I wasn't a big fan of the white backdrop, but at least the lighting now worked. Her skin looked peachy, and her eyes sparkled.

"Looks great!" The blond guy enthused, earning a glare from his bearded mentor.

"Thank you so much, Gus. If you could send me the footage sometime this week, that'd be amazing." Janie smiled at him.

Gus smiled back, his gaze roaming her chest, and my hands flexed from an overwhelming desire to escort him out of the house. "I can stay back and upload them now if you want? It'll take a while, but—"

Janie cast him an apologetic smile. "I'm sorry but I need to wrap up right now. I have a date tonight and I need to get ready."

"A date?" Gus glanced at me.

"Not with me. I'm just here to fix the fencing," I grumbled.

He relaxed a little. "Well, okay. We'll call it a day. How about those aerial shots in Esk Valley you talked about? Let me know what time suits."

Janie blushed, glancing at me. "Thank you. Emir offered to do those shots for me, so I won't need more of your time at this stage.

You've been very helpful, though."

Something on Gus's face shifted in a way that alerted my body to danger. He kept a smile on his face, tilting his head at Janie. "I'm not sure I'd be comfortable with relinquishing creative control in the middle of a shoot like this. I was under the impression that I'd get to shoot and edit the entire piece, as well as add it to my showreel."

Janie rubbed her forehead, eyes flashing with desperation. "We would credit you for the camera work, obviously. But there's very little editing. I can take care of that."

Gus folded his arms, lips pursed. "Fine. But I must put my foot down with the filming, Janie. Either you want to work with me, or you don't. Do I need to remind you of everything I bring to the table, free of charge?" He nodded at the impressive pile of gear his assistant was currently packing away. "Don't you think some high-quality drone shots would be useful for showing the devastation of the floods?"

The knot in my stomach wound tighter. I didn't have this kind of filming gear. All I had was my trusted camera. I'd do anything for Janie, but I couldn't turn into a drone.

"He's right," I said through gritted teeth. "If you want aerial shots like that, you'll need his help. I have a decent camera but no drone."

Gus straightened his back, vindicated. What a dick. The guy was so into his gear he'd probably upgraded his actual dick with some sort of high-tech equipment.

Janie's voice rose. "Okay, then. If it's not too much trouble. I'll call you about the time."

"I can do tomorrow," he informed us. "It's easier on the weekend."

She walked the men to the door, and we watched them load up their banged-up Hyundai with the camera gear. The younger guy waved us goodbye before hopping onto the passenger side.

"I don't like this," I blurted as their car disappeared.

Janie didn't miss a beat, her eyes boring into mine. "You suggested it."

"Well, if you want free drone footage..."

She shrugged. "We need something to show the devastation. Aerial shots might not even be the best choice. Maybe what we need is to zero in on one of the collapsed houses, bring the subject closer and more personal."

I stared at her mouth, holding my breath. I could hear the hurt behind her words. I hadn't fought to take over her project and replace those guys. I hadn't done what I'd promised, and I wanted to kick myself. Why hadn't I told the guy I had a drone and told him to leave? There was something fishy about him and I wanted him out of Janie's life, for good.

"Call him and cancel," I told her. "I'll do those shots. I'm sorry. I thought you wanted the drone shots. I didn't want to mess up your plans."

She crossed her arms across her chest and pinned me with a look I couldn't interpret. "Maybe it's best you stay away. That way, nobody gets hurt. I can't offer you any guarantees. I like you, Emir. I'd risk my heart for you. I'd take the hurt. But if you don't want to risk it, don't. Stay away and let me live my life." She glanced at the door. "I need to get ready for my date."

Her eyes flashing with fury, she traipsed back into the house, leaving the front door open. My arms flung out to catch her, too late. She was right. I was a coward. I wasn't protecting her. I was protecting myself. My chest aching, I returned inside and retreated to the guest room, throwing myself on the bed.

I must have left the doors open since Gru followed me, jumping on the bed. He curled next to me, burrowing under the blanket, and I stroked his scraggly fur, grateful for the company.

"Gru, listen. You're Janie's dog. You should be with her," I finally told him, patting him on the back.

The dog seemed to understand me since he jumped off the bed and zoomed away. I wished I could have sent a message with him. I just wasn't sure what to say. Apologize? Ask her to cancel the date? Now that I thought about it, the date bothered me even more than the useless film crew. But I couldn't ask her to cancel. What could I give her in return? A few short days of passion, followed by a grueling breakup? Because breaking up with Janie would be too painful. Being ten thousand miles away from her would be even worse.

I rubbed my forehead, groaning from pain. Why did I have to be like this? Why couldn't I be like my brother, throwing myself headfirst into whatever took my fancy. Cem went all in, ignoring red flags, disregarding consequences. And somehow, things worked out for him.

I'd always been the dependable, sensible one. I thought before I acted. Where had my approach taken me? I was currently without steady income, an overqualified, 35-year-old farmhand trying to keep my hands off my beautiful hostess.

Who was off to date another guy.

Fuck.

Outside, the afternoon light had turned warm and low—a sign of evening approaching. Janie would be out the door and away all evening. How could I keep sane, waiting for her to return? What if the date went well and she ended up staying with him? Did she sleep with guys on the first date? She'd kissed me back without reservations, melting into my every move, as far as I was willing to take her. I imagined laying her down on the bed. How would she have reacted? It wasn't like we could have done anything, with her film crew out there, waiting. But it didn't stop me from imagining it.

There was nothing coy about Janie. She'd told me what she wanted, plain and simple. She was willing to risk it.

I'd made my choice and I'd given her my answer.

Why couldn't I stop obsessing over this?

Desperate for distraction, I got up, threw on a jacket and headed out the side door to the deck. I spent some time fixing the awning which had partially collapsed. I was waiting on a shipment of materials for fixing the deck and the rest of the fencing. On my way, I noted that Janie's car was still parked in front. She hadn't left yet. I walked down the driveway towards the stables. On the way, I checked on the chickens, pocketing two eggs I found. The veggie garden behind the chicken coop looked dry, so I watered it.

I'd already learned Janie's daily schedule—when she fed the pigs, chickens and the horse, and the haphazard way she tended to her garden. The local climate seemed to help her out with daily bursts of rain, so most of the plants thrived regardless.

I walked around and pulled some weeds and searched online for a way to get rid of the white butterflies eating her kale.

Finally, I made it to the stables. I examined Molly's eye, which looked a lot better, and gave her the drops. She barely reacted this time, already used to my presence. The late afternoon sun was still warm and gorgeous, so I let her out.

I was watching her gallop up the hill when I heard the engine. Janie's car. She was leaving for her date. Everything in me tightened at the thought, and the headache returned like an internal hammer pounding my skull. What if they hit it off? Most people didn't get that far on the first date, but Janie would. She was in a vulnerable place, and brave enough to bypass the usual pretense. She'd done it with me. What if she turned to this other guy and confided in him? What if she fell in love with him? I would lose my chance with her if I ever had one.

I'd made all my decisions carefully, to avoid pain. But right now, my whole body ached. I rubbed my temples, trying to relax my shoulders, but it seemed to do nothing. What if this pain was even worse? What if Janie's new man wanted me out of the house and I'd lose her massages as well? I couldn't help the niggling realization that time was running out. There was an offer on the table, and it was about to expire.

I rushed towards the driveway, waving my arms to get her

attention, but her Lexus sped past me, leaving me in a cloud of dust. Had she not noticed me, or deliberately ignored my signal?

CHAPTER 16

Janie

I closed the front door behind me, my nerves buzzing like the coffee maker I'd cranked up to its highest setting to perk up for the evening. My own house had become a mood, one that was hard to shake. It had taken ninety minutes of preparation, including a bubble bath singing along to Abba, to get me into a state where I was ready to meet anyone else at all.

As I'd prepared for the date, I'd looked up Len online, trying to find out more about him. I was hoping to find something to pique my curiosity, or even an interesting conversation topic, but Len didn't have much of an online presence outside of his job. His name only popped up boringly and appropriately in context of weddings and funerals. Even in the rare photos, he stood in the background, out of focus, his black shirt and white collar the picture of service.

Before leaving, I'd once again walked from one end of the house to the other, hoping to bump into Emir in my pre-date glory. His door was ajar, his bed made with military style precision, but Emir must have been outside, possibly avoiding me.

It was easier this way. I didn't need to see his conflicted face or hear his opinions on Len. The guy who'd just kissed me and pushed me away could hardly be impartial. Still, I'd changed into a shimmering teal dress and heels, blow-dried my hair in soft waves and spent an hour on my makeup and was hoping to walk past him. He'd seen me at my worst. It didn't seem fair that when I finally pulled myself together, he'd disappear. All the effort I'd put into getting ready, wasted.

I unlocked my car, my inside contracting with shame. How could I think like that? I'd prettied myself up for Len, obviously. He was the one who needed to witness and appreciate my efforts, not Emir. Why couldn't I get this message through to my thick skull?

As I passed the stables, I noticed him, a fraction of a second that registered as a flash in the corner of my eye. It took me a moment to realize what I'd seen, and by the time I'd rounded the bend, turning onto the main road, it was too late to check in the rearview mirror. Maybe I'd imagined the whole thing. If I turned back, I'd be late for my date. So, I kept driving, wondering if I'd seen Emir or imagined him.

The sandwich board outside the restaurant advertised a quarter pound steak with various types of potatoes. As I stepped inside, I was greeted by the general hubbub of middle-aged men enjoying happy hour, a rugby game blasting on the TV above the bar. Not a quiet, intimate place then. Maybe that was for the best.

I scanned the wooden tables and sturdy chairs set under windows overlooking the busy downtown street. It looked like one of those middle-of-the-road places with nothing exciting about it. Traditional, yet without any Art Deco influences Napier was known for. I'd walked past many times and had never even noticed the restaurant. But maybe Len knew better.

Where was he anyway?

I edged closer to the dining side, turning away from the bar in case any of the patrons recognized me. It didn't happen so regularly anymore, now that I wasn't on TV every morning, but seeing the TV screen above the bar still gave me an uneasy feeling.

"Janie?"

I whipped around and found Len standing behind me, dressed in jeans and a beige jacket with no tie, his brown hair combed to perfection.

"Hi, Len." I smiled, accepting his friendly handshake.

He led me to the farthest table, obscured by a row of artificial plants, and I sighed with relief. Sitting here, nobody could see me from the bar.

"Nice place," I said, sliding into the padded seat.

Len smiled. "I'm aware it's probably not your speed, but their steak is great and there're never any tourists."

"You don't like tourists?" My mind jumped to Emir, and I focused my eyes on the dimple on his clean-shaven cheek.

Dimples were cute. Emir didn't have one. Or maybe he did. I hadn't actually seen him smile. Okay. I officially couldn't get the Turkish man out of my head.

Len shrugged, giving me a sheepish smile. "I find those tourist traps a bit disingenuous, and overpriced."

"For sure."

He leaned in. "I must confess I'm not well versed in fine dining. Or dating in general. I was afraid that if I took you somewhere fancy, I might commit a terrible faux pas and embarrass you. Or you'd get the wrong idea of what I can afford."

He had that self-deprecating, easy manner that made him instantly relatable, yet somehow teflon. It made me think of my colleagues on the morning show. There was a similar energy. On air, you had to be endlessly affable and witty, so most of us learned to smile and joke our way through life, always keeping the tone upbeat. I believed in smiling. It energized me even when my soul felt heavy, but now I wanted to lose the chitchat. I wanted to be real, even uncomfortable. The way I could be with Emir. Maybe it was possible with Len, too, if I was brave enough to try.

"It's all good," I told him. "I'm on a tight budget myself. The divorce left me out of pocket and I'm skimping on anything non-essential. So, I'm not much of a catch in that sense."

"Well, that worked out perfectly, then!" He let out an uncomfortable laugh, handing me one of the menus waiting in a stand. "The steaks are great. Order anything you like, it's on me! Wait..." He opened his own menu and pretended to pore over it in panicked frenzy. "Just checking they don't have any hundred-dollar lobster or something. I'd have to eat my words."

I laughed politely, browsing the list of hearty meals. No lobsters. "I think you're safe."

The waiter appeared with a jug of water and two glasses.

"Did you want a glass of wine?" Len asked. "I'm happy to order you a drink, but I like to keep a clear head. Especially on a first... date."

Oh, great. How could I drink if he wasn't drinking? I shook my head. "A clear head sounds good."

It was a good call. Neither of us evidently needed social lubricants. Although, one glass of wine might have made his jokes funnier.

He ordered the rump steak, and I chose the chicken salad, my second one today. Oh, dear. I could compare it to the one I'd made for lunch at home.

Len picked up the conversational ball, asking polite questions about my career, carefully avoiding the topic of marriage. After a moment, a swell of cheers carried from the bar, drowning our voices. The home team must have scored.

"Sorry about the racket," he said, glancing at the bar. "I forgot about the game."

"It's good," I assured him. "Like a smoke screen, right? Nobody will pay any attention to us." I risked a quick glance over my shoulder. "I bet these are all locals. Someone might know you."

His shoulders tightened. "You're right. But it's even more likely they'll recognize you. Sorry, I should have considered that."

"Well, we agreed to meet in public. There's always a risk. How are you finding it? Being known by people, I mean."

He smiled. "I'm not that well known, honestly. Most people don't go to church anymore. Even people I've married don't always recognize me. I prefer it that way. Fame is a double-edged sword, which I'm sure you know."

He peered at me, as if gauging my attitudes towards the subject.

"I know." I took a sip of water. "I'm hoping people eventually forget my face and I can live my life under the radar again."

"I saw your face in the paper on Thursday." He winced.

I nodded, remembering the article about Shaun. They'd put my face in the side column, in a little ex-wife explainer box. I hated this side of publicity, but did I truly want to get out? In the last year, I'd organized several interviews for myself, desperately trying to project a positive image out there. You could only do that by giving them another story, one where I was the main character. If I was completely honest with myself, I didn't want out as much as I wanted control. But it seemed I wasn't willing to be honest with Len.

The waiter returned with a tall candle and clicked his lighter over it several times until the flame finally appeared. So, he'd figured out this was a first date, and since alcohol was not consumed, soft candlelight would work as beer goggles.

When he left, I took a deep breath, reaching for my brave. "We're both old enough to say what we mean, right?"

Len cleared his throat and cocked his head, assuming an expression he probably used at work. The compassionate listening face. "And what is it you want to say, Janie?"

I narrowed my eyes, trying to see through the act. On the surface, he seemed genuine, but somehow impenetrable. Unshakable.

"What was your marriage like? If your wife hadn't died, would you still be together?"

Len jerked back, gripping the side of the table. "Um... yes, probably. It wasn't perfect, but divorce wasn't an option."

"So, you'd never divorce?"

He shook his head very slowly, holding my gaze. "I don't see that as an option. But I'm not judging you. Or anyone else."

"It wasn't my choice," I said, my voice small.

He reached across the table and took my hand, stroking it gently. "I know, Janie. I know."

My eyes threatened to tear up. Trying not to blink, I turned to look out the window. And that's when I saw Emir.

CHAPTER 17

Emir

I admit, calling an Uber to follow Janie into town wasn't the smartest decision I'd ever made. By the time I arrived in front of the Masonic hotel, the only landmark I could think of when booking the ride, I still had no plan, and no idea where Janie was dining with this guy. But for some reason, I felt better being here. Closer to her.

Maybe I wouldn't even tell her I'd been here. I'd just take a walk, eat something, and return. Hopefully before she did, although I hated the idea of her staying out late.

I walked around town, admiring the Art Deco detailing and signs, all perfectly representing the 1930s, watching the Saturday night buzz at bars and restaurants. Happy couples and groups of singles, dressed up so casually I felt overdressed in my dress shirt.

After ten minutes of walking, I'd convinced myself that I didn't want to find Janie. I didn't want to interrupt her date or embarrass her. I only wanted to see the guy she was dating. She'd told me nothing about him, not even his name, and my imagination was running wild.

I was passing another restaurant, about to order Uber to get back, when a flicker of light behind a window caught my eye. Someone was lighting a tall candle. I stopped, observing the scene. I should buy some candles, I thought. They were an excellent way to add ambience and take beautiful photos. I could snap one of Janie. As the flame on the candle grew, my gaze swept to the person next to it.

My breath caught in my throat. I was staring into Janie's eyes. Huge, bewildered eyes. She was so close I could have reached out to touch her arm, had there not been a glass in-between. Her eyes flicked across the table, at the man holding her hand. Wait? Why was he holding her hand?

Janie looked back at me, raising her brows, and I slowly shook my head, gesturing over my shoulder, then backtracked to where I'd come from, until my legs hit the outdoor table of the next restaurant. It was an Italian one, with checkered tablecloths. I took a seat, ordering a cup of tea and a pizza. There. Now I had a reason to be here. I was hungry, after all.

I sat at the table, my gut in knots, my eyes trained at the doorway of the neighboring restaurant. Would Janie make an excuse and come out to talk to me? Or would she tell her date she was being stalked by an unhinged Turkish man? Every part of that sentence was accurate, I realized, cold sweat prickling on my neck. Following her had been a huge mistake.

But I couldn't let go of her. Not yet. Was it possible to have this experience, let myself get swept into an affair that crashed and burned within two weeks? On the surface, it didn't seem that dangerous. Someone else might have considered it a bit of fun. But I wasn't a fun guy.

After the longest fifteen minutes of my life, everything arrived at once—my pizza, my tea, and Janie. She snuck behind me as my attention was momentarily on the waiter and grabbed a slice with the most capsicum and pepperoni.

"Thank you! I was starving. The salad I ordered was drenched in this disgusting curry sauce. So much mayo. Yuck." She grinned, sitting across the table. "Also, what are you doing here?"

"Please, help yourself." I pushed the plate towards her. "I—" I looked at her and lost the ability to speak.

Janie looked incredible. Her hair swirled over her shoulders in shiny, loose waves and her eyes hypnotized me. The dark green dress hugged her curves so perfectly my mouth went dry.

"You look..." The words had truly deserted my brain.

"I look...?" She prompted.

"Great," I finished lamely.

"Great," she repeated brightly. "You don't think it's too revealing?" She brushed her fingers down the plunging neckline of the dress, eyes mock innocent.

Yes. It was too revealing for dating someone else, but I couldn't tell her that.

Janie leaned in, her eyes serious. "What are you doing here, Emir?"

"I was feeling a bit stir crazy alone in the house, so I came here for dinner."

"So, you're not spying on my date?" Her eyes narrowed.

I looked her square in the eye. "I am." Honesty was the only thing I was good at. If I tried to keep up any false story, it'd unravel fast. "I'm sorry, Janie. I don't think I can do this."

"Do what?"

I gestured at the other restaurant, then at her and the sexiest dress ever. "This! You, in that... dating someone else. I can't."

This wasn't what I'd agreed on with my brain only moments ago. But as soon as I saw her, some primal part of me reared its ugly head, spouting these nonsensical, jealous words.

CHAPTER 18

Janie

I dropped my half-eaten pizza slice, my insides sloshing, a fresh lump in my throat. This man was impossible.

"You don't want to date me," I hissed. "Ergo, you have no say. You can't just barge in here in the middle of my date and tell me that. I had to lie to him. I told him I had a weird feeling I parked in a handicap spot. I don't think he believed me." I glanced over my shoulder, cringing at the thought of going back in there.

There was nothing wrong with Len, but there was something seriously wrong with me. I was spending time with another man during our first date. There was no coming back from this. Len and I were doomed. But that didn't mean I had a future with the dark Turkish man currently staring at me, his eyes like storm clouds, the crease on his forehead so deep he'd soon have to start cleaning it with a Q-tip.

I watched his Adam's apple bob up and down, chest rising and falling. The black dress shirt he wore made him look even more menacing. So sexy. So infuriating. "Why was he holding your hand?"

I blinked several times, trying to hop onto his train of thought. "Len? You mean Len?"

"His name is Len? Like... Leonard?"

"No, I think it's just Len. I'm not sure. Why?"

"It just sounds like half a name."

I rounded my eyes in mock outrage. "Well, he's not as tall as you, so he doesn't get a full four letters."

The corner of his mouth twitched, and I held my breath. Would there be a smile? Please, God, let there be a smile! But the twitching settled, and his eyes hardened again. "Why was Len holding your hand?"

My lungs deflated, irritation coiling in my gut again. "Are you seriously asking me that?"

He shrugged, maintaining the indignant look in his eyes. "It's a bit... forward on the first date, isn't it?"

"Forward?" My eyes rounded in disbelief. "He's a pastor. He practically has a degree in hand holding! I was upset and talking about my divorce. He held my hand. How is that forward? You haven't taken me out once and we've dry humped against my bedroom wall."

"He's a pastor?" Emir's eyes flashed with alarm. He pushed the plate of pizza towards me. "Please, eat."

I huffed. "This is not a date, Emir." I wagged my finger between us. "This is me blowing off my date. I have to go back there, soon."

He looked away, seemingly embarrassed. Then his gaze returned, burning with passion. "I don't think I'm making myself understood. What I'm asking is... how is it going? Are you enjoying this date? Is there going to be a second date?"

I briefly considered making him suffer, but he looked so desolate I couldn't bring myself to hurt him. "Emir. I ditched my date to sit here with you. There's no coming back from this. I can't build anything new with this guy when I'm acting like this. I'm angry with you, but I'm furious with myself."

He nodded. "I'm sorry I ruined it for you."

I got up. "I'm going to go back in and thank him for a lovely evening, make up an excuse, and then I'll give you a ride home. It'll be the second time I'm lying to a pastor. I'll be going to hell. I hope you're happy."

He stood up and blocked my way. "Don't lie. Tell him the truth."

"And what would that be?"

"That you're not available."

I took a step closer, placing my hands on his chest. "Why am I not available?"

"Because you're here with me."

I sighed. "I'm a stupid woman."

He pulled me into him, leaning his forehead against mine. "I can't believe I'm saying this, but I wish I was more like my brother. He's a leaper. But I'm not like that. I keep looking ahead, and

I can't figure out how to make it work. Which means we must prepare for the end."

I pulled back, giving him a pointed look. "How about we have the middle first? If you keep thinking like that, you'll never experience anything. It's like a self-fulfilling prophecy."

He threw out his arms, eyes thunderous. "Then, tell me how it's going to work! I fly back to Istanbul. You stay here. We meet up in the middle once a year?"

I dragged my bottom lip between my teeth, frustration coursing through me. I folded my arms, staring back at him defiantly. "I don't know. Sometimes life surprises you."

"How, Janie? Will the continents move? Will my parents suddenly embrace the idea that both of their children live on the other side of the world? What about your sons, Janie? I haven't even met them, but I bet they'd like to have their mother around."

I hung my head, defeated. Because he was right. All I had was an unfounded faith in things miraculously working out. That was my nature, just like the cold practicality was his. Yet, he wanted me. I could feel it, and the thought gave me hope.

"Maybe we could have a fling?" I winced at the words as they floated out into the warm night air. "People have flings."

"I don't." He shook his head, eyes drawn. "I mean, I haven't been with anyone since..." His voice fizzled out.

There was a story there, and I'd pry it out of him. I had to. I had to know what I was up against.

I handed him my car keys. "My car is just around the corner." I pointed past him at the next street corner. "Wait for me."

Bracing myself for impact, I stepped into the restaurant. Len sat at our table, browsing his phone.

"I thought you ditched me," he said with a wide smile as I appeared in front of him.

Len knew how to smile, I thought with a pang. His current grin was tinged with panic, but it was there. I'd seen his entire set of teeth during our first dinner.

"No, I'm not ditching you, but I have to go. I got a call from my son. He needs to talk… he sounded quite upset. I promised I'd call him back soon. Thank you for the dinner, it's been lovely." I took a step back, smiling like my life depended on it.

It wasn't a total lie. I did need to call my sons and check how they were doing with the idea of a new sibling. Shaun had insisted everyone was thrilled, but I had my doubts.

"I understand. Kids come first." He stopped at the bar to settle the bill, refusing my credit card, then followed me to the door. "I'll walk you to your car."

I nearly threw up in my mouth. "No, no! You don't have to. It's right around the corner."

"It's dark out there. Of course, I will." He held the door for me.

My stomach in knots, I led him down the street towards my car. How could I get rid of him before he saw the Turkish man in my passenger seat? There was absolutely no explanation I could give for the presence of Emir.

This was a nightmare.

I stopped a few meters away from my vehicle, gesturing at it. "Made it here safely, thank you!"

Len's eyebrows sailed up. "That's a nice ride!" He stepped closer to investigate my Lexus, its golden paint shimmering under the streetlight.

Why couldn't my car be a boring-as-fuck silver Prius? My stomach tightened into a hard ball as Len ran his hand along the roof, muttering something in appreciative tone.

From my vantage point, I could see the exact moment Emir noticed him. His eyes flashed and he knocked on the window, casting a furious glare at Len. The pastor yelped, stumbling backwards. "There's a man! Janie, there's a man in your car!"

"I know. It's Emir. My... farmhand."

"Farmhand?"

Emir stepped out, joining us on the footpath. "You must be Len."

He stuck out his hand, and Len shook it, looking like he'd seen a ghost.

"Emir Erkam."

Len introduced himself. Then he took a breath, turning to me. "Janie. I don't want to jump to conclusions, but I'm having a hard time understanding why your... farmhand is sitting in your car while you're out on a date." He scanned Emir's outfit, taking in the shiny, black shirt and dress pants. Absolutely nothing about him said 'farmhand'.

I winced. "He needed a ride back from town, so I said he can wait in my car. Sorry, I should have told you. I bumped into Emir outside when I checked on my parking."

Emir nodded. "I don't have a car. I'm only visiting New Zealand. From Turkey."

Len tilted his head, still confused. "Ah, okay. That's far."

"Anyway, we need to go. Thank you again. It was lovely to meet you." I offered Len my hand, but he pulled me into a hug.

Over his shoulder, I caught the look on Emir's face, and it made my blood chill. As Len released me, he caught my eye, and smiled.

Please don't say we should do this again sometime.

"We should do this again sometime." Len's eyes shone with hope.

"No, you won't." Emir's deep, low growl stole the air from my lungs.

I staggered away as Emir stepped in front of Len, towering over him. "You should stay away from her, for your own good."

"Who is this guy?" Len demanded as I retreated around my car and slipped behind the wheel. "Janie?"

I was too mortified to answer, and so angry I immediately decided to leave Emir behind to make his own way back. But he was quicker, catching the door handle as I released the handbrake, sliding into my moving car as I reversed and turned to get out of the tight parking spot.

My face burned as I sped down the road, tears streaming down my face. "Emir!" I screamed at him. "What the fuck was that?!"

"I'm sorry." His voice came out so strained I barely heard it. "I'm sorry."

"What are you? An ape? Who does that?"

"I'm sorry, Janie. But you were too nice. You were encouraging him. He would have kept calling."

"So what? You don't think I can turn him down if I want to? I don't need some prehistoric idiot with an underdeveloped frontal cortex protecting me! I'm not yours. You don't get to do that. Do you understand?"

He didn't reply, but from the corner of my eye, I saw him nod. In the light of the passing streetlights, I noticed his eyes glisten, and felt a weight on my chest. What was he doing to me?

"Even if we were together, I'd hate that caveman shit," I added, but my voice had lost its edge and came out more sad than angry.

"I don't know why I... I'm sorry, Janie. I just couldn't take it. I don't want this guy around you."

"He was perfectly pleasant and respectful and behaved a whole lot better than you. So, tell me, what is wrong with him?"

Emir looked out the window, his voice distant. "Nothing."

"So, you just don't want any man around me?"

"Stop the car, Janie."

Despite the rage shaking my body, I found myself slowing down and pulling over on the side of the road. We were just outside of town, with no more streetlights. Was he going to get out and slam the door? I waited; my muscles seized in a full-body cramp. As much as he riled me, I didn't want him to leave me alone.

"Now what?" I asked when he didn't move.

In the dark, I could barely see his face. After a moment, I noticed the crescent moon and my eyes adjusted to its low light, making out his features. The moonlight reflected off his eyes, begging me to keep watch.

He blinked, staring ahead, mouth a straight line.

"I want to be someone else. Someone who could take a chance

on this... whatever is happening between us. But I'm not. I thought I'd someday get back to dating, but not like this. Not here. Not—"

"With someone like me? I'm older than you, Emir. Is that a problem? My kids are grown. You must be looking for someone younger, to start a family with."

That was it. I could never have him, for real. The only thing I could imagine was a fling, and even that might not be in the cards.

His shook his head slightly, looking at his hands. "I never saw myself with a family. Even my mom knows that. She's pinned her hopes on Cem. But I've been burned before, and it's hard to take the leap when you know how much the crash-landing hurts."

I reached for his hand. His fingers curled around mine. "What happened?"

We sat in silence for a long time. When I'd all but given up hope, Emir spoke. "I was engaged to be married. Her name was Hande. She was beautiful, talented. An actress. I met her on set when visiting Cem. I should have known. She played a minor role on his show. I thought she loved me for me, but it turned out she was in love with my brother. I was the consolation prize. I mean, it makes sense. He's the movie star. I'm the brother who looks a bit like him. I only wish I'd found out earlier, before I proposed, and we got the families involved. We were only a week away from the wedding when I found the photos. She had an entire folder of Cem on her phone. Every fucking angle."

I held my breath. "How did you find them?"

"She'd been acting a bit odd. Everyone told me it was the wedding jitters or something, but then Burcu, my brother's co-star, came to see me. She said she'd noticed something on set, told me to look through Hande's phone. I didn't want to. I said I trusted her. But Burcu insisted. So, I did it, to prove her wrong. And that's when I found them."

"So, you confronted Hande?"

"She confessed immediately, like she'd been holding it in and was relieved to finally tell me. She'd been in love with Cem for years. That's why she'd taken the role on my brother's show and of course it killed her to watch Cem and Burcu become an item."

"How did she manage to hide it? You must have spent a lot of time together. I don't think I could ever do that. I struggled with keeping it together for one date."

"What are you talking about? You looked at him like he hung the moon."

"Did I?" I narrowed my eyes at him. "Or do you just feel like that because you saw him as a threat? We're pretty polite here in New Zealand and the way I responded to him would come across as not that keen. The way you responded, on the other hand..." I raised my brows and stared him down until he grunted.

"Yeah, I get it. Psycho."

"Well, I'm way too polite to say that, but thank you."

"Why do you have to smile at him, though?"

He frowned, biting his bottom lip, and the thought struck me. "That's what your fiancé did, right? She felt conflicted or uncomfortable and covered it up with a smile. Because that's what we do. We use our smile as a shield, to cover up how we're truly feeling, so we don't burden other people. We use our smile to put everyone at ease."

He stared at the dark windshield. "Or to mislead them."

"I'm sorry. I shouldn't psychoanalyze your past relationship. I'm not a professional."

"I acted psycho, so I think we're even. And she smiled a lot. She had a beautiful smile. When she smiled, I ignored everything else."

"Did you... smile back?" I leaned in, my heart lodged in my throat. The sheer privilege of hearing his story had me shivering.

He shrugged, giving me a rueful look. "I must have. Nobody complained about my face like they do now."

"So, it's in muscle memory," I said, brushing my thumb across the side of his lips, coaxing the corner of his mouth upwards. "Just hiding."

"Why are you so intent on me smiling? You said we use our smile to cover up what's really going on. I prefer honesty. Be yourself and anyone who's worth knowing will stick around."

I held his gaze. "I've never faked a smile with you. I smile because I'm fascinated. I smile because I want you to smile. And if you one day smile back, I'll melt into a puddle."

He huffed and his mouth tugged a little, until sadness invaded his eyes again. "You have a beautiful smile." He stroked my hand with his thumb. "You should smile if you can."

I felt my face flush and was grateful for the darkness that hid my blush.

"Everyone tells me I look like Cem when I smile. Hande always asked me to smile."

His dark voice made my insides coil tighter. "You think she was living out her fantasy of being with Cem?"

He turned to face me, a challenge in his glistening eyes. "Why else?"

"But you two are nothing alike."

"No, we're not." His voice broke and he cleared his throat. "If we were, you'd have already had your Turkish fling. But here you are, listening to a grown man cry."

"Oh, Emir. I don't want a fling. Nobody wants a fling. A fling is just love that fails the test of time. We all want something better, right? But it's not always available."

"Maybe not, but most women would choose a fling with my brother over anything with me."

His voice sounded rough as he turned to face away from me. I felt a flicker of understanding. He stood in his brother's shadow, believing he wasn't good enough. I squeezed his hand. "I know your brother is famous in Turkey, and I know how that distorts reality, but I don't fancy him. Honestly. Not every woman does."

He turned a fraction to give me a side eye. I let go of his hand.

"You're not into movie stars?"

"Not particularly. But I'm into you, Emir. I'm mad at you, but I still prefer you."

"So, you wouldn't prefer to be back in that restaurant, with Len?"

I shook my head, smiling a little. He had me there. "No, I wouldn't."

"Why are you mad at me, then?"

"Because this is a small town and rumors will spread."

"Because the pastor is such a gossip?"

I shook my head, letting out a sad laugh. "I don't know! He might talk to someone, and the word will spread. Everyone will talk about me sleeping with my Turkish farmhand."

"I object to being called a farmhand, but why is it such a big deal, otherwise?"

I weaved my fingers in tight knots, thinking about the question. Why was it such a big deal what Len said to his golf buddies or what Tabitha and the town gossip mill had to say about me? If the story got to the media, if they gave it the good old 'scandal' spin, did it matter? Did I truly care about the opinions of strangers? I didn't want to be the person who did.

"I don't know how this will play out, but I'm mad at you because that's not how I wanted to end that date. That's not what I wanted to say to him. I don't need anyone to fight my battles for me. I'm not a helpless maiden who needs to be protected. Promise me you won't do that ever again."

He returned my intense stare with an even more intense one. "If you promise me you won't date him."

Only if you dated me instead, I thought. But I couldn't say that. I'd made myself more than available. I wasn't a masochist.

Why did I have to fall for the damaged, grumpy Turkish man when there were wonderful, socially acceptable and sensible choices like Len out there? I was only going to get hurt. That was the one thing we agreed on so far—that we'd both get hurt.

I started the engine. "I'll make no promises."

I drove home and parked outside my house. Still angry, I got out without a word. Not waiting for Emir, I marched to the door and took out my key to unlock it. As I turned the key, I instantly knew something was wrong. "It's not locked. Did I not lock it? That's odd."

CHAPTER 19

Emir

Dread shot through me like a cold shower. Janie rushed in before I could stop her. I heard her voice from the living room. "Well, it doesn't look like I've been robbed."

I caught her by the kitchen counter, guided her behind it and whispered, "Stay here. I'll check the rest of the house, okay?"

Janie smiled. "Relax. I probably just forgot to lock the door. I was so nervous about that date. Maybe I thought I didn't need to because you were here somewhere."

I shook my head, giving her a stern look. "Think again. You gave me a spare key. I was the last one to leave the house and I double checked that all doors were locked." I kept my voice low. "If the front door was unlocked, it's because someone opened it.

Who else has a key?"

"My boys, but they're in Auckland." She checked her phone. "No messages. They wouldn't just turn up. They'd text me to pick them up from the bus stop."

"Listen. If someone broke in by picking the lock, and then left, wouldn't they lock the door behind them? It locks from the outside without a key, doesn't it?"

She looked up, her eyes now alert. "Are you seriously suggesting someone broke in, and they're still here?"

"Where's Gru?" Emir looked around, puzzled, and my blood chilled.

"If someone broke in, they would have been met by Gru." She looked up at me, eyes flooding with panic. "He's not much of a guard dog, but he'd be at the door, greeting them, getting in their way..."

I squeezed her arm. "I'm sure he's okay. Please wait here while I check the house."

"What if there's more than one person? What if they're armed?"

I grabbed the sharpest looking kitchen knife from a marble block and headed down the hallway towards Janie's bedroom. The living room was clear. If someone was looking for valuables, they might go for the master bedroom.

When I saw the pile of dresses and handbags on Janie's bed, I froze. Had someone been going through her stuff? Then I remembered she'd been getting ready for the date. Nothing else seemed out of the ordinary, but stepping into the room, I had a strange sensation of being watched. I raised the knife, almost as a reflex, and felt a cool breeze on my skin. The sliding door to her private patio was open. As I leapt towards it, I saw movement behind the glass. A dark figure pushed their way through the pot plants, disappearing into the night. It was only a flash, a fraction of a second, but I knew what I saw.

I burst outside, taking off after them. But it was so dark I could only follow the fading sound of footsteps on the grass. Taking a guess, I ran around the house towards the driveway, then the road. But they must have gone into the bushes.

When I stopped to listen, I only heard the high-pitched buzz of cicadas. The outdoor lights of the house didn't reach down the driveway. I pulled out my phone and turned on the flashlight, but it only showed a little further down the empty driveway. The intruder may have headed to the main road through the gardens rather than the driveway. There was no way I'd find him now. Or her. I couldn't be sure of anything.

As I climbed up the slope back to the house, I wondered what I should tell Janie. I had no visual description or anything else useful. I had no evidence of anyone breaking in, other than the unlocked door. Janie hadn't seen the burglar. Would she believe me? I'd acted like an overly protective, jealous jerk and the timing of this break-in felt suspiciously convenient. What if she thought I'd made up a burglar to justify my protectiveness? My insides tensed at the thought.

But I couldn't hide this from her, either. I couldn't compromise her safety, and I needed her to be on high alert.

When I got to the front door, I head a sharp bark. Gru emerged from the shadows, jumping at my feet. Relief flooded through me.

At least the dog was here, and alive. "It's okay, boy." I bent down the pat him. "He's gone now."

Careful of the knife I was still holding, I picked him up and stepped inside.

We found Janie in the living room, huddled in the corner of the couch under a blanket. The way her face brightened when she saw us made my heart swell more than I liked to admit.

"Oh, Gru! Thank you, thank you!" She rushed to meet me.

I spread my arms wide to avoid stabbing her. She took that as an invitation and wrapped her arms around both of us. I walked us to the kitchen, returned the knife into its holder, then hugged her back.

Gru was so excited he didn't know who to lick first, offering both of us a fair share of saliva. I set him on the floor and Janie lowered down, continuing to pet him. "Where did you find him?" She asked, looking up at me.

"He was just outside the door. The thief must have pushed him out of the house when he arrived."

"He probably licked the intruder," Janie mused, scratching Gru's ears. "You're not much of a guard, are you?"

"He's a good boy." I wasn't much of a guard either.

"Where did you go anyway?" She asked.

"I... chased him, but he got away. He must have gone into the bush. It's so dark out there and the light on my phone is terrible."

Janie stood up, her eyes huge. "You saw him?"

I shook my head in regret. "I only saw movement, and this dark shape running into the night. A man or a large woman. that's all

I can say."

Janie's brows pulled together as she stared at me in confusion. "But nothing's missing. There's no mess or other signs of burglary. Why would… How… This makes no sense."

I stepped closer, taking her hands in mine, holding her gaze. "I know it doesn't, yet. But I need you to believe me. I know I've been an overprotective, jealous idiot tonight. But I saw him. Your bedroom door was open a crack and they were just outside, getting away."

"And you chased them?"

"Of course. I would have caught them too if it wasn't so dark out there. I'm not great at Pilates but I'm a good runner."

She shook her head, her eyes huge. "You don't run after a burglar, Emir. That's dangerous."

"It was just one person," I argued. "And they were running away. People who run like that are not prepared for a fight."

"Maybe not prepared, but they're desperate and unpredictable, possibly high on meth. They could be armed. I don't like this. I don't want you to act stupid, even if it's to protect me."

My stomach flooded with warmth. "It was a calculated risk, I promise. I wanted to see which way they went, see if I could catch the license plate."

She seemed to accept this answer, turning her head to scan the room. "So, now what? Do I need to call the police? If they didn't take anything, it seems like an overreaction."

"We don't know that yet. Let's go through the house and do a proper check, okay?"

CHAPTER 20

Janie

"Nothing. I swear, nothing is missing," I wailed at Emir, staring at the contents of my wardrobe and jewelry box spread out on the duvet.

We'd spent an hour cataloguing the house contents like the world's most invasive insurance appraisers. I'd never realized how much stuff I had until I'd been forced to stare at each item through the eyes of a thief. What was it worth? How much did it weigh? I needed to organize a garage sale. Except I didn't want to invite strangers to poke around my house. I didn't want anyone around, except Emir. For some reason, I trusted him. Maybe it was his refusal to sleep with me, his direct manner, or the lack of smiles, but he was the one male I could tolerate right now. Barely.

"How can you know?" Emir demanded. "You have so many clothes."

"I know the designer pieces. Nobody would go after my farm clothes."

"What about your underwear?"

I blinked. "I don't have designer underwear."

Emir cleared his throat. "I mean, you have a laundry hamper in there." He pointed at the now nearly empty walk-in wardrobe.

My nose wrinkled. "You think someone took my dirty underwear?" I was so disgusted by the possibility I couldn't even look him in the eye.

"Just check, please," he pleaded, still pointing at the open doorway.

He turned away as I pulled piece by piece out of the hamper. At a glance, it didn't seem like anything was missing. I thought back to what I'd been wearing lately. The yellow lace! I'd worn a yellow bra and a pair of lacy yellow panties to feel sexier for the filming earlier today. The bra was here, but where were the panties? I dumped the contents on the floor and put them back one by one. No. The yellow lace panties were gone.

I paused for a moment, trying to remember where I'd undressed when getting ready for the date. Maybe that pair was lying under the bed or somewhere in the bathroom. If I told Emir about it, he'd flip out. The man was already on edge. I didn't want to see him any more agitated, or protective.

"All accounted for," I reported, stepping back into the bedroom.

"Okay. I'll check all the locks for signs of tampering. Do you have a flashlight I can borrow?"

I rummaged through the hallway closet and found the giant one Shaun had bought, complaining about the lack of outdoor lighting. It was heavy enough to knock someone out, which was probably a good thing right now. "Here you go."

Emir flipped the thing in his hands like it weighed nothing, and my stomach flipped. I'd never realized how phallic an object it was. The same lighting power could likely have been achieved without the size and weight, but I could imagine men choosing this product over anything pocket sized every time.

He held the flashlight at an upward angle, examining it. "You're wondering if mine's bigger, right?"

I burst out in nervous laughter. I'd never heard him talk like this. "Emir. Are you trying to lighten the mood?"

His slight half-smile had an embarrassed edge. "Is it working?"

I took the flashlight from him, measuring it in my hands. It'd be an impressive size. Too long for comfort, but nice and thick. I stifled another giggle, grateful for the momentary break from the terror I'd been feeling. "Thank you. Now I'll never be able to touch this thing without thinking about your... you know."

"I was willing to take that risk."

"And you're not going to answer the question, are you?"

He shook his head. "My only intention was to make you smile."

I smiled, relishing in the way his features softened and mouth twitched in response. It wasn't quite a smile, but it was still a miracle. In that moment, I felt deeply grateful for him, even his protectiveness. If I'd been home alone... I didn't even want to imagine how terrifying all of this could have been. It could have been me, walking into my own bedroom and finding the door open and someone behind the window. Someone who may or may not have stolen my used underwear. I shuddered.

"Are you okay?" Emir touched my shoulder.

I nodded, overcome by a full-body shiver I suspected he could detect with his fingers. "I'm fine."

I'll be back soon." Emir flipped the switch, casting a beam of light on the wall. Every other light inside was already on as I'd been desperately trying to chase away the shadows of the night. I'd told Shaun I preferred moody, atmospheric lighting and being able to see the moon and the stars. Now, I wanted industrial strength spotlights out on my yard and all the way down my driveway.

As Emir left to investigate the locks, I returned to the bedroom, desperate to rule out the possibility of someone stealing my panties. I searched under the bed, every corner of the bathroom and everywhere else I could think of. When I was certain they weren't in the bedroom, I jogged through the house to check the laundry, going through my pile of sheets.

The yellow underwear was gone.

What did this mean? Had someone broken into my house to steal a pair of used underwear? The thought turned my stomach so much I didn't even want to explore it any further. It made no sense. Maybe I'd put them in the wash, and they'd been swallowed by the same black hole that ate single socks? I hadn't run the washer, but maybe the black hole was getting stronger and able to suck in objects without water or mechanical rotation. I shook my head at the crazy thoughts. I'd never been burgled before and felt shaken to my core.

I returned to the living room and made us tea. I'd only picked on my dinner and was currently living off the slice of pizza I'd stolen from Emir's plate, most of which had been left there, uneaten. He must have been starving. I made us ham sandwiches and microwaved apple pies I found in the fridge. I needed something cozy and sweet.

When Emir came back from outside, I had the table set for two, the lighting turned down to my usual evening vibe and a candle flickering in the middle. It looked so homely and inviting, yet I couldn't shake the sense of dread.

"This looks nice," he said.

"I figured you might still be hungry. I am."

I poured him a cup of well-brewed tea and chose the seat next to him so that we were occupying the corner of the huge dining table. It must have looked odd, but I didn't care. I needed him close, otherwise I wouldn't be able to digest anything.

"Thank you. I haven't eaten anything in hours," he confessed, tackling the sandwich with gusto.

"I was thinking... It's only nine o'clock. If you hadn't interrupted our date, I might still be out. Maybe whoever was here knew I was going out. I don't know how, but it's possible, I think. And if they did, maybe they chose tonight for that reason, thinking I'd be out all night."

Emir swallowed, nodding. "I thought about that, too. Someone who knew about your date but didn't know about me. And then we walked in on him, and he had to flee. Maybe that's why nothing is missing. He didn't have time to take anything."

"You think he would have broken in right before we arrived?"

I felt better about that option. I hated to think of someone spending an hour at my house, touching and sniffing my things. Was that person now sitting somewhere, sniffing my underwear? I fought the gagging reflex and swallowed the piece of bread in my mouth.

"But even then, if it was a burglar, they'd go for the low-hanging fruit, like your jewelry. You had gold necklaces hanging in that little tree on your dressing table. It would have taken him seconds to grab those. It makes no sense." Emir slowly shook his head, the frown on his forehead deepening.

Unless they just went straight to the laundry hamper, I thought, my insides twisting. But there was still a chance I was wrong. Those panties would turn up, and I'd feel like a fool.

We ate in silence, both listening for any sounds out of the ordinary, but there was nothing going on, only the faint whirr of cicadas behind the window, like a static from a disconnected TV someone had left on. The night already felt cooler. I loved sleeping with my window open, and feeling that breeze, but how could I do that anymore? I'd have to close and lock every door and window.

"I know it's late, but I need to do some exercise," I said. "I'll just get changed first. Do you mind if I take over the living room floor?"

He looked surprised. "Why do you ask? It's your house. Or are you asking me to join you?"

I swallowed a lump. "I guess I'm asking you to stay close. I know that sounds stupid, but I'd feel better if—"

"Of course. I'll be here."

We cleaned up after our second dinner, and he settled on the couch with Gru and a thriller he found on my shelf. How could he read something like that after a day like this? I'd never understand men. They seemed to thrive on adrenaline, whereas I felt drained and shaky, desperate to return to my previous state of ignorant bliss, the time in the past when I'd never even considered the possibility of someone breaking into my house. But obviously, that option wasn't available, and I'd have to adjust to the new reality. What would that reality look like when Emir returned to Turkey, and I was left here by myself?

Taking deep breaths to quell the shivers, I retreated to my bedroom, constantly looking over my shoulder as I organized my clothes and changed into a pair of slacks and a T-shirt. This didn't change anything between me and Emir, I reminded myself. We had no future, and the harder I leaned on him to get through this, the harder I'd make this for both of us. I had to rely on myself. I had to be brave enough.

I hurried back to the living room, instantly feeling better when I found Emir exactly where I'd left him, seemingly engrossed in the book. But as I lowered myself to the floor, I felt his eyes on me.

I cast the exercise video from my phone to the TV, keeping the volume so low I could barely hear it. I was afraid the cheerful voice of the Pilates lady would drown out something else I needed to hear.

Would I ever feel relaxed again? Even though making my

muscles burn helped, it didn't soothe the roiling in my stomach.

I got up on shaking legs. "I don't want to keep you up, but would you like to watch a movie with me? I'll just take a quick shower."

Emir's eyes filled with understanding. "Are you nervous about going to sleep?"

That's exactly what I was feeling, but I'd promised myself I wouldn't do this.

"No. I'm just not that sleepy yet," I said brightly, stifling a yawn.

I wanted nothing more than to curl up in bed, as long as it was next to Emir in a windowless room with a bolted door. Or just next to Emir. I needed him close enough to feel his vitals. I needed a living, breathing male handy with a weapon between me and the rest of the world.

So, I'd been reduced to this? I'd accused him of caveman behavior, and now I wanted to sleep in a cave, protected by a particularly tall and strong specimen of the male species who was holding a club.

Come on, Janie! You're better than this.

"Actually... I'm starting to feel tired. I'll just go to bed. Sleep tight!" I yawned for good measure and gave him one last smile before skipping to my end of the house.

He'd be in the same house. The doors were locked. Tomorrow, I'd get better locks. Dead bolts. Chains. A security camera at every entrance. I'd sell some of my useless junk to cover the cost. I only had to make it through this one night.

CHAPTER 21

Emir

How could she go to sleep after all this? I'd been sitting down for a good hour, but my pulse remained elevated. Although watching Janie bend over in a pair of white tights likely had something to do with it. I should have kept my eyes on the book, but I struggled to focus on the story, my mind split between fantasies of her naked body and scenarios of the break-in. Neither activity helped me relax, and by the time she finished her workout, I felt like going for a long run, but I didn't want to leave her alone, even for a half an hour. Besides, I'd already done a run and a workout in the morning, which now seemed like a week ago.

As Janie headed to her bedroom, I grabbed the flashlight and got back outside, circling the house, checking every possible point of entry. I'd already closed every window and checked the locks. The front door did show some scratches that could have been made by a lock pick, but that was to be expected. I knew I hadn't left the door unlocked. I'd found no scuff marks on the other doors, which suggested the thief hadn't tried them first. Why the front door? The location was remote, with no neighbors watching, but it still felt too brazen. Why not even try the back door? That was usually the weakest link.

And why bother with lock picking? Why not just break the glass on one of the many sliding doors, flip the simple lock and let yourself in? It would have been a lot faster. After all, there was nobody around to hear the sound of breaking glass. Unless the intruder had planned to get in and out without being noticed. And in that case, what were they after? If they had stolen something, Janie would have noticed. She'd had a strange expression when checking her laundry hamper, but it might have been just the shock or sheer awkwardness of having to do it in front of me. If she said nothing was missing, I had to believe her.

But if nothing was missing, and the phantom burglar had planned to pop in unnoticed, then why break in at all? It made no sense. The whole situation was making me itchy.

I was so deep in thought, mulling over every scenario, that I never even considered I was approaching Janie's bedroom. The sliding door was now locked, and the curtains drawn. I rounded the corner.

I swear it never crossed my mind that she had a window on the other wall, right above her bed. It didn't have a curtain, maybe because it was quite narrow and sat relatively high. Not too high for me, though, especially as I stepped on a wooden bench lining her wraparound deck. I only did it to check a potential vantage point the intruder might have used to spy on her. To my shock, standing on the relatively low bench gave me a direct view into her bedroom, zeroing in on the bathroom door. I couldn't see Janie, but I pointed my flashlight carefully down at my feet, to avoid spooking her if she happened to look outside. Looking down at my feet, my eyes caught something shiny. A gum wrapper. It had lodged between the wooden slats. I hadn't noticed Janie chewing gum but maybe her sons did. Was it possible someone had been standing right here at night, peering into her house like I was doing right now?

I was about to step down from the bench, when the bathroom door opened, and Janie stepped out, wearing a towel. I turned off the flashlight, just to be sure, and should have looked away. I should have left. But when I saw her starting to unwrap the towel, my body seized. I couldn't look away. I stared, unwilling to even blink, as the towel came undone, falling on her bed. Janie, in the nude. I kept staring as she picked up a pair of black panties and pulled them on. She was so hot I gave up breathing along with blinking, my throat turning to sandpaper as my mouth hung open in the cool night air. All the Pilates had paid off. Her body was a work of art, one I desperately wanted to touch.

Janie reached under her duvet, digging up something purple. I was still looking as she pulled on pajama bottoms, then a matching camisole. When her pink nipples finally disappeared behind fabric,

I sucked in a sharp breath, lowered onto the ground, and shifted away from the window, leaning my shoulder against the wall. I tried to adjust the crotch of my pants. They felt too tight.

Focus, I ordered my brain. Check the rest of the perimeter. Make sure everything is in order. I shone the flashlight down to the bushes, but my mind replayed a highlights reel of Janie's curves.

Taking small, uncomfortable steps, I returned inside, locking the door. I highly doubted the intruder would try again the same night, but I still brought out one of the dining chairs, propping it against the door handle. If anyone tried to break in, they'd make enough racket to wake us up. Gru followed me around the house, jumping on the chair.

"Good boy. You keep watch all night, let us know if anyone tries to get in." I gave the dog a meaningful look and he yipped, settling on the seat.

I'd mostly seen him snoozing on his fluffy bed in the corner of the living room, or zooming through the house for no good reason, so it was good to see him looking alive. At least one of us was onto it and not too horny to think straight. Who would have thought it was the dog?

I grabbed the heavy flashlight and the book I'd pretended to read and retreated to my bedroom. It was going to be a long night.

CHAPTER 22

Janie

It's nothing, I told myself, for the thousandth time. But I knew I'd seen something behind the window. A flash of light. I stepped closer to look, my heart beating like a drum. I could only make out the faint outline of the bench by the deck. Everything I knew to be out there, the lawn and the bush behind it, disappeared in the blanketing night. I could make out the faint outline of the ferns against the sky, so subtle it only appeared after my eyes adjusted to the darkness. I held still, listening for any sounds, my limbs frozen with fear.

I couldn't go to sleep like this. I couldn't imagine ever sleeping again in this house. Not with both eyes closed. Not alone.

I was weak and pathetic, but I had no choice. Tears burning

behind my eyes, I gathered my pillow and my phone and marched through the house.

Whatever the emotionally damaged Turk thought of me, tonight, he was my only option. He'd have to deal with me.

I knocked on his door. "Emir?"

"Come in." His voice sounded a little strained, even through the door.

I found him in bed, under the covers, leaning on the headboard. Did he sleep in his dress shirt? I shook my head at the odd look, but fear had me in its grip, overriding other concerns.

I dropped my phone on the nightstand, threw my pillow on the bed and climbed in, burrowing under his blanket. "I'm sorry. I can't sleep in there. I feel like someone's lurking outside and I don't even have a curtain for one of the windows. It's creeping me out."

A shudder ran through me, and I dug in deeper under the blanket, and closer to him. As I did so, my foot brushed against something. His leg. His bare leg.

"Are you not wearing pants?" I whispered, looking up. "Why do you have a dress shirt on?"

Emir shifted away from my toes, looking embarrassed. "I was in the middle of getting changed when I heard your knocking, so I jumped under the covers."

I sat up, for the first time noticing his dress pants strewn across the bedroom chair. "You could have just asked me to wait."

He frowned in his usual way, pained and earnest. "But you could have been in danger."

"I promise, if I'm being chased by zombies, I won't knock. I will barge in."

"Okay, good." His shoulders dropped as he held my gaze, and I watched the miraculous transformation. The frown smoothed and his mouth tugged. "You could also give me a heads up by screaming 'zombies' so I can get my flamethrower."

My body flooded with endorphins, and I smiled back like an absolute fool, reveling in the miracle. Emir was smiling. He was smiling to make me feel better. For a moment, I held my breath, scared a sudden move might scare it away. But soon, I couldn't resist. "Emir. You're smiling."

"I am."

We'd been staring at each other for a while, and I could tell he was struggling to keep those lips curved. It was waning. I felt like I was witnessing the final moments of sunset as the last whispers of smile disappeared, leaving me with a warm glow.

"Thank you," I whispered. "I feel so much better here, with you. I thought I could be strong but—"

"You don't have to be strong, Janie. Not tonight."

His voice was velvety dark now, perfectly in sync with the night. I felt it deep in my belly, like he was drawing everything out of me I needed to keep hidden. I wanted to curl up in his lap and weep, and I hated myself for it.

"If you want to get changed, go ahead. I'll try to look the other way," I said brusquely, throwing a grin at him. "I might be tempted to peek, but I can use this blanket to build a barricade between us."

I started pulling the blanket off him, to pile it up in the middle of the bed, but he held onto his end. "It's okay. I'll just take my shirt off right here." He began unbuttoning it.

He looked so awkward I didn't know whether to laugh or cry. I'd highjacked his bed and he must have felt obligated to let me stay, after a night like this, even though he'd rather sleep alone.

"Do you sleep in the nude, or...?" I felt my cheeks warm up.

"Not usually."

"Then go get your pajamas. I don't want you to be uncomfortable."

I snatched the blanket off him to get him moving, and that's when I saw it. The huge, almost purple erection poking out from under the hem of his shirt like a big fat sundial. I stared at it, blinking.

Emir sighed. "As you can see, I'm already a bit uncomfortable." His voice sounded matter of fact, almost apologetic as he unbuttoned the shirt, peeled it off and threw it over a chair.

He was officially naked. I was in bed with a gorgeous, naked man who had an erection—one he was no longer trying to hide. He looked down at his crotch, then at me, as if resigned to the fact that the cat was out of the bag. And what a large, thick, veiny cat it was.

Look away, Janie. Away. Away is not his crotch.

As I turned to stare at the door, my mind finally connected the dots. He must have been touching himself. I'd walked in on him masturbating, yet he'd still let me in, worried that I was in danger. It was unbelievable.

I brought my hand to my mouth, trying to stop the nervous giggle. "I'm so sorry! Were you...? Did I interrupt you...?"

"It's okay," he said. I felt the blanket shift as he pulled it up to cover himself again. "I was trying to keep it to myself."

Heat bloomed between my thighs at the thought of him stroking himself. Up to this moment, I'd never even imagined him masturbating. Of course, he did. Everybody did. But Emir seemed so controlled it didn't fit my image of him. Who did he think about? What did he look like when he came? What happened to that crease on his forehead? I needed to know all these things, and more. The feeling grew like a crazy tickle in my throat, one I couldn't shake, and words coughed their way out.

"I know you don't want to sleep with me, but I'd be happy to help," I swallowed against the roughness in my throat, casting my eyes at the teepee in his lap. "I mean, we need to do something about that."

There. I'd officially begged for sex. Good one, Janie. If there was a way to go even lower, I'd find it.

He gave me an odd look, his eyebrows twitching. "You think I don't want to sleep with you?"

Was he for real? I stared back, my eyes dry from the prolonged gawking. "Well... I keep throwing myself at you and you keep turning me down."

He let out a deep sigh, turning to face me. A vein pulsed on his temple as he searched for words, his gaze circling the room, then returning to me, sweeping down the loose hair that spilled over my shoulders, hiding the hardened nipples that tried to poke through the thin camisole, as the rest of me hid under the blanket.

"Janie." His gravelly voice sent tremors through me. "What we should or shouldn't do has nothing to do with what I want. I'm hard because of you."

"Because of me?" I squeaked.

He shifted closer, pulling on the scrunched-up blanket until it was taut across our laps, and we sat side by side, him naked underneath, me in my pajama bottoms. As he pivoted to face me, his knee poked my leg and I caught sight of that erection again, partially hiding under the covers. "I'm sorry." He raised his hand and brushed it down my cheek, his fingers curled, like he couldn't quite bring himself to touch me. "I'm not practiced at this."

"Me neither," I admitted, turning to match his posture, my legs folded in lotus pose.

"How do you do that?" He gestured at the way I sat, trying to do the same while awkwardly pulling the blanket to cover himself.

It wasn't even vaguely the same posture, his knees sticking up under the blanket, arms looped around them to keep from kicking me. Long, muscular, painfully stiff legs. Poor guy. Who was hard because of me. Had he meant to say that? The words vibrated in my body like aftereffects of a massage, releasing shiver after shiver. I never wanted it to stop.

"It's a bed," I said, biting my lip to keep from smiling too hard. "Maybe we can just lie down rather than try to sit up properly like we're at a tea party."

"Feels more like a Pilates class," he grumbled, but accepted my suggestion.

I lay down on my side, leaning on my elbow, so I could see his face. "Why did you say you're hard because of me?"

He turned to face me but avoided eye contact. "I saw you naked. It was an accident."

My breath hitched as I tried to rearrange my thoughts. "When? How?"

Emir rubbed his forehead and blew out a deep breath before finally looking at me. "I was walking around the house earlier, to check the grounds, and I saw you coming out of the shower. I should have looked away... sooner. I'm sorry."

My heart pounded in my ears. "It was you! The light I saw behind my window."

He winced. "Probably. I'm sorry."

"And I got so spooked that I finally just grabbed my pillow and ran to your room." I didn't mean it as criticism, only observation, but from the way he rubbed his face with his giant hand, groaning, I could see he took it that way.

"It wasn't my plan," he said. "I wasn't trying to get you into my bed."

I pushed that hand off his face, forcing him to look at me. "I know, Emir. I was already scared. I'm sure I would have ended up at your door either way."

"I would have never tried anything."

"I know."

He swallowed and his voice turned darker. "But, now that you're here, I can't stop imagining all the things I want to do..." His hot breath grazed my shoulder as he leaned closer, his voice even darker. "Janie. If you have any doubts about this, you must leave. You're not safe with me anymore."

"I feel safe with you, Emir. And I want you. If we both want it, what's the big deal?" I attempted a carefree smile, but I couldn't shake the feeling he'd somehow transmitted into my brain, of this being a big deal. That if we slept together, everything would change.

He placed a kiss on my collar bone, letting out a frustrated growl. "I have a lot of self-control, Janie. At least I thought I did. Until I met you."

"I'm going to take that as a compliment," I whispered back. "Self-control is overrated, anyway." I reached for his forehead, itching to touch that frown.

"You think?" He buried his face between the mattress and my hand, letting his fingers trace my shoulder, and slip down to my breast.

He wouldn't meet my eyes, like he was embarrassed to be touching me this way, yet his hand kept moving, his thumb brushing across my nipple, rough and tender. Half of his beautiful face peeked from behind my hand, one brown eye begging for mercy.

I held still, terrified that he'd change his mind and pull away. I could feel his internal battle, yet I didn't want him to stop. Part of me believed that if I could only make him lose control, something would shift. He'd begin smiling and singing on a regular basis and the world would fill with rainbows and unicorns.

I was an idiot. This man had set rules for himself. If he failed his own standards, he'd likely hate himself and hate me by extension. But my body had already decided, and it seemed my mind was happy to follow.

I wiggled my camisole over my head and threw it on the floor. "Touch me, Emir. I don't want to be alone tonight."

He stared at my breasts, mouth ajar. "You're so beautiful, Janie. It's impossible to look away."

"Why would you look away?" Smiling at him, I peeled off the rest of the blanket, exposing his toned chest. "I'm not going to."

I ran my fingers down the hairy middle, down the narrow trail leading to the hard-on that, if possible, was even bigger than before. Holding his gaze, I wrapped my fingers around his length, eliciting a rough gasp.

"Janie. I..."

I gave him a good stroke, watching his eyes roll back. "What? Do you want me to stop?"

"No. But you must. Or..."

He removed my hand to catch his breath, and rolled me onto my back, holding his weight over me, his face inches from mine. "Janie. I don't do casual sex or casual relationships. So, if you want this, you're mine. You don't date other guys. I don't look at other women."

"You can look, frowny face." I smiled, rubbing my thumb on his forehead. "But I won't date anyone else. How could I? You scare them away."

I tried to hold onto my smile, to keep my tone light, but he wouldn't have it. Emir's dark eyes bored down into my soul, simultaneously chilling and heating my blood. Hot. Cold. I couldn't decide. It was the strangest feeling.

His hand tightened around my arm. "I'm ready. I want to take the risk, even if I can't see the road ahead. I want to believe it's still there, and I'll do everything I can to keep you."

The words left my mouth hanging, and he kissed me, slowly and deliberately. Whatever I'd had in mind, it wasn't this. I'd thought I could drive him over the edge, tease him until he snapped and fucked me against the wall, giving us both a moment of release, finally. But this man was after my heart, like he was preparing to not just have sex but... make love? Seriously? That hot cold feeling intensified, filling my chest. What did he mean he was ready? How was he going to keep me?

But as the kiss deepened, his tongue sweeping in to meet mine, I forgot my questions. And when his hand trailed down my belly, I forgot all the rest. He kissed my lips, then my ear and neck as that hand travelled further south. Brushing over my hip bone, he retreated, then made his way down again. My legs trembled from anticipation, and I fought the urge to push his fingers where I craved them. I knew he was teasing me, and it was working. I'd never been hungrier for more.

Lowering to snatch my nipple between his lips, he finally stroked across my pubic bone. Stars burst behind my eyelids, and I felt the surge of hot liquid inside me, rushing down to my core. A pulse of pleasure built up between my thighs, so sweet and perfect it pushed away everything else, not leaving behind a single intelligent thought. His fingers had finally arrived, teasing me lightly over the fabric. Diving between my pajama bottoms and panties, he drew circles through the soaked cotton, his touch as light as a gust of breath, and I arched my back, moaning from frustration.

"You like that?" I heard the smile in his voice, or maybe I imagined it.

"Yes," I gasped, moving in sync with his hand like we were dancing, enjoying the way my body responded to everything he did. "Don't stop."

As I pushed against his hand, he drew back, but only so much, gradually increasing the pressure as my hips moved up to beg for more. The fingers kept moving, slowly and deliberately, like he could go on forever. Somehow, I believed he could, and the thought relaxed me further, my head sinking deeper into the pillow, my body surrendering, cell by cell. I was finally leaving my head, entering the sweet oblivion. Without the rush. Without the expectations.

It was just me and him, and the night. And I was safe.

Emir rose to my eye level, kissing my cheek.

"You're perfect, Janie. So perfect."

My heart squeezed, sending dangerous signals all over my body. He wasn't only turning me on and taking me over the edge. He was disarming me. There was no turning back. I'd crossed that bridge some time ago, and now I'd follow this path to its very end.

Emir leaned on his elbow, his eyes roaming my bare breasts, dark and glassy, unhurried. "In my fantasies, you were always naked," he murmured. "But you look even better than I imagined. So sexy."

Holding my gaze, he slipped his hand inside my panties, finally his skin on my skin, gasping as he discovered the pool of slick and wet that had already formed. His relentless teasing had transformed me. If my usual aroused state resembled a landscape of dewy grass, this was the wetlands. "Oh, Janie."

He tugged the waistband a little lower, then over my buttocks. "This sweet ass...," he panted into my ear. "Let me see you."

Pulling my pajama bottoms and underwear down to my knees, then completely off, he lowered between my thighs, landing his tongue between my swollen folds. My pulse throbbed like a heavy drumbeat, drowning all other sounds. He pulled back, teasing and teasing, until I trembled all over. That light touch was so much better than any grinding I'd felt in the past, so careful and precise. Emir didn't do anything sloppy, and I'd never appreciated it more.

I'd started this. I needed this. But how would I ever survive this? His thumb sunk inside me, and his tongue pressed once again on the nerve endings ruling my body. I felt the unstoppable force of orgasm gathering momentum. I cried out, tilting my pelvis at his face and grasping the crumpled sheets as involuntary dance moves took over. A wave after wave shook me, flooding my body with such intense pleasure I feared nothing would ever compare.

I took deep breaths, opening my eyes for a moment to confirm that yes, the ceiling was indeed spinning. As the pulsating settled into a breathable rhythm, I reached for him. Where was Emir? My hand landed on his arm, and I turned to face him, laying side by side just like we'd been earlier, eyeballing each other with nervous energy. Now, my eyelids dipped, and a dazed smile hung on my lips, every part of me relaxed, yet so alive.

"I lost touch with reality."

It was an experience I'd cherish for the rest of my life. Dating was awkward. Everything was hard work. But these moments with Emir were easy and light.

I pushed him onto his back and stroked him, then took him into my mouth, enjoying the momentary power shift. Emir was mine, and I'd make him come. I'd highjacked his bed. It was only fair. Except as I touched him, the need between my thighs bloomed again, hollow and demanding.

"I want you inside me," I whispered.

He pulled me up to his chest and rolled me over.

I couldn't even fight back for show as he pinned my wrists against the mattress and lay half of his weight on me, nuzzling his rock-hard erection between my legs. It slid along slick skin and the pulse of pleasure traveled up my spine felt like a heatwave. He moved against me, holding my gaze, and a wobbly moan rose from my mouth. Oh, God. I could come again right here.

His eyes darkened. "I don't have a condom."

I blinked, feeling stupid. It had been so long since I'd slept with anyone that I'd evidently lost my sex license.

"No, wait! There might be one in the drawer." I pointed to my left and Emir reached for the nightstand.

Before he'd moved out, Shaun had moved into this room, taking the nightstand with him. I'd never thought I'd be grateful for anything he did, but here we were.

"Phew," he said, pulling out a strip of condoms. "I was prepared to run through the house naked."

"No, you weren't!" Laugh bubbled in my chest.

"Anything for you Janie. Even my dignity."

I stroked him and the smile turned into a hungry look.

He'd been holding back, taking care of me, waiting...

"Take me, Emir." The look I gave him held an open challenge. "Don't hold back."

Something in his eyes shifted. Darker. Hungrier. "You sure?"

"Positive."

He turned me around, lifting my bottom up until I was on my knees, ass in the air.

"Oh my God, Janie," he bit out, and I heard the condom wrapper, before he drove into me, emptying my lungs. Whatever control this man had held onto, I could no longer feel it. His hips pumped and he filled me again and again. The tightness in my core built up, releasing new ripples of pleasure.

I'd finally pushed him over the edge, and it drove me wild. I responded to each push with a moan, offering myself to him, yet losing myself in the sensation of absolute fullness.

"Janie, I can't hold it."

"Come, Emir."

"Not without you."

His fingers traced circles between my legs. Softer, then harder. I moved with him, chasing my second wave. When I heard his low growl and felt the pulse of his release inside me, my body followed, unraveling again. I felt it deeper, a hot wave that rose inside of me like magma from inside the earth.

He held onto my hips for a moment longer, locked into me,

then eventually pulled away, letting me drop onto the mattress.

I sucked in breaths, trying to gather my fragmented thoughts. But my brain was mush. I wondered if the afterglow would last for days or weeks.

He discarded the condom and lay down next to me, pulling the blanket over us. With concerned eyes, he brushed a strand of hair from my face. "Was that too rough?"

I smiled. "I'll be walking funny for a week."

His eyes filled with regret. "I'm sorry. I... lost control for a moment."

He looked so distraught and adorable I had to take his face into my hands. "Emir. That's what I wanted. It was perfect."

"Perfect," he repeated, in disbelief, yet relieved.

Almost perfect. Maybe spank me next time. I wanted to say something brusque to lighten the mood. But his eyes were too soft, exploring me, his fingers playing with loose tendrils of hair, and something in me broke. I couldn't put on a smile. I couldn't deliver the clever lines.

"You took care of me like... no one ever has." That was the truth, and it came out a little strangled as my eyes misted, making his face blurry.

"Don't talk about me in past tense. I'm here and I'm not done with you."

"You're not?" I blinked away the stubborn tear, trying to smile.

"I don't think I'll ever be done with you, Janie."

I stared at the mix of pain and awe in his eyes, feeling the same terrible cocktail in every part of my body. Emir had been clear about one thing. He didn't do casual relationships. I'd skipped over that part, only processing half of what he was saying, storing it for later. And now it was later, and those words were back, pouring out of his eyes, straight into my soul.

I couldn't think of him casually. Whatever I wanted to call this, it was too late to walk away unscathed. I was attached, tethered, dependent, and oh-so-satisfied. Maybe I could call it a fling later when the dust had settled. That would fall into some sort of socially accepted framework that made sense to other people. But it didn't make sense to me. I'd always known we were more than that. We could go our separate ways, but would we ever be done with each other?

Hormones shift and fade, I told myself. You'll recover.

"I don't want to think about the future," I whispered. "Not yet."

His eyes burned. "I don't want to think about the future without you."

My phone beeped on the nightstand, and I reached for it, relieved for the momentary distraction.

"It's Gus," I said. "He wants to know if I'm ready to do the drone shots tomorrow. Apparently, there's bad weather coming next week so this is our only chance."

Emir's eyes narrowed and he shifted closer, making me his little spoon. "Only chance? The weather changes five times a day in this country."

I chuckled. I loved that he'd noticed New Zealand's changeable ways. "I hope it's not terrible all week. That'd be awful for Cem and Aria."

"I've fixed the awning on the deck so unless there's a hurricane—"

"Cyclone."

"What's the difference?"

"We only have cyclones on this side of the hemisphere. We can have typhoons…" I huffed at myself. Why was I educating him on all things New Zealand? "It doesn't matter. Thank you for fixing the awning."

My phone pinged again. It was Gus suggesting a time.

"Do I even need drone shots?" I sighed onto the screen. "I don't want to get up at seven."

"Why seven? Afternoon light will work just as well."

I turned to him. "Really? I love you!"

The words collided with reality, instantly taking on a new meaning, and I froze. His hand on my waist froze. Nobody breathed for seconds.

"I mean…" I finally wiggled around to look at him. My unsure smile wavered. I couldn't let myself go there.

"I know." He buried his face in my hair.

We lay in silence, and he held me so tight there wasn't room for words.

When my phone pinged again, he spoke in a darker voice. "I'm coming with you."

I didn't argue. That would have been pointless. Instead, I melted against his wide chest, enjoying the weight of his arm around me. The fear had vanished. He'd chased it away with his presence, his attentiveness, his… I stopped myself right on the cusp of another

L-word, shaking from soft laughter. A couple of mind-blowing orgasms, and I was losing my mind.

Yet, I didn't move. I made no attempt to distance myself from him. I listened to his breathing deepen as he fell asleep, enjoying the way he held onto me, even in his sleep. It was a fleeting moment, but I'd memorize it. I'd keep it forever.

My mind was a whirlpool of scary questions, my body loose and tender. But my heart glowed like a bioluminescent creature, lighting up the darkness around us, and I fell asleep thinking of him.

CHAPTER 23

Emir

She was in my arms, I registered through a haze of sleep. I'd dreamed of us, right there, sleeping side by side in her guest room, my arm resting on her hip. It made sense. There wasn't anything better to be dreaming about. Sure, we could have both sprouted wings and been able to fly, or breakfast items could have materialized out of thin air, but I couldn't see that hugely improving reality.

Daylight seeped in through the crack between the heavy curtains, serving as a gentle reminder of the outside world. Janie stirred against me, her breathing shortening as she woke up.

"Emir?" She wrapped her fingers around my arm and my heart expanded.

"I'm right here."

"You stayed with me." I heard the smile in her sleepy voice.

She turned to face me. Gazing into her sleepy eyes, I marveled at the absence of pain. Every part of me felt rested, my head light on the pillow. I think she saw the difference in me, because her fingers climbed up to my forehead and her smile widened. "You look different."

"I feel different. Good."

Her smile widened, and she traced her finger to the corner of my mouth. "I've been so obsessed with making you smile." She blushed.

She looked so adorable I didn't even realize I was smiling back until her finger touched my incisor. "It's magical, you know?" There was a hint of teasing, but also that warmth I'd come to associate with her. Janie gave everything meaning.

"It's not that I don't want to smile. I just haven't had a reason."

"Oh, Emir." Her eyes filled with compassion, and she sunk her fingers into my hair and massaged my scalp. "I didn't massage you last night. That was our agreement. I'm so sorry."

I wanted to tell her I wasn't in any pain, but her touch released a sweet sensation, flowing like liquid down my spine, paralyzing my tongue. I wanted to stay right here, forever.

"It's okay, Janie." I finally closed my hand around her wrist, holding it down. "You haven't broken our agreement."

"I have," she insisted. "When I checked on Molly yesterday, her eye looked so much better. And I saw you cleaned the stables, too. And my veggie garden looks amazing. Have you been weeding it?"

"I have a lot of time on my hands," I said evasively. "But it doesn't mean you owe me anything."

"But I promised to massage you! And yesterday..." Her eyes darkened.

"Yesterday was a shit show, that somehow turned into the best day of my life." I leaned in to kiss her. "That's the part I want to focus on."

"What time is it?" She lifted her head to peer over my shoulder.

I reached for my phone she was eyeing on the bedside table and raised it to check the time. "Eight thirty. What time is that drone shoot?"

"We're meeting Gus by the harbor at 3pm. But Aria and Cem are coming to work on the decorations. Or I think Aria is on that and Cem is..."

"Annoying me full-time," I finished.

She giggled into my chest, then her voice turned serious. "Do you think they'll notice there's something between us? Should we tell them?"

"Why wouldn't we?"

"I don't know. Because it's so new?"

"But what if I can't hide it?" I asked.

My brother would probably take one look at my face and call it.

"Then I guess we have no choice."

"It might be good to have them on our side," As much as my brother annoyed me, I needed him onboard. This was going to be a hard sell for my parents.

She bit her lip, her eyes peering at me from behind the strands of hair. "Okay, maybe."

"So, what time are they coming?"

"At around ten."

"Which means we have time for…"

"What did you have in mind?"

My gaze fell on her breasts, peeking from underneath the blanket, and I pulled it a little lower, watching her cheeks color and eyes crinkle with a smile. I was already hard, having woken up that way, and more blood rushed in to complete the job. "You've taken over my mind, Janie. I dreamed about you."

Tears sprung to her eyes, making her smile sparkle. "I was worried you'd be too hard on yourself for failing your own standards… I mean, you had it all figured out and you decided we shouldn't get involved. Your logic was flawless." She gave a sad chuckle. "I was worried you'd wake up and regret this."

A smile spread across my face, effortlessly, and I let it. I dropped the phone back on the table and turned my attention on her, enjoying the way her face lit up in response. I'd never get tired of her smile. "I was relying on logic for years but look where it got me. I was in pain. I was miserable. Now I feel… good. How could I regret that? I tend to expect a lot from myself, but I'm human. We make mistakes…" Her eyes flooded with worry, and I instantly regretted my word choice. "Not this! *This* is not the mistake. I meant what I said last night. Let's make this work."

A shadow of fear crossed her face, and I held my breath. Would she accept my change of mind? Would she give us a fighting chance?

"Emir. I can't see that far ahead. But I want you right now. Please?" Her apologetic voice turned breathy, and she leaned closer, placing her lips on mine. I didn't need another invitation. I'd stay and love her, for as long as she'd let me. I knew better than to freak her out with confessions she wasn't ready for, but deep in my heart, I knew what I felt. Something that hadn't happened in years, something that I thought would maybe never happen again, had come over me like a meteor shower, changing the color of the sky. There was no room for anything else on my mind as I put my hands on her warm skin and my tongue surged to meet hers.

She shuffled closer, skin to skin. The way we fit together left no room for anything and it gave me hope. We kissed like it was Sunday, with nothing else on the agenda, lost in the moment. Nothing felt familiar, even my own body or face. I'd become unrecognizable to myself, but I was willing to overlook anything to stay in that bubble with her.

Janie, out of control, was better than anything I could have captured with my camera. The halo of morning sun in her hair, eyes rolling back, mouth ajar. Her body was controlling mine, commanding every cell.

We made love, losing track of time. Afterwards, she collapsed on my chest, out of breath. "Emir. Your smile is kryptonite. You have to be careful."

I stroked her hair, inhaling deeply. "I'll keep that in mind."

What if I couldn't keep this stupid grin hidden in public? My family would think I'd lost my mind. They'd ship me away to an institution. A laugh bubbled up in my chest. First a low rumble, like the distant sound of earthworks, slowly turning into an earthquake.

Janie jerked up, staring at my face, blinking.

My laughter settled into a soft chuckle. "You think I'm a miserable, grumpy bastard, right?" I wiped my eyes, shaking my head. "I can't blame you. I'd forgotten how to feel... light enough, I guess."

Her eyes misted. "I... I don't even know what to think of you, Emir. You keep surprising me."

We stared at each other for a moment, both unable to speak. I could see it in her eyes, the weight of what had happened between us. The implications. There was no going back to what we'd been before, yet we had no words for what existed right now. It was too fresh.

As the waves of pleasure settled into gentle laps, the reality re-entered our world. Janie rolled off me, checking her phone for time. "I have to feed the pigs and check on Molly, let her out..."

She leapt from the bed, and I followed her, finding her camisole on the floor. "I'll help."

"Only if you want to. I also need to get new locks and some kind of security system and maybe report the break-in to the police. But I don't want to turn my home into a crime scene."

She looked so distraught, standing before me in her underwear, hair mussed. "You don't have to go to the police if you don't want to. We can just secure the property."

"Okay."

"I'll call Cem right now and ask him to pick up a few items on the way. We can add a deadbolt to the front door and secure the latches on those sliding doors. How does that sound?"

"I'll pay him back! But nothing hi-tech or super expensive," she pleaded.

"Okay." I had no control over Cem's spending, but I also knew he'd never accept a penny from Janie.

"Thank you!" Her smile was adorable when she kissed me on the cheek and skipped off to get dressed.

CHAPTER 24

Janie

With Emir handling more than half of my morning chores, we were back in the dining room in half an hour, preparing eggs on toast. I'd insisted on a light breakfast so I could focus on baking something for Cem and Aria's visit. I couldn't believe how much had happened since the last time I'd seen my friend. This was the longest weekend of my life.

Emir cleaned up our breakfast dishes, casting dubious glances my way as I ransacked the cupboards to find ingredients for spicy apple muffins.

"You don't have to cater for them," he said.

"Isn't that the Turkish way, though? Catering and cleaning like your life depends on it?" It was a phrase one of my Turkish interviewees had used years ago.

Emir grinned. "We're in New Zealand."

Seeing that smile on his face, my insides did a series of flips. I focused on mixing the muffin batter. "I know. I'm just getting ready for the culture shock."

He stepped closer, forcing me to look up. "Are you planning to follow me to Istanbul?"

Logic caught up with my flighty heart, and I laughed. "I don't know what I'm saying. I'm all high on... you know."

His smile faded and my laughter fizzled out. We couldn't make any plans or promises.

His gaze snagged on a photo on the fridge. Me and my boys on the day we'd moved to Napier. I'd asked Shaun to take the photo after a lunch in town. He'd hated the food, and complained about everything, and I'd been happy he wasn't in the picture, ruining our fresh start with his foul mood. Alex and Josh both smiled— the sort of polite half-smile they knew would be passable with me. They looked so handsome in their new shirts. With all the expenses on the farm, I'd have to work twice as hard to provide for them. I couldn't let them down.

"Tell me about them," Emir said softly, following my gaze.

I shook my head and smiled. He didn't need to know about my kids. This was a fling. Whatever he'd told me. Whatever I'd felt last night... nothing could change my reality.

"They both look like you. The younger has your eyes," he said, studying the photo. "What are they like?"

"Alex is eighteen. He's artistic, easy-going... an extrovert. Josh is only thirteen. He's a thinker. Very smart. Quiet. Always thinking of others." I sighed, looking at the photo. "I miss them so much."

Emir rubbed my shoulder. "When are they coming to visit?"

"In a couple of weeks."

"I bet they miss you."

I smiled. "Alex would never admit it. Josh does. He's my baby."

Emir brushed a strand of hair behind my ear, his eyes sad. "I know you can't leave, but maybe you can visit? Maybe I can come back. We won't give up hope."

I nodded, staring at him, hopelessly trying to freeze time.

When I had the muffins rising in the oven, Gru shot towards the door, signaling the arrival of our guests before anyone even knocked on the door. He was such a good boy. What had happened during the break-in? I couldn't see any signs of harm or injury on him, yet he'd somehow ended up outside. Had my dog been trying to protect the house or just wagged his tail at the criminal?

Judging by his reaction to Aria and Cem, he'd likely drooled from enthusiasm.

"Welcome!" I called from the kitchen as Emir opened the door to his brother holding several paper bags.

"We brought decorations," Aria announced, placing two more bags on the dining table. "And muffins."

I gave her a pained grin. "Excuse me but I'm baking muffins!"

Her mouth hung for a second, then stretched into a smile. "We'll have a muffin tasting! Yours will win and you get a trophy."

"I can live with that."

As Cem and Emir unpacked the decorations, Aria met me in the kitchen, peering into my oven. "They smell amazing. So much better than store bought. Store bought are awful."

"It's okay," I assured her, smiling to myself. "How was the premiere?"

Aria let out a long, dreamy sigh. "Incredible. Seeing myself on the big screen in a real film like that... I can't even describe that feeling. And seeing Cem! He did so well. He's going to get more English-speaking roles because of that, I know it."

"What about you? Do you want to do more acting?"

"Yes... and no. I'd do a film like that any day, but I'm not desperate to take any role, you know? I'm happy to wait for a good one."

"As you should!"

After a moment, she gave me a concerned look. "How are you? The break-in sounds scary! I hope Emir is looking after you."

All the blood in my body surged into my cheeks. For a moment, I was convinced our sexy times were playing on my forehead like a dirty film cast by a tiny projector. But as I tried to wipe the wildly peculiar expression off my face, I realized she'd only picked up on a vibe. A strong one, though.

"Oh, my God, Janie. Has he... did he... sorry, I'm not sure why my mind's going down these tracks." Aria fanned herself, giving me an apologetic look.

"It's okay. It's been good to have a man around." I focused on finding oven mitts, to buy time.

We'd agreed on telling Aria and Cem, but now I felt reluctant to do so. Whatever was happening between us felt too fragile and too important. I was afraid putting it into words would flatten it, making it sound insignificant or cheesy.

Aria looked over my shoulder at Cem and Emir, and her eyes widened. It took me a moment to realize what she was reacting to. It wasn't Cem pulling turquoise paper ribbon out of a bag, unravelling it as he went. It was Emir, laughing.

Aria turned to me in shock. "What have you done to him?"

I decided to start with the easy one. "I... gave him a massage. Helps with his headache, apparently."

"He had a headache? It was all a headache?" Her volume rose.

"All what?"

"You know... that miserable fuckwit act." Aria's eyes flicked back at the men, busy untangling the ribbons, until Cem simply ripped the thing in half.

I peeked into the oven and decided I liked my muffins a little gooey. Before I met him, I'd known Emir as the side character in Aria's love story. The heartless manager who had stood in the way of their happiness. But that wasn't the Emir I knew. They felt like two different people, and I found myself oddly offended on his behalf.

"He's been in pain," I said, setting the muffins on the cooling rack.

The middles sank a little. I'd probably have to call them lava cakes. And forfeit the trophy.

A sudden burst of alarmingly loud Turkish made us both turn around. Cem talked to his brother, his eyes wild. His animated hand gesturing reminded me of road rage incidents I'd witnessed in the Middle East.

My throat squeezed. Had he told his brother about us?

"What are you guys shouting about?" Aria asked, cautiously approaching her fiancé.

Cem blew out a breath, eyes wide. "Just... our parents. Mom called me when she couldn't get hold of Emir. They're supposed to be enjoying Lake Tekapo but all she talks about is the wedding."

"Engagement party," Aria corrected.

"No, the wedding," Cem insisted. "She's having a hard time with... stuff."

"Hi! I'm Stuff," Aria raised her hand, eyes cast at the ceiling.

"It's not you. She likes you. But she keeps asking where we're going to live and where the grandchildren will grow up and what language they will speak and what religion they'll be and if they'll become 'foreigners'." He rolled his eyes. "It's exhausting!"

"Not to mention a little uncomfortable." Aria winced.

"What did you tell her?" I asked Cem, trying to keep my voice neutral.

Cem shrugged. "I just deflect. I keep reminding them they'll always have Emir." He jerked a thumb at his brother. "He might still marry a Turkish lady and have Turkish babies, right?"

Emir glared back, unimpressed.

Aria laced her fingers, leaping forward to theatrically pray to him. "Please, Emir! You're our only chance. If you let the ladies see that smile of yours, you won't be single for long. Just make sure you save the smiles for the Turkish ladies."

Emir scoffed, back to his usual frown. "Why do I have to smile for anyone?"

Aria turned her palms up to the ceiling. "I suppose the Turkish ladies don't mind. I've been watching these Dizis with Cem and there's this one mafia saga where the guys never smile. So, you're good. You remind me of the lead actor..."

I turned around to plate the muffins and hid my smile. I couldn't stop imagining Emir as a Turkish mafioso. He had the looks.

Cem lowered his voice. "Seriously, though, man. We need you to give them some hope. Call Mom. Remind her that you'll be around, that they're not losing you and maybe hint that you're open to dating in Istanbul."

"Like, a teeny, tiny hint!" Aria chorused. "Five percent chance you'll someday marry and have babies."

I took a breath, trying to relax. I was getting a decent ab workout from all the dating and baby mentions. I brought the muffins to the table. "Can I take coffee orders? Emir?"

"I don't want babies in any country," he grumbled. "You do it!"

Cem sighed. "I'm not asking you to have a baby. I'm asking you to give them hope, remind them that you're there for them."

"Why do I have to be there for them? Can't you? Split the year in half—summer in Turkey, then summer in New Zealand."

I held my breath as Emir and Cem entered a staring match. Air sizzled.

"Oh, the joys of international relationships." I smiled,

attempting a light tone I couldn't quite deliver.

Aria gave me a sad smile, tucking into one of the muffins. "Ahhh. I needed this," she mumbled, mouth full.

"But you're the responsible one!" Cem finally cried. "You're always reminding others... me... It's not like you'll ever move away from home. You have the shop, and the... why are you being like this? Stop torturing us! We're just trying to keep the peace and get through this engagement party and the wedding without Mom losing her mind."

Emir lifted a shoulder. "Parents cry at weddings, that's totally normal."

"You know Mom. She won't just dab her eyes with a tissue. She'll bawl and cause a scene."

"And I'm responsible for her emotional stability?" Emir stared back defiantly.

Cem groaned from frustration. "I swear... You act like a dick most of the time, and I ignore that, and I remind myself of your good qualities. You're dependable. You're smart. You're always there for Mom and Dad. You can turn that stupid shop around. If it was up to me, I'd sell that shit, but you know what it means to Dad. Are you saying I can't count on you anymore? That we can't count on you?" He glanced at Aria, drawing strength from their union.

Aria took another bite of the muffin, opting for silent chewing. A wise choice.

Emir looked away, twisting a paper ribbon around his finger until it was as fat as a toilet paper roll. "I'm just... considering my options. Am I not allowed to have options? Only Cem the movie star can take off and fall in love and change the course of his life?" He looked up, jutting his chin forward, voice cracking a little.

The hurt and confusion on Cem and Aria's faces made me feel ill.

Emir's gaze landed on me.

Not now. Please. I don't want to be the reason. They'll hate me.

"I'll make coffee," I announced brightly, skipping to the kitchen.

On the way out, I grabbed one of the muffins, and grimaced as my teeth hit the gooey middle. Not just gooey. Undercooked. Why was I so impatient? Was that why I'd slept with Emir? Because I couldn't wait until the chemical imbalance in my brain settled and good sense prevailed. And now I'd caused this drift between him and his brother, and probably his parents.

How could we ever tell them about us? Did we have to? A hundred years from now, all this would be irrelevant.

Solid logic, Janie.

Emir followed me a beat later and stood by the coffee maker. I knew he was waiting until I had the milk steamer hissing to disguise our voices.

When the rhythmic whistling filled the room, he leaned in. "We need to tell them. They'll just keep pushing, expecting us to play along and... I don't want to have babies in Istanbul!"

"No," I hissed over the steamer. "They're stressed about the engagement party and the wedding. If we tell them, they'll be even more stressed. They're already worried about how your parents will take it. Imagine what they'll say..."

"My parents will wail and moan no matter what. I'm not sacrificing—"

"This party is not about us and I'm not going to make it about us. I can't do that to Aria." I gestured at the dining table.

Aria babbled about creating some sort of backdrop and garlands to hang outside on the morning of the party. I could tell how nervous she was, but also excited. Maybe she'd be one of the lucky ones who only did this once and lived happily ever after. Either way, this was about her and Cem. I'd make sure we stayed in the background, much like those streamers hanging on the wall.

Emir sighed. "Okay. We won't tell them, yet. But after the party..."

He trailed off, looking even more distraught. Because we both knew that was our deadline. He'd fly back the next day.

"I'd change my flights but there's a fee, and Mom and Dad will need help—"

"Please take these." I handed him two coffees. "I'll make two more for us and then we'll devote our time to party decorations. Okay?"

He took the coffees, grumbling something under his breath.

I sighed, watching his receding back. He was tough. Proud. Obstinate. Yet, I knew he'd heard me. He would do as I asked. He'd respect my wishes. A dangerous warmth poured through my entire body, and I shivered. Damn it, Emir! He was supposed to be a disagreeable, miserable sod, who happened to be hot. He was an incredible lover—perfect fling material. Yet everything else about him had caught me off guard, and I already knew one thing. This was going to hurt.

CHAPTER 25

Emir

I was not a crafty person. Fixing fences, wiring electronics, or even repairing antique radios, sure. But ask me to weave fragile strips of paper, and things got ugly. Thankfully, my brother was even worse, and more vocal about it, so we were soon excused from the world of streamers.

"You can help me install the new deadbolt," I told Cem, taking the bag of supplies he'd picked up from the hardware store.

Janie had made up her mind, and I had to respect that. If I told my brother about us, I might ruin any chance I had with her, and nothing was worth that risk.

"You saying someone picked the lock?" Cem examined the door, eyebrows drawn.

"That's the only explanation I have. Plus, you can see the faint scratches on the metal." I guided him to look at the other side.

I freed the new deadbolt from its packaging and got the power drill ready. It wasn't very powerful but when fully charged, it had just enough kick for ten minutes. Maybe something to upgrade within the next year or so, I thought before catching myself. I couldn't think that far ahead.

Cem peered in, confusion clouding his eyes. "Why go through the trouble? A house in the middle of nowhere, no witnesses... It'd be so much faster to just break one of the million windows."

"I know. I agree. And I can't explain it."

And it bothered me.

Somehow, if it had been a simple smash and grab with the telltale mess and missing valuables, I could have breathed easier. Something about this felt personal and sinister. And the more I thought about flying back to Turkey and leaving Janie here, by herself, the worse I felt.

"I'm glad you're looking out for her." Cem held the door as I marked the placement for the new lock above the old one. "I didn't even know you could do this yourself."

"Why not? Seems to be the way in this country. DIY."

I kept seeing that advertised everywhere, like it was a great privilege to do everything yourself.

I'd never installed a lock before, but I didn't want Janie to spend money on a locksmith when she was already struggling. A couple of YouTube videos had told me the basics. The lock packet even came with a paper template to show you where to drill. If only everything else in life had been that straightforward. Follow the instruction to a guaranteed outcome.

The only thing I didn't have were safety goggles, but once we got to drilling the larger hole for the cylinder, Cem lent me his designer shades.

"You're adapting to the ways of the country," Cem mused. "You look more at home here than I do, and I've been shooting a film here for two months, and I'm marrying a local."

"You mean I look at home doing maintenance?"

Cem folded his arms. "No, I mean... you look different. Something's different..."

He leaned in to establish eye contact, as if I was hiding something. Which I was, obviously, but I fixed him with my best scowl.

"Or maybe not." He shrugged.

My face hurt from frowning. Was that what I'd been doing before? The headaches were starting to make more sense.

"I didn't say it was bad, different." Cem's voice was thoughtful as he handed me the power drill. "You seem more relaxed. Happier."

"Just keeping up appearances. It's the Kiwi way."

"Well, if you're doing it for me and Aria, we appreciate it. I was worried about you getting along with Janie. She seems so—"

"What?" I ground out between lips holding two screws.

"So... bubbly. Friendly. I thought that might not mix too well with yours truly. I was worried you'd end up offending her."

"You think I'm that obnoxious?" I asked, knowing full well that

I was. I had been, at least.

"No," Cem said, to my surprise. "You have a good heart, deep down. Way, way down. And she's probably figured that out, judging by the way she looks at you."

My head whipped around embarrassingly fast. "What do you mean?" I turned back to the lock, deliberately slowing my movements. "I mean... how do you think she looks at me?"

Way to sound less needy, man.

Cem chuckled. "If I didn't know better, I'd say you like her."

Just like him to not answer the question. He'd make me beg and reveal all my cards.

I lifted a shoulder. "She smiles too much, but she's not as fake as I first thought."

An image of Janie in bed, her eyelids fluttering, mouth ajar but still somehow smiling flashed behind my eyes. There was nothing fake about her. About us. I may have offended her, just like Cem had predicted, but I'd also surrendered to whatever was growing between us. I didn't feel the same. I wasn't the same, and having to hide it was making me increasingly uncomfortable.

"Done," I said, tightening the screws.

"Really?"

Janie's bright voice shot straight to my heart. Light streaming from kitchen doorway gave her a halo as she stepped into the entry hall, smiling so brightly I had to fight the urge to smile back. With Cem's suspicious eyes on me, I'd never hear the end of it.

"You do the honors." I handed her the new key and closed the front door.

"Oh, wow." She joined me at the door.

I should have moved back, to make sure I didn't raise any suspicion, but I couldn't. If there was a chance to inhale her scent, I was ready to risk everything.

Janie stepped outside, locking and unlocking the door, letting out a rapturous gasp as she stepped inside and turned the latch, locking the door again. I'd never seen anyone quite so enamored by a door before.

"That click," she explained, turning the latch again, "is so satisfying. Thank you."

"Are all Kiwi women turned on by locks? Asking for a friend." Cem sneered behind me.

Janie whipped her head, casting him a brilliant smile. "Totally. I recommend a new deadbolt and a panic room for your wedding night."

She turned to me and her exaggerated smile morphed into a grateful one, eyes glossy. "Thank you, Emir. You have no idea what this means. I feel like I've been tensing muscles I didn't even know I had, and they just relaxed."

"That's good." I wanted so badly to hold her that my entire arm twitched.

What was my brother still doing here? A quick glance in his direction answered my question. He was assessing us, his eyes flicking between us, a sly smile tugging at his lips.

I cleared my throat and started packing up the tools. Once done, I fetched the vacuum cleaner from the hallway closet, ignoring another look from my brother. Yes, I knew where she kept cleaning supplies. So, what?

Janie tried to take the vacuum. "That's my job, Emir."

"I made the mess, I'll clean it."

She stepped back and took Cem with her as I cleaned up the sawdust. Maybe she'd sensed it, too—The longer we spent together, the more we risked revealing. If she didn't want to tell them about us, she had to stay away from me.

CHAPTER 26

Janie

I pulled up to a half-empty parking lot overlooking the ocean. "This is it, I think. I'll just double check Gus's message."

As I mentioned the filmmaker's name, the crease on Emir's forehead reappeared. "I can't see his Hyundai."

"How do you remember his car?"

He shrugged. "I just do."

After a moment, we spotted the car approaching us. "Promise me you'll behave."

His face softened. "I don't like him, but I'll be civil."

I blew out a breath, reaching for the door handle. "Good enough. I don't like him either, but he has major GAS and we can use that to our advantage."

"GAS?"

"Gear acquisition syndrome," I clarified. "It's a common condition within the film and TV industry."

My heart leapt as a short laugh rumbled out of him. "I thought it was short for gaslighting as that seemed to be his special talent."

I burst out in full laughter, still holding onto the door handle. This was too good. I didn't care how stupid the jokes were, or at whose expense. All I cared about was that connection between us.

We met Gus by his vehicle. His collar shirt seemed fresh out of a packet, with the creases from folding still visible.

"Hello, Gus!" I shook his hand. "Thank you for meeting us. Are you ready to go or do you want to grab coffees?"

"Hi!" Gus smiled back, until he noticed Emir behind me. "Oh. I didn't realize you brought... who's he again?"

I forced my smile a little wider and voice chirpier. "Emir's helping out at the farm and offered to get some B-roll."

"What kind of camera do you have?" Gus glared at Emir.

"Black one," Emir deadpanned, and I had to engage my entire core, Pilates-style, to stop from cracking up in snort-laughter.

Gus rolled his eyes unappreciatively. "I meant the make and model, but whatever."

"It's good enough," Emir said evasively, gesturing at the cars. "Shall we?"

Gus wouldn't budge. He shifted his weight from one leg to the other, his voice turning into a reprimanding drone. "I know you're trying to be clever or whatever, but I'm only asking since Janie said she'll edit. That means she'll have to match your footage to mine and deal with the different ratios and frame rates and completely different color profiles."

Emir raised an eyebrow. "It's B-roll. She can take it or leave it. Shall we?" He took a step towards my car.

Gus folded his arms, sticking out his chin. "I have to say I'm not entirely comfortable—"

"Would you like to grab coffees before we leave?" I asked again, quite forcefully.

My stomach punctuated my words with an audible growl. With all the party crafts, we'd lived on undercooked muffins. Coffee might help.

Gus's face brightened. "That's not a bad idea."

Ignoring Emir's frown, I led us to the nearest cafe along the beach road.

Emir followed at our heels like a hovering bodyguard, stopping to wait at the doorway of the cafe. I ordered a flat white for him as well. I could feel his eyes on me, piercing and protective, just like before, but it no longer made me nervous. As mortifying as it was to admit, it excited me. Like I'd tamed a dragon who everyone else feared. He was mine. He'd never hurt me.

"So, you've got yourself a WWOOFer?"

I jerked at Gus's question. I was familiar with WWOOF, a local organization that connected travelers with organic farms, to work for room and board.

"I suppose it's hard to find people who work for free AND speak decent English," he continued. "Where is he from, anyway?"

"He's Turkish, but he's not a tourist. A friend of a friend."

"Turkish, huh?" Gus rubbed his beard. "Heavy smoker?"

"No."

His eyebrows shot up. "For real? Never met a Turk who didn't smoke."

I shrugged. "Well, now you have."

"I quit two months ago. Makes it harder to keep the weight off, but I guess it's better for my health." Gus adjusted his belt, tucking the shirt a little tighter over the bulge.

"For sure. How did you do it?" I asked, grateful for a safe topic.

"Willpower." He thrust out his chest, grabbing his coffee without a thank you.

Picking up the rest of the coffees and sandwiches, I thanked the barista for the both of us and gestured at the door. "Wow. No hypnosis? Not even gum? You must have amazing willpower."

He put on a self-deprecating act. "Well, gum doesn't count, right?"

As we reached the cars, I snuck another look at Emir over my shoulder, and caught him staring at me with such adoring eyes my stomach flipped. Oh, God. I searched for the sense of panic, but only felt that wobbly flip-flopping of my insides, like my organs were playing musical chairs.

I felt Gus's questioning gaze on us. I hadn't given him an answer. Emir wasn't a WWOOFer or a farmhand, but he was hardly a 'friend of a friend' either. Why couldn't I find the words? Why was it this hard?

If I wanted to keep Emir, I'd have to tell people. I'd have to tell my family. If I wanted to hang onto this happiness, and there was no other word for what my heart was doing right now, I'd have to go public with a younger Turkish man.

"Should we take two cars, or—" Gus gestured at his Hyundai.

"Yes." I pointed at a bag on his back seat. "You have a lot of gear."

I was speaking way too brightly, probably annoying Emir. Hell, I was annoying myself, but I couldn't be trapped in a car with this guy, his gear and his gear obsession.

Gus nodded, finally getting behind the wheel. "Do you want to ride with me? We can discuss the shoot? Would save time."

I swallowed hard but gave him a sweet smile. "I would, but Emir can't drive." I shot Emir a sharp look, silencing the protests that clearly hovered on his tongue.

Gus eyed him with mock sympathy. "Oh, no! That's too bad. How do you get around?"

Emir gritted his teeth but played along. "I don't. It's a pain."

Casting me a half-menacing look, he slid into the passenger seat of my car, slamming the door. Teasing him gave me a thrill I wasn't entirely proud of.

"Just follow me, I'll drive to the first location I had in mind. You can tell me if you think it's any good." I smiled at Gus before getting behind the wheel.

"I *can* drive," Emir grumbled as I started the car.

"Sometimes it's best to tell a white lie, trust me. Let that douche feel all smug because he thinks you can't drive, and he thinks that gives him the upper hand somehow. He'll be easier to work with. It's all bullshit anyway. It's not like driving or having a nice car adds inches to your dick—"

"Nice car? *Nice* car?"

I laughed. "I'm not talking about his Huyndai!"

"Thank you."

I couldn't stop chuckling at his indignant expression. What was it with men and cars? I couldn't have cared less about mine.

Entering Esk Valley, my mood shifted. This is why I'd wanted to do the documentary. Nature had already done its thing, new growth taking over the layer of silt that had settled over the landscape, transforming it into a drained ocean floor, but the evidence of destruction was everywhere. I tried to imagine the waters that had poured through, my mind wandering to Emir's home country.

"Have you visited the affected areas after the earthquake in Turkey?"

"No. But my uncle sent pictures of their house and neighborhood. Nothing but rubble." He sighed.

"Natural disasters are so unfair, aren't they?"

I parked by a dilapidated house, with only one of its retaining walls standing upright, perfectly illustrating my argument.

"Don't get too close," Emir said. "That might collapse."

He took out his camera and fiddled with the settings. Gus parked behind us and I met him at his car. "A good spot, eh?" I gestured at the desolate location.

"Very 'The Road', isn't it?" Gus popped his trunk and opened a case containing his precious drone. "Have you seen it?"

I had but shook my head. I didn't feel like gushing over the photography.

I spent the next hour and a half directing Gus, who flew the drone over the landscape. Meanwhile, Emir walked up and down the road, recording footage on the ground. When he returned, Gus had just set up a field monitor on the hood of his car to view the shots.

Throughout the shoot, he kept dropping movie references, either to connect with me or test my knowledge, I wasn't sure. I stuck to my excuse of knowing nothing and not having enough time for movies, until he moved to such old, mainstream titles I could no longer claim ignorance. So, I nodded along as he preached about the importance of wide-angle shots and symmetry in the Shining, grateful that he kept the tone and content professional, even if he stood a little too close, accidentally brushing my shoulder every time he gesticulated with his hands.

He was clearly passionate about filmmaking, and I couldn't hold that against him. Maybe I needed to re-evaluate my first impression.

As Emir approached, Gus stiffened. He shifted closer to me, pointing at something on the screen. I leaned back as much as I could while still paying attention to the clip of aerial footage, which honestly didn't look that different to an earlier clip he was comparing it to.

In different circumstances, I might have flirted a little, to keep him at ease. But I felt Emir's gaze on me. He was fighting hard to not show his reaction, but the air fizzled with tension.

"Thank you, Gus. We'll be in touch."

My smile was genuine as I shook his hand and guided Emir towards our car. I held my breath until I sat behind the wheel, doors closed.

"Are you okay?" Emir's voice was low, filled with concern. "Did he try something? I should have stayed with you, but I was afraid I'd end up slapping that beard off his face." The muscle in his jaw ticked.

I gave a shaky laugh. "No. He's just passionate about films, waffled on and on. Honestly, I think I may have been too hard on him. He's not a bad guy, just a bit awkward."

Emir scoffed. "I get that you try to see the best in everyone, but he's—"

"Obnoxious, yes. But so were you when we first met. If I didn't choose to see the best in everyone, I would have missed out on those smiles you were hiding."

I glanced at him, and my stomach wobbled at the mix of emotions on his face—jealousy shifting to embarrassment, then a ripple of joy. I wanted to bottle it.

"You shouldn't assume everyone has good intentions." Emir smoothed his indigo dress shirt.

He seemed to dress up rather than down, on most occasions. In my linen top and jeans, I felt almost too casual to be seen with him. Yet I wanted to be seen with him. The thought hit me out of nowhere, followed by a smack of nerves. Could I risk a public outing?

"I'm starving," I said tentatively. "Should we stop for lunch somewhere?"

He gave me an intense look. "Let's. I need to talk to you."

The way he said it immediately released every winged creature hanging about in my stomach. Bats. They were probably bats, hanging upside down in a hollow dungeon. The butterflies of my youth wouldn't have survived.

I wasn't ready for this talk. We had to keep things casual, at least on the surface, for as long as possible. On a whim, I pulled over at a cheap little roadside bakery. With the afternoon sun hanging low, we were approaching dinner time, and I couldn't let this turn into a romantic dinner.

Casual. I could do casual.

"Let's grab pies or something."

He cast a suspicious look at the peeling vinyl stickers on the shop window. "If that's what you want."

I skipped out of the car and into the bakery, trying not to show my distaste as I saw everything in the cabinet was packaged in glad wrap. I wasn't a big fan of pie, either. Or rather, my digestive system wasn't. But I had to feed those bats—they were going crazy in their hollow cave, making me feel far too much.

An old guy sitting by the door in dirty boots perked up. The sneer on his beefy face told me he'd recognized me. As seen on TV, buddy. Except I was older now, thus looked older, which some idiots felt like they needed to mention to my face. I hoped he wasn't one of them.

People who watched me on TV felt like they knew me. It was an occupational hazard I couldn't change. Normally, I would have been careful, smiling just enough to not seem rude. I knew how to deal with it. I'd been doing it for years.

But that day, I stepped into the bakery with a Turkish bodyguard in tow. I felt volatile, yet somehow invincible.

"Janie Andrews! As I live and breathe!" The man bellowed at me, standing up as if he'd been sitting there, expecting me all day.

I grinned back and curtsied. "Here I am. Excuse me…" I circled his rather large form to get closer to the glad-wrapped food items.

Emir stopped at the doorway, observing the situation.

"What do you want?" I asked over my shoulder.

"Anything."

His tone was cautious, his gaze on the gentleman who'd followed me to the sandwich cabinet. I felt Emir's protective presence, only a few feet away, and it made me brave. A wide smile spread across my face.

"So, you're keeping it tight," the man said, nodding appreciatively as his eyes swept down my body. "That's a spankable ass right there."

Who said skinny jeans were out of fashion? Playing along, I glanced over my shoulder as if noticing my own ass for the first time. "Is it? Well, thank you, sir." I slapped my own butt for good measure.

"You're welcome!" The man laughed so hard his stomach shook.

He stepped closer and I caught the whiff of alcohol on his breath. I grabbed two egg sandwiches and slammed them on the counter. The young girl behind the register gave me a curious look.

Taking my sandwiches, I hurried to the door, past Emir's furious face and rigid body. "Come on. Let's drive somewhere."

To my horror, the drunk guy followed us outside. He must have been too wasted to notice Emir, because one look at his face would have sent a lesser man running.

I reached my car door when the pair of muddy work boots entered my field of vision.

"So, you like being spanked?" He drawled.

"No, thank you." I said brightly and I tried to open the car door, but he leaned his weight on it.

"Janie Andrews." He breathed my name like a prayer.

"Can you please move?" My heart hammered in my chest as I saw Emir approaching him from behind. "I seriously recommend you do."

Within seconds, Emir had him in a headlock, making choking sounds. "If you like spanking so much, that can be arranged."

"No, Emir! Let him go," I pleaded, until he released the man, shoving him away.

He clambered away, coughing, boots dragging against the pavement.

I drew a shuddering breath, feeling like a fool. This was my fault. I should have never responded to that creep. I owed Emir an apology. And a proper dinner, I thought, looking at the sorry sandwiches in my hand.

The sandwiches fell on the ground as Emir backed me against the car door, locking me between hard muscle and sunbaked steel. His voice was a low growl. "Never do that again, Janie. I mean it."

"I was just... humoring him." I tried to keep my tone light, but my whole body throbbed, inexplicably turned on. "He's a drunk idiot."

"A drunk idiot who's twice your size. What if I wasn't with you?"

I swallowed a lump, embarrassed. "Then... I wouldn't. I'm sorry." I finally looked up, catching his concerned, menacing eyes. Jaw tight, muscles on his arms ticking like they wanted to fight something. Hot coals danced inside me because that's what I wanted. I'd teased him, on purpose, and this was my reward. I was sick.

"I feel safe with you, Emir. So safe that I'm acting recklessly."

My breath felt hot and heavy against his neck as he bent down to kiss me by the ear. "I'm acting recklessly, too. And that's why I need to talk to you."

Okay. I officially couldn't make him eat egg sandwiches in the car.

"Let's go to a restaurant."

"I can take you out? On a date?" The hope and tenderness in his eyes were my undoing.

"Yes. Take me out on a date, Emir."

CHAPTER 27

Janie

I spent the entire drive explaining to myself why this wasn't a big deal. Emir had that weird intensity about him. That's how he talked. It didn't mean anything.

It was only a dinner. Nothing flash, nothing particularly attention-grabbing. If someone saw us and rumors started spreading, so what? I'd deal with it later. Besides, nothing was going on, at least on the outside. He was helping me with a documentary. We had a reason to be seen together, not that it should have mattered.

I parked along the beach road. Napier was beautiful on an average day, but that evening, the scenery was dramatic. The darker clouds had rolled in, but the golden sun still streamed through, like arguing with the impending storm. I could have chosen a more secluded spot to avoid running into anyone I knew, but my heart won.

"This is my favorite place," I told him, gesturing at the unremarkable brown building.

I led Emir towards the beach, thinking we could slip in from the ocean side, unnoticed. But I didn't account for how recognizable my car was.

We were halfway across the stretch of grass when I heard the shrill voice. "Janie! Janie!"

I turned around and found Tabitha picking across the grass in her heels, waving her hand. Having caught my attention, she stopped, sinking one ice pick heel into the soft ground, awkwardly tilted to one side.

"She's the lady that visited you, right?" Emir hissed. "I recognize her voice."

"Yep." I cast him an apologetic look. "You can go ahead if you want, and I'll talk to her. It won't take long." I wouldn't let it.

"You don't want to be seen with me?" Emir smoothed his hair and shirt, as if something might be wrong with his impeccable presentation.

I felt the sting of shame all through my being. I couldn't treat him like this. It wasn't right. "No. I just wanted to spare you."

My stomach wound itself into a tight ball of nerves as I approached Tabitha. By the time we reached her, she'd managed to extract her heel and tiptoed back to the concrete path, smiling sheepishly. "That'll teach me," she grumbled, pulling a packet of wet wipes from her purse to clean her shoes.

"I know. Those things sink in like tent pegs." I hid my smile, thinking that her metallic heels looked a lot like tent pegs.

"I was waving like mad and calling your name, but you didn't hear me."

"Sorry."

Her heels cleaned and back on, Tabitha wiped her hands and brushed her flowery blouse, turning to my companion. "I don't think we've met."

She made it sound like an accusation.

Emir stuck out his hand like a true gentleman, leaning in to kiss Tabitha on both cheeks. "Emir Erkam. Pleased to meet you."

An odd flush of jealousy darkened my thoughts. I'd seen his family greet each other like this, but he'd never done it with me. When we'd first met, he'd been holding that camera, though.

Tabitha tried to cover her blush by fussing with her hair. "Tabitha Tubbs. I'm Janie's friend."

"Me too."

"Oh. I haven't seen you around. Heard a rumor, but..."

My heart drummed in my throat. "What rumor?"

Tabitha turned to give me a tired look. "Oh, come on. It's a small town. So, this must be the mysterious stranger?" She threw a sideways glance at Emir.

It was a small town, but that didn't make any sense. "Did Len tell you about our date?"

I'd relied on his discretion, thinking that as a pastor he was used to keeping confidences, even though I hadn't specifically asked. I hadn't texted him at all since the date, which was terrible of me. But so much had happened since then that I'd all but forgotten about poor Len.

Tabitha's mouth opened a couple of times before any words came out, her tone defensive. "He played golf with Adrian early this morning. They always do on Sundays, well before church. You didn't reply to my text so of course I asked Adrian to find out how the date went. You must understand why I'm curious. I know both of you and I set you up. I feel invested." She cast me a hurt look.

I drew a deep breath despite the elephant sitting on my chest. "Of course."

Tabitha's eyes flicked at Emir again, even more hurt. "I just thought you and Len were so compatible. He's so lovely."

"He is. Absolutely. We had a nice dinner."

Tabitha smiled back, thawing a little. "Well, that's good. And I wasn't expecting an update from you, immediately. But in due time... I thought Len might cancel the golf game this week if the date went well." She wiggled an eyebrow.

I folded my arms, the feeling of betrayal gnawing my gut. "So, he told your husband all about it this morning?"

Tabitha's eyebrows stopped wiggling and flew up. "Oh, no! Len is very discreet. Adrian said it took a lot of prying to get a few words out of him. He said that there was someone else in your life."

"Someone else?" I tried to look sufficiently confused. "Nah... It just didn't... I'm sorry it didn't work out." I glanced up at Emir, wishing we could both step through a portal and enter another dimension, where I could properly apologize to him. I could feel his eyes on me, trying to understand my evasive words. But he didn't know Tabitha.

I shuffled my feet, looking for the right parting words, when Tabitha zeroed her interest back on Emir.

"So, Emir, where's that accent of yours from?"

"Turkey."

Tabitha turned to me, lowering her voice. "Is he in the country legally? Permanently?"

"Yes and no," Emir replied on his own behalf. I could tell he was irritated.

"He's visiting his brother, who's engaged to my dear friend. I'm hosting their engagement party," I explained, hoping this was enough information to satisfy Tabitha's boundless curiosity.

"Oh, that's nice of you, Janie! And how's it going with Gus? Has he been helpful?"

"Yes, very helpful. He just did some drone shots for me this afternoon."

"Good. Good." Tabitha nodded, looking pleased. "I just knew he'd be a good fit. I've been told I have a gift when it comes to matching people. I can always tell who'll hit it off."

My face hurt from the effort of maintaining a friendly smile. "Sure. If you'll excuse us, I promised to shout Emir dinner since he also did some filming for me."

Tabitha's eyes brightened. "Oh, so he's working for you. That's wonderful. How's the documentary coming along?"

"Great. I'm putting together a little teaser to pitch it to a few people, to secure some funding."

Tabitha's mood improved even more. "So, it may not go ahead then? Because we missed you at the Art Deco Gala meeting."

I sighed. "Pete from our film office was interested in it, too. I might send him in to represent me if that's okay."

I could tell from her face that it wasn't okay, but she gave a courteous nod. "It's just that we need people who're good on camera for the social media bits. Helen and Barb were hoping you'd be available to present, even if you can't make it to every meeting."

"I'll... check my schedule."

Tabitha plastered on a wide smile. "You do that." She turned to Emir. "Very nice of you to help Janie on a Sunday like this. So, you're a filmmaker?"

"No."

"But handy with a camera, obviously?"

"Yes."

"And... are you staying in town with your brother?"

"No."

Emir's monosyllabic answers threatened to erode Tabitha's brilliant smile, but she fought to keep it up. "I trust you're enjoying Napier?"

"Yes."

At this stage I knew he was doing it on purpose. I did my best to hide my amusement.

"Well, that's good at least. How long are you here for?" Tabitha propped a hand on her hip, eyes sharp. No more yes/no questions it seemed.

"Two weeks."

"And are you traveling around New Zealand? I mean… what's your itinerary?"

"No."

I had to clamp my lips together to keep from laughing. I tracked backwards until I entered the grass. "I hope you excuse us. We're both starving. We didn't have a proper lunch and our breakfast wasn't that filling either."

"*Our* breakfast?" Tabitha followed us to the edge of the lawn, her eyes flashing with interest, and I wanted to bite my tongue for misbehaving.

"No… I mean it's been a long day…" I glanced at Emir for confirmation.

"Yes," he said.

A vein in Tabitha's neck ticked like a time bomb. Catching me with a strange Turkish guy must have been the scoop she'd been hoping for all year. The juiciest piece of gossip in town, especially as she connected the dots with whatever Len had revealed about our date. I could tell she was desperate for more and we were about to slip out of her reach.

Worried that she'd follow us to the restaurant, I took a step closer, dropping my voice to sound like I was speaking in confidence. "Let's have a proper catchup soon, okay? I'll call you."

She answered with a meaningful nod, eyes wide and animated. "Perfect. Let's."

Casting one last look at Emir, she sailed away with her head held high.

I gazed up at him too, feeling terrible. "I'm sorry about the third degree. She's relentless."

Emir's face was unreadable. "She wanted to know if we're together."

"I know." I looked away, feeling squeamish under his gaze. Was he hurt I hadn't announced us sleeping together to the worst gossip in town?

"And now she's going to go through her contact list to find someone else to set you up with." Emir nodded at Tabitha's trim figure teetering on the sky-high heels.

I opened my mouth to protest, but immediately ran out of steam. Because he was right. That's exactly what Tabitha would do.

"Well, you told her you're here for two weeks. If I told her I'm dating you, it'd be like announcing a holiday fling. Is that what you want?"

Emir studied me for a moment. "No."

I groaned. "What is it that you want then?"

He didn't smile, but somehow, his eyes smiled. "I want to have dinner with you."

We stepped into the restaurant. All the tables were taken, but I spotted a couple of couches and a coffee table on the terrace.

"Mind if we sit here?" I asked him, plopping down on the couch. "You can say no, I'm just testing the cushions." I grinned up at him.

"If this is your favorite place, I would expect you're pretty familiar with the cushions already." He sat across from me, grabbing one of the menus the quick-moving server thrusted on us.

We ordered the daily special, whiptail.

"Are you sure it's fish?" Emir asked when the waitress left. "It's not like… lizard?"

I chuckled at his expression. "I'm pretty sure they don't serve lizard anywhere in New Zealand."

We sat at the restaurant until sunset, ordering desserts and talking. I could tell he was building up to something, but taking his time, drawing it out. I didn't mind. I wanted the evening to last forever. I never wanted to arrive at the hard questions—I already knew they'd steal away this mellow feeling brought on by a glass of wine and the peachy hues of sunset. I loved listening to his deep voice and those throaty consonants of his accent, the eloquence of his speech. We talked about anything safe. Books. Movies. Language. Culture. I loved his carefully considered opinions, balanced views and references to data. Emir didn't base anything on a hunch. He read and studied and seemed to absorb everything. I thought of myself as well versed in current affairs, but he kept surprising me. Where my knowledge was broad and light, Emir's was digested and deep.

After he finished explaining the ins and out of Turkey's dreadful economy, the conversation came to a lull. I saw the shift in him before he even opened his mouth.

"How are you, Janie?" He asked, leaning forward. "I know I've caught you right after a divorce. You've been hurt."

"So have you."

He nodded. "But mine's not that fresh."

I thought about it. He was right. We were all products of our environment and circumstances, and what a product I was. "It's true. You caught me at my worst. The last two years have been tough. I feel like I've gone from one low to the next. And maybe that's why I've been acting so out of character. I don't jump into bed with my house guests... I don't even have house guests, or flirt with drunken idiots... I'm not proud of how I acted. It's not okay." I hid my face behind my hands, trying to compose myself.

We'd had such a lovely time, moments I'd never forget, but he could see how out of control I was. Up and down. Fragile. I was in no condition to date anyone.

"That's not what I'm getting at, Janie."

I sniffed behind my finger wall. "But it's true. I should work on myself before I even dream about dating again."

"When is that magical time going to come? When is anyone ready? You can't work out your issues in isolation and then present yourself to society all healed and perfect. If it worked that way, I'd be healed and perfect." He huffed, looking away. "I met you at your most vulnerable, and I'm forever grateful for that, because at any other moment in your life, you wouldn't have looked at me twice."

My head jerked up at the suggestion and I dropped my hands to my lap, revealing the tears I couldn't hide. I couldn't hide my smile, either. "I would have! You're very noticeable, Emir. You know that, right?"

He looked sad. "I'm used to working behind the scenes. People don't ask me questions about my life, or my thoughts on anything.

The way you look at me and talk to me…" He rubbed his forehead, and my heart wobbled. "This probably sounds lame, but I feel like I'm trying to make sense of who I am. I haven't told these stories about myself. I've told them about Cem. I could talk about him for hours because that's what everyone wants to hear. But I don't talk about me. And every question you ask me, every thought we exchange that doesn't involve my brother, I struggle, because I'm answering it for the first time."

I noticed color rising to his cheeks and his eyes burned with sincerity.

"It gets easier. I'm interviewed all the time. I know how to recite these stories about me. Once you tell your story a hundred times, it rolls off your tongue without a second thought. We end up becoming the stories we tell about ourselves. If you haven't told your story for a while, you have a chance to tell a new story."

"That's what dating is, isn't it? Packaging yourself in some kind of digestible format."

I let out a deep sigh. "And that's why it's so exhausting."

"The things that happened to me… the engagement, managing Cem, even the family business… I've been thinking of them as things I failed at." He picked up a saltshaker and placed it on the table between us, staring at it. "Things I put in this silo in my mind that I never wanted to think about again. But they led me here. Maybe everything had to happen that way, in that exact order. Because I feel more alive than before, like I'm breathing in more air." He held my gaze almost desperately. "I can't go back to how things were. How I was."

"Then don't. I love seeing this side of you. It's a privilege to peek inside your silo." I grabbed the saltshaker and sprinkled some salt on my palm, then swiped it with my finger and had a taste. "You are endlessly fascinating, Emir. Back in the day, I would have loved to interview someone like you."

He scoffed so softly it was half-way to laughter. "I'm glad I never saw you on TV. I would have dismissed you. I don't trust... actresses. I didn't trust you at first. I thought your smile was fake."

I had to laugh. "I think it is, sometimes, but I can make myself feel better by smiling."

"I can see that now. I wish I could do the same."

"Maybe you just need practice."

His mouth curved a little and I cheered. But I felt the truth in his earlier words. There was so much faking in this world. "I don't particularly trust people in the media either. There are some good ones but twice as many with giant egos. That's partly why I wanted out. I wanted something more authentic."

"Me, too."

"What was it like," I asked, "all that media circus around your brother? Life of luxury and celebrities?"

"We didn't grow up rich. Cem... he's our goose with the golden eggs. I saw the potential and I wanted to see if he could be the one in a million. I never imagined it would turn out that way. And when it did, I think I got caught up with all that. Growing it. Maintaining it. Maintaining him. You must understand that Cem is, he always was, a bit sheltered. He didn't have to worry about money. He probably doesn't even remember the time our father's business nearly went bankrupt. He was pretty thrown by the sudden fame. It was a lot to deal with. So, I dealt with most of it. I saw the ugly side, the leeches, and the inflated egos. It's a tough business, I'm sure you know."

"I do."

"So, why is this place your favorite?" He asked, examining the array of fingerprints on the glass table.

I bit my lip, staring at the pile of paper napkins. It wasn't the fanciest place, but that was part of the charm.

"I think it's because of the view, as much as the food." I nodded at the horizon where the last glow of sunset still lingered. "And the fact that it's within my budget. Anything with tablecloths is out of the question right now."

"I completely understand." He leaned his elbows on his knees, running his fingers through his hair. "I need to sort out my finances, which means turning my father's antique business around. It's turning a profit, but only just. The whole place needs an overhaul."

"And it's in Istanbul." It wasn't a question, I just needed to hear that sentence out loud.

"It's in Istanbul," he repeated, voice heavy, eyes full of regret as he turned to stare at the vast ocean.

Maybe he needed to hear himself say it, too.

I picked up one of the paper napkins and started folding it into a swan. "I could try to make the farm more profitable. Grow more food, keep more animals. I just don't think I have it in me. Maybe that's why I jumped on this documentary idea. If I can sell that..."

I sighed because I hadn't thought any of it through. "I don't know. I can live on my salary from running the film office. It's easy and fun. But it doesn't pay enough for travel." I glanced up at him, holding my breath. "I'd have to move back to Auckland, try to get back on TV."

I shuddered at the thought of those early mornings. The constant stress and scrutiny. Even with all the uncertainties of my current situation, life was a lot more relaxed right now. "It took me decades, but I've finally learned to value my own wellbeing. I might have some clout left I could capitalize but can't go back."

"I understand." He turned back to me, his mouth a straight line. "I'm not asking you to uproot your life. If I had a place like yours, a life like yours, I wouldn't move back into the city, either. I don't even want to think about going back to Istanbul. The people. The noise." He exhaled a low growl. "But I have no choice. I have to get my affairs in order. I have to make something of myself. I can't ask you to marry me like this, with nothing to my name."

Someone must have whacked me with an invisible ping pong paddle because my lungs suddenly flattened. "M-marry me?" I choked out, blinking like an idiot.

He reached across the table to place his thumb on my forehead, just like I'd done on him. "Don't look so confused. I told you this is not casual." It was only when he stroked my skin that I realized how deeply I was frowning.

"But you're going back. I'm staying here. Whatever you want to call this, it's not... marriage material."

"Our time might be short, but I'm not giving you up. I couldn't."

"Are you saying you want a long-distance relationship?"

His headshake was swift, eyes hard. "No. I don't want that. But it's the last option on the table."

I nodded, blinking away tears that threatened to spill on my floppy napkin swan. I set it on the table between us. "Apart from breaking up."

What had felt so possible at night, fell apart in daylight. I'd known it yet refused to see it.

He picked up the swan, gently supporting its floppy head with his finger. "You can break up with me, Janie. I won't break up with you."

CHAPTER 28

Emir

I'd always had the ability to mask my reactions. Often, I didn't bother. But as I watched Janie's erratic driving, I opted for freezing those facial muscles. After all, I'd obviously scared her. She was processing things I'd said.

I had to be patient with her.

"Are you sure you're okay?" I asked again as she hit the brakes, sending us both forward with such force both seatbelts locked simultaneously.

"I'm fine. Sorry. I didn't see the light."

I'd seen the red light from afar, glowing as the only beacon in the night.

"Do you want me to drive?"

"No. It's okay. I just have a lot on my mind." She cast me a look that suddenly turned furious. "You… You can't drop that kind of bomb on me. This is a fling. If that. It's fun and exciting and… many things, but it's not real and I—"

"Janie."

"Don't 'Janie' me. It's one thing to have chemistry, or whatever this is. Or physical attraction. Or… to like someone…" Her voice turned quiet, exasperated. "Respect someone. Or to find a man who isn't dumb as a doornail—"

"Thank you." I couldn't help the smile she drew out of me. I'd never get used to what my face was doing around her.

Janie's knuckles sharpened as she squeezed the steering wheel, but I could see little cracks in that fury. Sunshine peeking through. "I mean it's all great, but it doesn't mean you start talking about marriage. I just got out of one!"

"I know." That's all I could say. I couldn't take back my words. I couldn't soften them. But maybe I could give her context. "I know it's not the same thing in your culture, but I was brought up this way. If I'm serious about a woman, I have to do the right thing. It's about respect. You can say it's a fling, but that doesn't change the way I feel. And I think you feel it, too."

She let out a heavy exhale, her eyes on the road. "We're both high on dopamine and serotonin and whatnot. I can tell you have this habit of driving people away, and that's why you haven't connected with anyone. You didn't give anyone a chance. And I somehow broke through, and…" She sighed, still not so much as glancing at me. "I love seeing the real you. It's magical. But if you didn't drive people away, they'd see what I see, and you could connect with anyone. You could charm anyone."

I leaned a little closer, mindful of the fact that she was still driving, but I had to say it. "Here's how I choose to see it: You're the reason I had to drive away everyone else, and I'd do it all over again. If you don't drive away the wrong people, you'll never find the right one. The one you'd risk everything for."

There. I'd said it.

"Goddammit, Emir. I can't see the road." She blinked away tears, struggling to stay on the lane.

I rested my hand on her thigh, speaking as calmly as I could. "There's a gas station coming up on your left. Pull over."

She managed the car off the road, parking sideways across two white lines. Killing the engine, she wiped her eyes and stared at me. "It's too early, Emir. I can't…"

"I know."

"I have kids. A life. It's in pieces. I'm in pieces right now. I'm not young and free."

"I know that, too."

She smiled. "Thank you for not saying I look young."

"You do, but that's not the point. You're talking about where you are in life. And I know it's complicated. But it doesn't mean we can't try."

"But we haven't figured out anything!"

"But we will."

I pulled her in for a kiss. It tasted of tears and something unspeakably sweet. I never wanted it to end. Finally, she pulled back, glancing over my shoulder.

"There's nobody out there."

"I know. I just…"

She didn't feel safe, and I hated that. I wanted to fix that.

"It's dark outside. I must get back home…" Her eyes flashed with panic. "Molly! Did you let her out this morning? Is she still out there?"

"She'll be fine. It's not even raining."

Janie started the car and drove back to her house. The security light I'd installed at the front door shone in the darkness as we snaked up the driveway.

When I saw the human shape by the door, adrenaline shot through my heart. My muscles tensed and a hundred thoughts rushed through my mind, none of which matched with Janie's soft words.

"That's my son."

CHAPTER 29

Janie

He looked so tall and broad-shouldered, yet small. Stooped. My lovely 13-year-old baby boy stood under the pale security light, a big bag at his feet, eyes on his phone.

I didn't bother driving to the parking bay. I simply stopped in front of the door, startling him. Casting a quick look at Emir, I scrambled out of the car. He understood, hanging back as I rushed to my boy and hugged him.

Hug first, questions later. That'd been my philosophy all these years, and Josh knew it. I hit my forehead on his sharp collarbone, but I didn't care.

He sniffed. "Mom. I tried to call you. You weren't home and I... panicked."

"Oh, my God! My phone must be still silent. We were filming earlier, and…"

My phone was mostly silent. I hated its sound. I hadn't checked it for hours, too preoccupied with my dinner with Emir. "How did you get here? Is it just you?"

"I took the bus, then Uber."

"It's not school holidays yet." I drew back to study his drawn face. "What happened?"

His chin jutted forward, green eyes almost black in the low light, voice wavering. "Can I live here?"

I felt air leaving my lungs, deflating like a punctured tire.

"Yes, of course. But why? Do you not like the school? Are you having problems?"

"No. I just don't want to live there anymore."

"With Dad?"

"With Dad and *Kelly.*" He bit out the name like it tasted vile. "I don't want to be there anymore."

"Okay." I unlocked the door, taking a tad longer with my brand-new key, then led him inside the house. "I'll be right with you, and we'll talk this through, but I have someone in the car. He's a friend of a friend who's been staying here, helping on the farm. You know my colleague, Aria? I'm hosting her engagement party in a few days, and this is her fiancé's brother." I took a breath, feeling like I was babbling.

"What? Who?" His brow wrinkled. The low lighting threw shadows under his sulking eyes, making him look simultaneously younger and older.

"His name is Emir. He's Turkish. I like him." I sucked in my lips, waiting for his reaction.

His lips puckered defiantly. "Don't tell me you're having a baby and starting a new family, too?"

"Dear Lord. No." I patted his arm. "I'm just saying... he's my friend, so be nice." I tried to smile instead of wincing. There was no way to save this, probably. I could have been hosting Santa Claus and Josh would still be wary of the other guy in the house. He'd come here for his mom and didn't want to share. "Why don't you take your bags to your room and get settled. I'll make us all some tea. Then Emir can go to bed, and we'll talk."

I looked at him until he nodded, took his bags and dragged them down the hallway. I ran back outside and found Emir leaning on the car door, browsing his phone. He looked up, worried. "What happened?"

I lifted my shoulders. "Not sure. But it sounds like he needs some Mom time."

"Of course."

"I told me I'd make us some tea and then have a chat with him."

"I don't need tea. Don't worry about me. Go talk to him."

He gave me a look full of compassion and something in my chest tugged, hard.

"I'm... sorry." I turned around, but he grabbed my arm, forcing me to turn back.

"You're not sorry. I'm not sorry. We both have lives. We both have... non-negotiable responsibilities. That's no reason to back down. We deal with it."

"Like adults, you mean?"

"Yeah."

"I hate adulting." I made a face and laughed a little. He didn't join me but nodded in confirmation.

Giving him a grateful smile, I slipped back inside. I found Josh in his room, lying face down on his bed spread, with Gru nuzzled by his side.

"Hey, Josh." I guided the dog on the other side and sat on the edge of the bed, rubbing his shoulder.

He turned his head enough to allow for some red-rimmed eye contact. The crescent moon shaped night light cast a glow over his face.

"Dad doesn't see me anymore. It's just baby this, baby that. And Kelly... she's buying and buying these... baby things. I can't even walk through the house anymore; I stumble over all this sh... crap."

I nodded. "Well, she's pregnant. It's called nesting."

"What, like a bird?"

"Yeah, like a bird." I bit my lip.

"Well, if she's a bird then she's a big, fat, dumb... chicken."

I had to a smile at his sulky pout. "Chickens are not that dumb. Mine are hiding the eggs so well I think I miss half of them."

"I'll help you find them, Mom. Just let me stay."

I sighed. "We need to sort things out with your school. You can't just disappear. Does your dad know where you are right now?"

"I left a note."

I reached into the handbag still perched on my hip and

plucked out my phone. Five missed calls from Josh, none from my ex-husband.

"He hasn't called."

"He won't notice until it's bedtime and he comes to check that I'm not on my screen." Josh's resigned voice made me shiver.

"What?"

"Yeah, he's too busy with work and Kelly and the baby."

"What about Alex? Does he check on him?"

"No. Alex loves that. They got him a tiny house in the backyard so he can listen to his music as loud as he wants. The neighbors called noise control once."

Alex was eighteen and enjoying his freedom. But Josh... Josh was my baby, and my heart went out to him. Nearly five years younger, he'd always been the baby. And now, he was having a little sister or brother. I'd barely processed the news of my ex-husband's new family. I hadn't even thought about what it meant for my boys. The last time I'd talked to Alex and Josh, both had been playing it cool. But how much could you expect to get out of teenagers via text messaging? If I called, they always sounded distracted, probably playing a game on the laptop as they offered one-word answers to my prying questions.

As I listened to Josh's words, I felt grateful he could confide in me, yet increasingly upset. I knew Shaun's shiny new thing syndrome, but I'd never thought it would extend to his children. The whole thing made me sizzle with anger, yet inexplicably sad, like I'd accidentally jumped to the end of a book, skipping something important. My story with Emir was only beginning.

And now, reality came crashing down, washing away the dreams, leaving only responsibilities.

"I should call him," I said, but my fingers made no effort to dial.

I didn't want to talk to Shaun.

"Where did you leave the note? What if they haven't found it? They might have already called the police."

"Well, then the police will come into my bedroom and find the giant piece of paper I left on the bed."

"But if you didn't make the bed, it might be obscured by the sheets—"

"Mom! I made the bed. There's nothing but a giant note on it."

The phone rang in my hand. Shaun. I took a deep breath. "Hi Shaun."

"Is he there? Is Josh there?" He sounded out of breath. Irritated.

"Yes."

"Well, send him back, will you? He's got school tomorrow."

"It's late. Let's discuss this tomorrow, okay?"

"There's nothing to discuss. We agreed the boys go to Auckland Grammar."

"Shaun. He's here. He was unhappy enough to spend seven hours on a bus. Let's discuss this tomorrow."

"What are you trying to pull? You're not in zone for anything out there! There's no plan B."

I felt like protesting, but I knew Shaun didn't count Napier's schools as contenders. Not when he had access to the one with the highest grade average, the one that had produced the most All Blacks in the country. Shaun considered his house in the Grammar zone as one of his best assets. Kelly probably agreed and had gotten pregnant just to access that damn school.

"I'm not trying to pull anything. I'll call you tomorrow."

I ended the call and turned off my phone. There.

"It's okay. We'll figure it out," I told Josh.

"Dad will never let me switch schools," he whined. "But I hate it there. Everyone's flexing about their iPhones and gaming setups and birthday trips to California."

"California? Dear Lord." I shook my head.

I knew the school was elitist, but I'd chosen to focus on the opportunities and resources it offered. When would I learn to look reality in the eye? I was way too old to be this naive. Just like I was far too old to fall for a Turkish man and imagine that things would somehow magically work out.

Josh hung his head. "I can't ask anyone over to our house because it's full of baby stuff and Dad won't get me a new computer and we only have Netflix and none of the others like Callum and Logan have. And if I go visit them, they want to come visit and I'll be so embarrassed. Our house is so small!"

"It's huge," I argued. "You have your own room."

But I knew what he meant. When you hung out with the rich kids, the bar was so much higher. I didn't want that for him. That constant comparison, perpetual feeling of inadequacy. It had followed me in Auckland like a bad smell. Poor Josh was only thirteen. He didn't have the maturity to look at the big picture. At that age, your friends were your world.

"Having a bigger house or better computers won't fix anything.

You know why?"

"Why?' He rolled his eyes.

"Because it's a game you can't win. Someone will always have something bigger or better. If you hang out with people who measure your worth in that way, you're not with true friends."

"I miss Benji. I want to go back to Napier Intermediate."

I patted his arm and laughed. "You can't go backwards. And I'm pretty sure Benji is in high school now too."

His eyes lit up. "He's at Colenso! Can I go there?"

I sighed. "I don't know."

Colenso was a good enough school, an easy choice that wasn't too far. If I could somehow get Shaun onboard, maybe Josh could finish high school in Napier. Small town schooling wouldn't open every door, but he'd still have a life ahead of him. And maybe a happier last year of his childhood.

I'd fight for it. I had to.

"Are you hungry?" I asked.

Josh nodded and followed me into the kitchen.

"What's that?"

Josh pointed at the dining table, and I did a double take. A tray filled with nuts, dried fruit and small sandwiches sat in the middle next to a pot of steaming tea.

"Oh. Emir must have made these."

"For you?"

"For us."

Josh stared at me, then the table again. "Is he like a butler or something?"

I burst out laughing and somehow got tears in my eyes. "He's just very considerate."

"Sweet." Josh sat down, filled a plate and tucked in.

"Should I get him? I should introduce you guys since he's staying here. It'll be less awkward."

Josh shrugged, his expression non-plussed, which was teenage speak for enthusiastic agreement.

I found Emir in the guest room, sitting in the corner, reading the thriller he'd picked up the previous night.

I stood in the open doorway, waiting for him to notice me. I loved that he'd left the door open but retreated to the far corner of the room. For someone scathingly honest who never sugarcoated his words, Emir seemed to consider others in a way not many people did. It was easy to be offended by his manner and words and miss those actions. The more time spent with him, the louder they seemed. Much louder than the words.

"Janie. Are you okay? Is your son okay?" He stuck something between the pages and dropped the book on the nightstand.

"Yes. Josh is a bit upset but he'll be fine. Thank you for the snacks you made. Have you eaten? Come join us. I'll introduce you."

He stood up, but hesitated. "Introduce me as..."

The question hung in the air as his eyes implored me.

"A... friend?"

He looked a little defeated but nodded. "Okay."

As we reached the dining room, Josh looked up, eyes wide. He blinked a couple of times, mouth ajar.

I introduced them, and I urged Josh to get up and offer his hand. Emir shook it, then popped into the kitchen to fetch a teacup.

"Is he in the mafia or something?" Josh asked under his breath.

"No. He just looks like he is." I bit back my smile, sliding into the seat next to my son. "To my knowledge, he's not involved in anything illegal."

Emir returned to the table and poured himself a cup of tea. He gave Josh a look, as if assessing his mood, then turned to me. "I have something to tell you, Janie. But I want you to not worry, because it'll be alright."

My breath seized. "What?"

"I went outside but couldn't find Molly. I checked the stables, and walked around and called for her, but it's so dark out there I may have missed her. We have to wait until it's light outside."

I opened my mouth to protest, then closed it again. It was my fault. I'd been too preoccupied to even check on my poor horse. "She usually comes back to the stables for the night, even if I let her stay out."

Emir nodded. "And she usually comes when I whistle. Not this time."

"Maybe she's hiding?" I swallowed a lump of fear.

"We'll go first thing in the morning. Josh can come with me. He's young and fit and Molly knows him, right?"

Josh nodded. "Don't worry, Mom. We'll find her."

I didn't miss the sharp focus in his eyes. Emir had given my son a purpose.

"What time is sunrise?"

"6.25 a.m." Emir answered, looking at his phone.

"I'll set my alarm for 6 a.m." Josh said, getting to his feet. "I better get some sleep."

He followed Emir to the kitchen and stacked his plate and cup in the dishwasher. I watched in awe as he said good night and retreated to his room.

Worried that he was putting on an act for the sake of our house guest, I trailed him to his room. "Hey, Josh." I stopped at his doorway.

"What?" He stood in the middle of his room and stared at me; eyebrows raised.

"I wanted to check you're okay. I know it's weird that there's someone else here. Had I known you were coming..."

Would I have sent Emir away? I wasn't sure of anything anymore, but the situation felt forced. I wasn't ready to introduce Emir to anyone, yet I wanted to hold onto him. I was such a mess.

"Is he your boyfriend?"

He looked me straight in the eye and I gave the slightest of nods.

"Okay." Josh unzipped his bag and dug through it, pulling out wrinkled T-shirts and underwear.

"Just, okay?"

"Yeah. I mean, he seems okay. If you say he's not a mafioso, I guess I'll have to believe you."

"I appreciate that." I pulled a face, watching him gather his toiletries and shuffle to the bathroom.

I left him to it and popped my head into the guest room, where

I found Emir holding a toothbrush.

"Janie." He paused, toothbrush in midair, kindness and pain in his eyes. "How is he?"

"He… he wants to live here, with me."

"What happened?"

"I'm not sure. I think he feels neglected, with the baby coming. And the new school is a bit prestigious."

"You mean elitist?"

I smiled. "Yeah."

"Sounds like he needs you."

It wasn't a question, just a simple statement. A statement that sealed our fate. I swallowed and nodded.

"Good night. I'll see you in the morning."

"You okay to sleep alone in there?" He half-whispered, nodding towards the other end of the house.

I didn't feel great about it, but I had to stop leaning on Emir. The guest room was right across the hallway from Josh's bedroom. He may have known we were an item, but I couldn't risk him hearing us. "I'll be fine."

"If you feel unsafe… if you need anything, text me." He gestured at his phone on the nightstand.

"Thank you."

I glanced over my shoulder. Josh was still in the bathroom. I heard the shower running and tiptoed to Emir. He opened his arms, and I snuck in. One last hug, I told myself. Those strong arms snapped around me and he kissed my forehead. "I'll follow your lead, Janie. Whatever you need."

A giant lump rose into my throat, and I sniffed into his shirt. "I told him we're... together. I don't want to hide. The little time we have left—"

"Time is a creation. We don't have to accept it."

"Really? How do I reject it? Because I'm sick of the minutes and hours and days marching forward."

He stroked my hair, his warm breath landing on the top of my head. "First of all, we can agree to not measure the experience of us, together, using units of time."

"So, we haven't had a two-week relationship?" I said to humor him.

We had a few minutes, whether we measured them or not. Josh would step out of the shower, and I'd be forced to move away.

"No. We've had an intensive education on each other. A thousand moments."

"A thousand?"

"I used to waste time. I think I lost a year at some point, just working. Like I wasn't even there. But I'm here now, with you, and everything counts. Time isn't linear. It stretches and contracts and bends."

I couldn't stop the glow that spread across my chest, like I'd been plugged in. "I'm starting to think you've been fooling me and you're actually very good with words."

"I'm honest. Sometimes, that works out."

My eyes burst full of tears. "I want this to work out, so badly. But—"

"Let me love you... just let me, Janie. I know life is complicated.

I know you're scared. But we can figure it out. If you feel anything for me, anything at all—"

My heart leapt from my chest, and words out of my mouth. "I love you more than I know what to do with, you fucking idiot!" As my brain processed the runaway truth, I recoiled, stumbling backwards. I couldn't take it back.

"Janie." His eyes were the warmest I'd ever seen, voice gentle.

I heard the bathroom door. My arms flailed about, gesturing at the exit I had to take.

"It's okay. Go."

Clamping my mouth shut and all but swallowing both lips so that nothing else escaped, I ran off, all the way to my own bedroom. I closed the door and leaned against it, heaving deep breaths. I was developing feelings that were harder and harder to dismiss, or even contain. They were spilling over, and what was worse, they were spilling all over him. Emir. The man who didn't do casual. The man who'd already decided to marry me, or something equally dramatic and ridiculous and impractical.

I'd only just gotten divorced, and it hadn't even been my decision. I wasn't ready for this. Shaun must have been planning his exit for a while, I knew that now. He'd been ready to move on and build a brand-new life the minute he returned to Auckland, while I'd been desperately clinging onto our old life. I'd sold him the dream of country living, but it had been a second-hand dream for him. Easy to let go, especially when the reality of it slapped us both in the face.

Gru jumped into my bed, burrowing under the blankets. I

hugged him, grateful for his eternal clinginess.

As much as I wanted to reject the concept of time and measure our relationship in thousands of moments, I couldn't. Timing sucked. This couldn't be more than a fling. I had to talk to someone and clear my head. Tomorrow would be Monday—the day known for its ability to whip you with reality. But it also meant returning to the office.

I texted Aria.

Janie: Are you coming to the office tomorrow? I need to talk to you. In person.

Did it sound too ominous?

Aria: I'll be in around 9. Coffees at the Pier?

Janie: Perfect.

I'd deal with it all tomorrow. The runaway horse, work, emails, the feelings. It was all an unholy mess, yet I felt blessed. Someone loved me. I imagined the energy of it, like radioactive waves permeating every wall between us. His attention on me, mine on him. It was beautiful, scary and intense, and I wouldn't let anyone tell me otherwise.

CHAPTER 30

Emir

Sunrise spread its buttery glow across the horizon as I trudged up the grassy hill, my most casual slacks getting damp from morning dew. Josh traipsed ahead of me, clearly keen to show off how fit he was. He'd mentioned playing cricket and running track as I'd asked him about sports, and shrugged several times when I asked about school.

The way he'd jumped on finding a missing horse told me the teenager needed a distraction. He seemed at peace here, probably happier in rubber boots and a hoodie than in the preppy school uniform I'd seen in one of Janie's photos.

I could tell Janie was trying to deal with this alone, and it bothered me. I didn't know how, but I wanted a future with her.

Josh was her family, which meant he'd be my family, too. But it was way too early. I had no right to butt myself into the situation.

When we made it to the back of the property, something caught my eye. Part of the fence had been flattened.

"Do you think Molly went through this?" Josh asked, pushing the loose fence post with his foot.

"If she did, she must have been very spooked."

I remembered this part of the fence had been leaning a bit, with one fence post in an awkward angle. The weather had been fine, which meant that something or someone had pushed on the fencepost, hard. Horses were strong and could probably bust through any fence they chose. But why? She hadn't taken the opportunity when the fencing had been in a much poorer condition.

"She must have gone through here. Do you know the area?" I asked. "We could split up here. You go closer to the road, I'll go up the hill and around that bit of bush, and we meet at the next house."

I knew the neighbor's mansion was somewhere there, behind the greenery. I'd seen it enough times when driving past, even if I wasn't sure of the distance on foot.

"Mr Pattison's house?" Josh pulled a face. "If she's gone there, he's going to be mad! That guy came for a visit when we first moved in and had a go at Mom about keeping the animals in check. Apparently, whoever owned our house last used to let them wander over and they'd destroy his garden."

"Did your mom buy the house with the animals?"

"Yeah. The horses... there used to be two but the other one was old and sick. They didn't tell us that. And then the chickens, but they had mites, and they didn't tell us that either. Dad wanted to..." he motioned across his neck, "but Mom wouldn't let him. She spent so much money trying to treat them."

I nodded, imagining Janie despair. "What about the pigs?"

Josh glanced to his side, thinking. "Uh... I don't know where she got those. It was later. Why?" His gaze snapped to mine, and I knew what he was asking.

Why was I gathering information on his mother?

"I'm in love with your mother. She told you we're together, right?"

Josh nodded, regarding me with a wary look. I couldn't blame him.

"I want to be straight with you. Because I can't stay here. I have to fly back to Istanbul soon. And while I'm gone... your mom is here by herself. Two days ago, someone broke into the house. We walked in on them. I went after the guy, but it was dark, and I lost sight of him."

Josh glanced at the broken fence, suddenly alert. "Do you think they went through here?"

He was a sharp guy. "Possibly. I went the wrong way, down the driveway."

"So, we should keep an eye on any other broken fences or snapped branches or something, to see which way he went?"

"It's a long shot, but sure. He might have had a vehicle of some kind."

"A dirt bike maybe? It leaves tracks."

"Okay. Good. Check for those."

For the first time since I'd seen him last night, Josh looked fully awake.

"I've changed the lock and installed a security light. I don't think the burglar is coming back, but I need you to look after your mom. Especially when I have to leave."

"I will."

I wondered if Janie would have protested about me telling her son about the break-in, but I felt like I had no choice. Something about the whole thing still bothered me, like a niggling stone inside my shoe. If Josh was going to be here, I needed him to keep watch.

I picked my way through the flattened fence, gesturing for Josh to follow. "I've changed my mind. Let's go together and come back along the road. I might need a local guide."

Josh's smile was a little lopsided, but still reminded me of Janie. "I only lived here a few months."

"Well, it's more than me."

We walked in silence for a while, my shoes getting wet from the dew.

"So, what happens after you go to Istanbul? Do you come back?"

"I hope so."

"I mean, you want to come back to New Zealand?" He looked at me with suspicion.

"Why not?"

Josh shrugged. "I don't know. Istanbul sounds cool."

"I guess."

We waded through long grass and reached the edge of the bush, walking alongside of it. I could see the neighbor's mansion peeking from behind the next hill. In a strange way, it reminded me of the houses lining up the beachfront in the suburb of the rich and famous of Bebek, Istanbul. Only, this one wasn't rubbing walls with the house next door. It stood in the middle of nowhere, declaring its owner's wealth to the hills around it.

It didn't take long before we spotted Molly—deep in the vegetable garden. She'd made a mess of it and was munching on a large cabbage head. Still, I was relieved. Losing her beloved horse wasn't something I wanted to add to Janie's list of worries. And maybe I wanted to be the hero who brought her back.

Josh gave me a wide-eyed look.

"I take it Mr. Pattison's not going to be happy about this?"

He shook his head in slow motion.

I gestured him to follow me towards the front of the house, stopping behind a large tree. And there he was—Mr. Pattison in the flesh. A stocky, greying man in khakis and a puffer vest, waxing a vintage Ford parked outside the triple garage. I saw a glimpse of at least two other cars. A vintage fleet.

I turned to Josh. "Okay. I have an idea, but I need your help. I'm going to walk back to the road, come up the driveway and distract him. Meanwhile, you go to Molly and lead her away. Pick some lettuce or whatever she likes and use that as bait. I'll meet you back at the house."

"Which house?"

"I mean... home. Back home." It was Josh's home, even if I couldn't claim the word.

Josh nodded, his face a picture of concentration, and headed back to the veggie garden, hiding behind bushes. I tramped down towards the main road and cut to the driveway, brushing my shirt and slacks. Once I was within talking distance, I raised my hand at Mr. Pattison.

"Hello! My car broke down and I'm waiting for a tow truck. Could I trouble you for a glass of water?"

The man jumped, then narrowed his eyes, regarding me with suspicion before throwing on a hospitable smile. "Hello. Where's that accent of yours from?"

"I'm Turkish."

"Are you the Turkish fella staying with Ms. Andrews?"

I jerked back at his question, fighting to keep my voice neutral. "Ms. Andrews?" I knew he was talking about Janie, but I hoped confusion would buy me some time.

"Yes. Janie Andrews. I keep hearing she's found herself a Turkish fella. Is that you?"

I met his challenging gaze. "I suppose so."

I'd never been called a Turkish fella, courtesy of having lived my whole life in Turkey. Did it bother me? I took a breath, taking note of the odd feeling in my stomach. This is what we'd always be with Janie—the odd ones out. Either me in New Zealand, or her in Turkey. She'd be the New Zealand woman. Would it bother her?

From the corner of my eye, right behind his back, I saw Josh walking Molly, a huge head of cabbage under his arm. No, not just the head. The entire stalk and roots hung off the thing. Mr. Pattison would be left scratching his head at the damages. I had to say something, to keep his eyes on me.

"I'm helping on Janie's farm. She's hosting my brother's engagement party and we're trying to get the place fixed up by then. There's quite a bit of... what's the word..." I waved my hand, as if searching for the right term, making him wait as Josh coaxed the stubborn horse through the gardens.

"Work?"

Did he really think I was struggling with the English word for 'work'?

Josh and the horse finally disappeared behind the bushes, and I exhaled.

"Yes, work!" I smacked myself on the forehead.

Cem should have seen me. There were two actors in the family, now. A movie star and an idiot who wasn't good enough for community theater.

"Must be a lot of work. She's let the place go since the divorce. Fencing is down here and there. It's a wonder her horse hasn't escaped."

I forced a smile on my face. "Don't worry. I've been fixing those fences, making sure the horse stays in. Anyway, I should get going. The tow truck will be here shortly."

"What about that glass of water?"

"I just remembered there's a water bottle in my trunk." I thanked him, lifted my hand in goodbye and turned around, hurrying down the driveway. The last thing I saw was Mr. Pattison scratching his bald head.

CHAPTER 31

Janie

It was amazing how stepping into your favorite café could ground you. The moment my buttocks touched the worn wooden chair and the aroma of roasted coffee beans hit my nostrils, I felt like the old Janie Andrews—the one who made things happen and did it with a smile.

"You look different," observed Aria, rendering my momentary sense of control completely void. "What's going on?"

"What do you mean?" I attempted to ooze inner strength as I took a sip of my espresso. The way it hit me on the way down induced an involuntary shake. "Oh, dear. I haven't had one of these in a while!"

"We were here last Thursday." Aria looked a little baffled.

"Yes, that's right. It just feels like a long time ago."

Everything prior to my relationship with Emir felt like a long time ago. Would I start marking time as 'before' and 'after' that man? Or would this all fade, like most things did? Even the divorce.

Aria waited, looking at me expectantly. I considered us friends now, but I was still technically her boss. She would never pressure me to open up, even if she suspected something.

"So, I'm looking at finishing work at the end of May. Cem has a new job in Istanbul, a local movie. They're filming over the summer there, so I'll tag along and escape the winter here."

"Sounds like a good deal."

She'd talked about quitting a few times, and I'd told her to follow her heart. It was a weird piece of advice—so easy to give, so hard to take. The only time I'd ever attempted to follow my heart was when moving to Napier. But my stupid heart had led me astray and left me lonely and broken.

"If the timing's not good, I can stay a bit longer. If you need me to train someone new, or—"

"It's fine. We'll figure it out. You need to go with him. Be with him." I waved a hand, but despite my best efforts, a lump swelled in my throat. I was losing my best friend.

Shit. She *was* my best friend. I'd left everyone behind when moving here. I had no friends of my own age. Nobody else I even truly liked. I'd been too preoccupied with my marriage to find new friends of my own or even stay in touch with the old ones. And then I'd lost all the couple friends. Everyone but Tabitha and Maree. But Aria had been there, sharing the office with me, sharing her tumultuous love story, seeking advice, and listening to my occasional life updates. She knew a lot about me, even if I tried to keep it light and not cry at work.

And if she was my best friend, why wasn't I being honest with her? Was I so hung up on being this admired, relentlessly positive and resourceful woman that I couldn't show my ugly, wobbly side to anyone? Except Emir, I thought with a start. I'd revealed my internal mess to Emir, and the world hadn't ended. Instead, I'd found a connection. I'd found someone I desperately wanted to hang onto.

"I'm in love with Emir." The words slipped out, almost without warning, followed by a stunned silence.

Gradually, a deranged, bubbly laugh rose from my belly, shaking my chest. "I'm not joking, it just sounds crazy. I've known him for a couple of weeks."

Aria's forehead wrinkled. "Why is that crazy? Is falling in love somehow time-based?"

I shook my head, staring at the fast-moving clouds outside the window. "That's what he said. That we shouldn't measure it in time... And I think he's right in a way. Time is not linear. Years pass in a blink of an eye, and maybe nothing changes, but then there're moments that change everything. It's like they ripple the fabric of time and nothing's ever going to be the same."

Now I was basically quoting him.

"You're serious," she stated, staring at me wide-eyed. "I thought something was going on, but... holy shit!" Aria grinned, still staring at me. "This is amazing!"

"Amazing? No. This is a disaster! It's impossible."

Her smile wavered. "What do you mean?"

"My life, my kids, my farm... everything's here. He must go back to Istanbul to sort out his father's business. He's not loaded like Cem, and neither am I. Our lives are not compatible."

"Why not?"

I hung my head. "Josh just moved back home. I need to deal with that first. I need to put my child first."

Aria let out a deep sigh. "Of course, you do."

I tried to smile. "But that's okay. Once you get to this age, especially if you go through a divorce, you realize a happily ever after is not a once and for all. Life is a series of seasons. People come along and they walk with you for a while. Maybe it's not for that long, but it might still be important. And Emir's so important. I know that."

The pain on her face reflected in my chest, like she was giving me a permission to feel it. "And... how does he feel about it?"

Heat blossomed across my face. "He... uhm... he's very serious. Talks about marriage. Silly man."

Aria's eyebrow lifted quizzically. "Okay. Emir is many things but he's not silly."

I smiled, rubbing my warm cheeks. "No, he's not. But the idea of marriage when I've only just divorced..."

"But if he wants to marry you, he must have figured out how it could work. It can't be that impossible. Sounds like he has a plan."

"More like wishful thinking." The same wishful thinking I saw in her eyes and felt in my heart. How we all wanted to believe in the fairy tale ending.

Aria took another sip of her coffee, her eyes pleading. "But... you can't give up! You fight for love, right?"

I shrugged, gently drumming my nails against the espresso cup I'd already drained. For the first time in years, I wished I'd ordered a flat white. Something softer on my taste buds, slower to drink. For me, an espresso was all about efficiency. A quick caffeine hit, no time wasted. I'd lived my whole life at maximum speed, doing as much as I could. Taking on the next challenge when I was half-way through the previous one. Even moving to the countryside hadn't truly slowed me down. I hadn't turned into a laid-back person who took luxuriously long breaks. If anything, I was striving harder than ever on a tight budget, to prove to everyone I didn't need any help.

"I don't want to give up. I don't even want to imagine a future without him. I want to slow down so much that clocks stop moving and the future never gets here. But I bet it'll still find me."

She nodded solemnly, but her mouth kept twitching and eyes sparkled. "I'm sorry, I just can't help getting excited! The thought of you and Emir... I don't know why it feels so right! Why does it feel so right?" Her brow wrinkled. "I mean, I hated him at first. He was so adversarial. Scary. But there's something about him. He's like this big, scary mystery to me and I always cringe when I see Cem teasing him... Like he's sneaking into a dragon's lair." Aria blushed, suddenly looking horrified. "I'm sorry, I didn't mean like that. I know he's not going to fire-breathe you to a crisp."

I let out a wobbly laugh. "It's okay. I know what you mean. He has that... quality."

She cocked her head. "It's weird, though. You're the only woman I can think of who can rock up to a dragon and be okay." She winced. "I'm so sorry. I have to stop using that metaphor!"

"If Emir decides to marry me, you should definitely speak at the wedding."

I cringed at my own joke, which made laughing a little difficult.

Aria didn't laugh either. Instead, her eyes filled with tears. "I'm sorry, I can't help picturing it, and it's beautiful." She dabbed her eyes with a paper napkin. "But don't mind me. I'm just terrified to move to Istanbul where I don't know anyone and can't speak the language... so I guess I'm clutching onto straws, hoping you'll love him so much you'll follow him there and I won't be alone."

"You'll be with Cem!"

"You know what I mean. He'll be working and I'll be sitting in his giant house, hiding from his parents, trying to learn Turkish."

"You'll learn quickly! And I'll miss you," I said quietly. As much as I wanted to, I couldn't make any promises.

"And I honestly think I misjudged Emir. Yesterday, it felt like we were seeing behind the curtain, the way he looks at you... how he's helping. I saw him vacuuming!"

"I know!" I shook my head, smiling at the memory.

"There's nothing hotter a man can possibly do."

"He's also cleaned my kitchen and cooked for me."

Aria looked like she'd seen a ghost. "Seriously? You've tamed the dragon. Okay, I'll stop now. I promise."

"It's okay. I don't feel like I've done anything, though. I feel like that's who he is. He's hellbent on doing the right thing, being helpful... maybe that's why he's talking about marriage. Because it's the proper thing to do and it'd be disrespectful to not offer that level of commitment. Turkish men are more conservative."

"Well, Cem doesn't think like that. And that's a good thing. I don't want him to propose to me because he's worried about my reputation."

"He's a celebrity, though. It's a weird space of its own, even in the cultural context. A bit of a la la land, where people can get away with not following the rules."

"Maybe... I'm just saying that he's Turkish and wants to marry for love and not out of responsibility."

"Of course! I'm sorry," I said, seeing the hurt in her eyes. "I'm not implying anything like that. I can see he loves you. Truly."

Her jaw jutted forward, and eyebrows lifted. "I saw Emir looking at you like that, too. I wasn't sure if you liked him too or if he was just pining for you, but it was clear as day."

My chest washed with warmth, and I expelled a breath. I couldn't explain away Emir's words or feelings, but did I want to?

"Do you know when Cem's parents are coming back to town?"

"You mean Emir's parents?" Aria gave me a knowing smile. "They'll be back tomorrow. Why?"

"I'm thinking of taking a bit of time off this week. Work is quiet right now. The house is in good shape so we should be ready for the party. I'll just fire off some emails today and I'll be contactable—"

"Of course! Go, spend time with Emir. And your son! How is he?"

"He's not happy in Auckland and wants to move here. Which means I have to deal with his father." My lungs deflated with a deep sigh. "The timing couldn't be worse."

"Or maybe it's good? You can do a test run of living under the same roof with them both." She gave me a cheeky smile.

"Oh, dear." My heart squeezed and I fought to keep the emotion contained. I couldn't let myself dream that far. It'd hurt so much more.

I got up. "We better get to work."

Aria followed me. Once we made it to the sidewalk, I stopped, turning to face her. "Thank you for listening to me."

"Any time."

We hugged so tight my lungs flattened. I was a little jealous of her easy happiness, her freedom to travel and plan her life with Cem, yet I was so lucky to have someone to talk to who understood. I wouldn't let us drift apart.

I spent a couple of hours in the office, returning phone calls and emails. Around lunchtime, I drove back home. Turning on my driveway, I saw Josh outside the stables, brushing Molly. Relief flooded my body as I stopped the car and lowered the window. "You found her!"

He waved at me, shouting back across the gooseberry bushes.

"She was eating cabbage in Mr. Pattison's garden. But he doesn't know. Emir distracted him and I snuck her out."

"Wow. Great teamwork!"

Josh's proud smile shone like a beacon, even across the distance. It was the first one I'd seen on his face since he'd arrived.

"Are you hungry?" I asked. Come up and I'll fix us something."

"I think Emir's cooking. But I told him I'd be back in fifteen, so I'll see you soon!"

Emir's cooking? I glanced at the digital clock on the dashboard. 12:04 p.m. I'd told him I'd be back around lunchtime to feed Josh. I'd even picked up some groceries on the way, to make sure I had ingredients for my son's favorite meals stashed for the week.

An uneasy feeling brewed in my stomach. Looking after my son was my job. I couldn't let Emir settle in and become someone we relied on, only to leave behind a crater when he left.

CHAPTER 32

Emir

I set down the blender pitcher as I heard the door, wondering what it would be like to be a husband. A house husband. Far from home, with no one around to cast judgment, it didn't feel that odd. I wasn't embarrassed. I only wanted to make her smile. Nothing could beat that feeling and I kept seeking it like a high.

"Lunch is served," I announced as I met her at the doorway.

That definitely sounded odd.

"What?" She blinked at me, dropping her handbag and a bag of groceries next to her shoes.

She wore a pale purple wrap dress I wanted to unwrap like a present. But her expression told me she wasn't in the right headspace for any of that. So, I picked up the groceries before

Gru could investigate them further.

As she saw the bread and dips on the table, she turned to me. "This is too much." Her gold earrings swung as she shook her head in disbelief.

"It's just lunch."

"Emir." Eyes wide, she took a step closer, examining the hummus and beetroot dip. "You made these? You made these!" Her voice rang with warning.

I shrugged. "I found chickpeas in your pantry. There was beetroot in the garden. It's no big deal."

"This is so nice, but you can't... I can't..." Her face contorted in pain and eyes filled with tears.

I heaved the groceries on the counter, crossed the floor and pulled her into my arms. "If I could have one wish, it'd be to keep cooking for you until you take it for granted. Until you just smile, sit down, and eat." I stroked her hair, feeling like I'd won every contest on earth, only to be told I had one day to live.

"Nobody should ever take this for granted." She hiccupped.

"Maybe not but imagine being able to rely on someone to be there. With no end in sight. No sadness."

"When's your flight?"

I tensed, despite my best efforts. "Next Sunday."

"Are you going to take it?"

My jaw tensed. "I have to."

There it was. Our end, very much in sight. I released her and pulled out a chair. "Josh should be back soon. He's great with Molly."

Janie wiped her eyes and smiled. "I know! I'm so glad you found her! He said you got her out of Mr Pattison's garden without him noticing."

"He'll notice the damage, but unless he has cameras pointed that way, there's no hard evidence."

"I guess we'll see."

The front door clicked, and Josh appeared, hovering over the table. "Wow! What's this?"

He reached for a piece of bread, but Janie slapped his hand away. "No grazing! Wash your hands, then come and sit at the table."

He flashed us a cheeky grin and disappeared down the hallway.

"He looks so happy." Janie threw me a questioning look. "What did you do?"

I took a breath, wondering what I should say. How she'd react. Last time I'd had to choose my words this carefully, I'd been negotiating a multimillion-dollar deal.

I sat next to her, keeping an eye on the doorway for Josh. Words rushed out of me, quiet yet strained. "Janie... I don't want to cross you, but I wanted to get to know him. He's family. And he was happy to talk to me."

"He was?" I saw the internal conflict twitching her facial muscles. "What did he say?"

"He told me about school and Auckland. It sounds like bullying. Not physical, but almost worse. These mind games the guys are playing about who has what and who's being cheap. I think it comes from the lives their parents are leading. It's so competitive. The kids reflect that, but more blatantly."

She nodded, looking miserable. "I should never have let Shaun take them up there."

"For what it's worth, it sounds like his big brother is doing well. I think he fell into a different crowd with arts. It's not so brutal I suppose. Less showing off with the latest toys and labels, more weirdos, like Josh says." I smiled, thinking back to our conversation.

"He told you all this?" Janie's voice wobbled with hurt.

"Sometimes, it's easier to talk to a stranger."

"But Josh has always been—"

"What?" Josh stood at the doorway, his sharp eyes regarding both of us. "What are you two whispering about? Sounds sus."

Janie turned to face him. "Sorry, Josh. I'm just worried about you."

Josh took a seat. "Well, if it's about me, I get to be part of the conversation, right?"

"I think he takes after you," I said with a wink. "Coffee?"

"Yes, please!"

"Yes, please," Josh echoed.

Janie glared at him. "Since when do you drink coffee?"

"Since Dad banned energy drinks from the house. Kelly's addicted to Monster and she's not allowed any during pregnancy. And since soda rots your teeth and the sugar free stuff has neurotoxins..." He drew out the word, rolling his eyes. "We only have decaf coffee."

"But I don't have decaf! Regular coffee has twice as much caffeine as any energy drink. Not that I want you hooked on those, either."

"I'll make him a single shot," I offered, and she gave me a reluctant nod.

"Sounds like Kelly's on a bit of a health kick?" Janie muttered. "Good for her."

I retreated to the other side of the kitchen island, as Josh launched into a detailed account of his stepmother's eating habits. "...and we can't have any dairy in the house because apparently it makes her bloated even if she's looking at it in the fridge. Like... it couldn't be the baby making her bloat? Has to be the dairy! And since she has zero self-control, we can't have anything in the house because she will accidentally eat it. Once, I hid a bag of Milky Ways in my room and she found it and went nuts."

"She got angry with you for having chocolates?" Janie's voice rose in concern.

"No, she ate all of them! I found her on the floor with the empty bag, crying."

"Oh, dear Lord."

I turned on the coffee machine, happy to drown out their voices. This was none of my business, as much as I disliked Janie's ex-husband and his new partner, based on that newspaper article.

But I had to admit I liked her son. He reminded me of myself at that age—observing the adults' crazy behavior, trying to make sense of the world. Longing to fit in, fighting a growing realization that I wasn't destined to. And it was okay.

CHAPTER 33

Janie

I was grateful for the long time Emir took preparing coffees, the hiss of the milk steamer creating a sound barrier between us. I listened quietly as stories and details of Josh's life in Auckland poured out, painting a picture I hardly wanted to look at.

"Dad wouldn't get me new trainers because the baby needs all this stuff... and Caleb and Logan and all the others are making fun of me for having these super old shoes."

"Your shoes are not old!"

"No, but they're not like... everyone else has these new Air Jordans and I have the last season's stuff. They're obsessed."

"Well, that's stupid. Besides, aren't you guys wearing identical school uniforms?"

"Not on the weekends. And last weekend, we went to Logan's birthday party, and he had a hot air balloon and a pool party and—"

"Oh, my God! What happened to pizza and movies?"

Josh let out a long sigh. "Dad said if I want a big party, I have to pay for it myself. But everyone knows my birthday is coming up and they're all expecting skydiving or something."

"Why?"

"Because I told them." His mouth twisted in shame. "I didn't know we were out of money."

"I'm sure you're not out of money. But that does sound excessive."

Josh hung his head. "I know."

I didn't mind that he'd decided to open up to Emir, but I also wanted to have that moment with him, alone. That's how it had always been. Me and him, chatting at bedtime. I'd missed him so much.

I wrapped my son in a tight side hug. "It's okay. I know how easy it is to get sucked into that world and feel like you need to compete with everyone. But you don't. And maybe it's better for you to live here for a while and hang out with friends who wouldn't expect that much."

He nodded. "Benji just wants pizza and a movie." I heard the smile in his voice and squeezed him even tighter.

"Benji is a good friend."

"I text him every time I sneak out to get a Big Mac," he confessed. "But I don't bring it into the house," he added. "I promised Dad I wouldn't do anything to upset Kelly."

Poor Josh had been sidelined by Shaun's new family. I knew Josh. It was his nature to be supportive. He stretched and bent every which way to accommodate others.

"Well, I bought your favorite cereal and lots of milk," I said, gesturing at the bag of groceries sitting on the counter. "You're a growing young man. You shouldn't be on a restricted diet designed for a 35-year-old pregnant woman, just because it's more convenient for her. I'll talk to Shaun."

"No! Don't make me go back! I'll work for my keep. I'll look after Molly and all the animals if you let me stay." His voice cracked.

Tear sprung into my eyes. "Oh, Josh. This is your home. You don't have to work for me! It wasn't my decision to send you to Auckland. I went along with it because your dad insisted the schooling was so much better and I was tired of fighting. I wanted a truce. I thought... I hoped it'd all work out. I miss you guys so much I've been miserable, but I thought I better get used to it because you're growing up anyway and will move away from home. And you'll have more opportunities in Auckland."

The milk steamer quieted down, then started again. I glanced over Josh's shoulder and caught Emir's eyes. A hint of a smile on his lips. Understanding. My heart wobbled, everything inside me resembling jelly.

"I don't care about the opportunities! I mean... I can always go back when I'm older, right? When I'm old enough to rent a house with some friends or something. Don't make me live with them. With her." His face twisted in pain.

"You're going to have a little brother or sister, soon. They might need you."

"Yeah, maybe. I promise I'll visit. But can I go to school here?"

Emir arrived with the coffees. Josh's posture straightened as he sipped his 'adult' drink. My heart squeezed. There was something so grown up about him, yet so fragile and vulnerable. I didn't want to miss these moments. I remembered Alex going through the same phase, although he'd always been more boisterous and outgoing. He walked his own path whereas Josh tried to fit in. I recognized that quality in myself. Maybe that's why I'd needed to move here and create a bit of distance between myself and the immersive world of media. Despite my age, I was just as vulnerable, just as easily sucked in, afraid of sticking out or being judged. Being called a cougar.

I cringed at the thought.

Emir joined us at the table, and we sipped coffees, taking turns to pat the excited Gru who jumped against our legs. The dog was beside himself having three people in the house. He must have been feeling lonely with me, just like I'd been. A few years ago, dealing with two growing boys in a smaller house in Auckland, I would have considered this level of solitude and space an absolute luxury. It was weird how quickly your perspective changed.

"So... I talked to Aria, and I think I'll take some time off work this week. We're in between productions so it's not a critical time. And I think we're ready for the party now, so we could do a day trip or something?" I studied their expressions.

I wanted us out of the house, somewhere nice and neutral where none of us had the home advantage or chores. If I kept working,

Emir would be here, cooking for us and looking after my son. I knew he'd do it, but I couldn't put him in that position.

"Day trip?" Emir repeated, lifting an eyebrow.

"Where?" Josh asked.

"We could go to the beach, or on a bush walk."

"I can stay back and look after the animals if you want to go for a longer trip." Emir gave me a tentative look.

I didn't want to leave him behind. I didn't want to miss a single moment with him, but I appreciated the offer. "I... I'll think about it."

Josh's eyes flashed with caution. "As long as you're not driving me back to Auckland."

I drew a deep breath. I had to talk to his father. I couldn't put it off any longer. It was Monday, and he wasn't at school. We'd texted a couple of times, only to confirm Josh was with me and he'd stay over the weekend. They'd informed the school about his absence, but Shaun still expected him to return.

"I'll call your dad," I told Josh. "I have an agreement with him. If he wants you in Auckland, you have to go back. I can't afford to go to court over this."

It was the truth, and it was best he knew it. Josh's mouth hardened into a straight line. I could tell he was fighting tears as he nodded. "Yeah, okay."

I excused myself and picked up my phone from its charging station on the kitchen counter.

"Don't fight with him," Josh urged. "Be nice. You know how he gets."

I nodded. I'd stroke his ego, even if it killed me.

When I got to the bedroom, with the door closed, it hit me. My new relationship hung in the balance. Whatever Shaun decided would seal our fate. If he agreed to let Josh move back to Napier, I'd have one son during school terms and the other one, or maybe both, during holidays. I'd be tied to this house with no chance to travel. If Emir couldn't come to me, I'd never see him again. Not that I'd been planning to chase him across the globe, consciously. But it seemed my unconscious mind had made such plans without telling me, because the images of airplanes and suitcases flashed before my eyes as my phone-holding hand trembled.

"What is it? I'm busy." Shaun barked.

"We need to talk about Josh."

"Yeah. When is he coming back? He's going to have to Uber himself from the bus station. I have no time to drive around this week." His voice oozed irritation. "Honestly, I didn't expect him to pull this sort of crap. It's so out of character. Teenagers, eh?" He attempted a lighter tone, and my stomach tightened.

"How is he doing at school?"

"Fine. He made friends straight out of the gate, already got invited to some birthday parties and all. They got to go on a hot air balloon. The family owns a hotel chain, they're a great connection."

"So, you have no idea why he suddenly packed up and left?" I kept my voice neutral, even if my own irritation was quickly reaching the boiling point. "There were no signs at all?"

"No... I mean... no." I heard the hesitation now, along with defensiveness.

He had no idea. Josh was the quiet one. He didn't seek you out to share about his life. If you didn't pay attention and give him time to talk, you missed everything.

"Sounds like you have a full plate, with the baby coming... congratulations, by the way. How's the business?"

"Good. Yeah... It's busy." The silence stretched between us, punctuated by heavy breaths. "It's been a bit stressful. We've avoided layoffs, so far, but it's a bit touch and go. Long days. So I haven't had a chance to catch up with Josh every day but Kelly is here twenty-four seven."

"She must have a lot on her mind though, with the baby coming."

I couldn't believe how understanding I managed to sound, given the way my stomach turned at the sheer mention of her name.

"She's pre-diabetic so she's having to watch her diet."

I steeled my nerves. "Ouch. That's tough, especially with pregnancy cravings."

"She's handling it. It's hard since she loves her sweets, but Kelly is so committed. She'll do anything for the baby."

I ignored the poorly veiled dig. I hadn't been committed enough to follow him back to Auckland, committed enough to give up the farm and our country lifestyle. Not committed enough to sacrifice my dream and be the perfect wife he wanted—the one on TV with celebrity friends and a face held together with Botox. I'd wanted out, and I'd fought tooth and nail to make it happen. In my own way, I was just as responsible for our divorce. I'd held onto the house I loved, the animals, the peace and quiet of a small town. I had begun to relax, and nothing could make me return. We'd been stuck, both waiting for the other to yield. Eventually, I suggested a compromise—a place just outside Auckland, a job that didn't stress me quite so much... but Shaun had already found a new woman to fill my role.

"That's great," I said, dragging myself up the high road by my bootstraps. "But it seems Josh has found it stressful to keep up with his new friends. Sounds like they're expecting the latest gear, expensive parties, and gifts. If you're having to tighten the belt, do you want him hanging out with these kids?"

"I'm sure it's not that bad—"

"And he misses his friends down here. He wants to stay and finish the school year in Napier."

"But... We agreed on Auckland Grammar. It's the best in the country."

"Sure. But, what if it's not best for *him?*"

There. I'd made my argument. My heart pounded like after a half-hour Pilates session. I wanted to win this argument, yet I could barely take the pain that came with it.

After a long silence, Shaun spoke. The bullishness had seeped out of his voice. "So, you'd have him on school terms and..."

"And you could take him over the holidays. Or every other holiday, so that the boys can see each other here over some breaks. Whatever works best. Sounds like Alex is doing well?"

"He's great. He's loving the classes. They have so many extra-curriculars to choose from. He's doing game design, animation, lots of things. I think he wants to play ice hockey. Can't do that in Napier."

"No, he can't," I conceded. I didn't expect to get my firstborn to move back to the middle of nowhere. He was more like Shaun, who thrived in the city. "I'm glad he's settled in so well. And believe me, this is not for me. I'm only suggesting it because I think it might be best for Josh."

Shaun's harrumph suggested he thought I was full of crap. "Obviously, I need to discuss this with Kelly, but if Josh is also keen to stay there, maybe we can work something out."

His words punched me in the heart. "Thank you," I choked. "I'll look into the details and let you know."

I ended the call, feeling the weight of the world on my shoulders. This is what it was to be a mother. It was time to send flighty dreams to the back of the queue and accept my lot.

CHAPTER 34

Emir

I scooped the last bit of horse poop off the stables floor and threw it on the wheelbarrow, leaning on my shovel. Molly nudged my shoulder and circled me, and I rubbed her mane. She was acting a lot more affectionately. Her eye looked better. Maybe the pain had made her skittish. I could certainly understand that as I rolled back my shoulders and raised my eyebrows, noting the absence of pain. It was amazing what fresh air and peace and quiet could do to your body. As well as falling in love, added a whispering voice inside me. Even if the last one would bring more pain down the road. I'd exchange the tension headache for a heartache.

I never thought I'd feel so emotional about scooping up excrement, but it was my last day on the farm. The last workday before the party. Before all the people arrived and my inner turmoil was drowned by the noise and chaos of celebration. I couldn't have been less of a party person if I'd tried, but I didn't want to ruin it for everyone else.

The week had been swallowed by responsibilities. My parents had returned from their trip, forcing me to rent a car and drive them around Napier, as well as hang around Aria's parents' place to translate for them, leaving out some of the stupid things they said to keep the peace. It was the least I could do for my brother. So far, everyone seemed to get along. My parents were sufficiently in love with New Zealand scenery and possessed enough average quality photos of mountains and lakes to torture our relatives back in Istanbul for years to come.

I'd slept three agonizing nights in Aria's parents' guest room, my legs hanging off the end of a short mattress, before I'd laid out my excuses for why I needed to spend the last day and night on Janie's farm. She needed help with the farm chores. The trellis on the deck was still unfinished (it wasn't) and I was tall enough to reach for things from the top of the cabinets, saving valuable time. I don't know if they'd bought any of my excuses, but Mom understood the pain of sleeping poorly, so she let me go and Aria's mom gave me a ride, dropping me off on her way to work.

Janie had been gone most of the day yesterday, driving Josh to visit the school he would transfer to, buying a new uniform and then reuniting him with his best friend. She'd given me an update late at night over the phone, sounding both happy and sad. I lay in bed for a long time after that, aching from the distance between us and the terrible mattress underneath me, wondering how badly it would hurt once we were on opposite sides of the world. Finally, the cooler night air lulled me to sleep, and I dreamed of us, together.

It had to be possible, I told myself as I dumped the pile of horse manure on a compost heap. But I had to talk to her, in private, before the party, and time was running out.

I glanced up at the house, watching for signs of life. It was 9:30 a.m. Janie must have been up already. I'd stopped at the stables to check on Molly—a habit I couldn't shake. And seeing her floor hadn't been cleaned, I'd got to work, giving myself a moment to think.

The house seemed quiet, but I noticed movement inside the greenhouse. A flash of peachy orange. I walked closer until I caught her scooting between the strawberry plants, slipping ripe fruit into the pockets of her bathrobe. Seeing her in that robe reminded me of the moment in the forest and I froze, waiting for her to notice me. She looked so sad. Defeated.

This was not how I wanted to leave her. I had to go away, but I needed us to have hope. I brushed wayward bits of straw and hay off my slacks and shook my shirt. I needed some farm appropriate clothes. I'd already destroyed two shirts and one pair of pants.

She jumped to her feet, letting out a shriek as she saw me. "Emir! Oh my God, you scared me!"

"I'm sorry," I took a tentative step closer. "Are you okay?"

She stared at me, breathing heavily, her hand resting on her rising and falling chest. "I don't know." For a moment, her gaze flicked from the strawberries to her bare feet, then back to me. "I mean, I'll have to be."

The hot and humid greenhouse air enveloped us into its suffocating cloud. Everything smelled of strawberry. I picked off one particularly red and ripe one, offering it to her. "Your pockets aren't big enough."

I'd taken on watering the plants twice daily but had missed the last couple of days. The soil looked dry.

Janie's laugh was a little wobbly and nervous. "I forgot to bring a container." She looked at her feet again. "I forgot to wear shoes."

"You've had a lot to deal with lately." I guided her out of the greenhouse. It was too hot to think.

"I didn't know you were coming back before the party. When did you arrive?"

"A little while ago. I left my bag by the back door and went to checked on Molly."

Her face fell. "Oh, Molly! Yes, I haven't cleaned the—"

"It's done," I said, catching her by her bathrobe as she lunged towards the staples. "All cleaned. Let's go."

"What? You shoveled shit in clothes like that?" She shook her head, scanning my outfit.

"Most of my clothes are like this. I didn't exactly come to New Zealand to work on a farm."

"And it doesn't make sense to get a new wardrobe for a temporary job," she finished, her mouth a straight line.

We stopped by the small orchard, under a plum tree heavy with ripening fruit. "Nothing about this is temporary. Or a job. When something changes the course of your life, it's a forever thing. You're my forever thing, Janie. I'll never be the same."

She looked at me from under wet eye lashes. "In a good way?"

"In a very good way," I confirmed.

"I... I love that. But it doesn't mean we can build a life together. I can't leave, and I can't ask you to drop everything, tear up that flight ticket and stay... can I?" She blinked and tears spilled, uncertainty and hope flickering behind the gloss of emotion. "I mean, if you could imagine that I'd share everything I have. It's not much, but I think we could have enough. We could live off the land. Maybe we could sell that documentary and work on it together. I downloaded the footage on my laptop yesterday and started playing around with it. There're some compelling shots, especially yours. They're beautiful, Emir. You could build a career as a photographer..."

My stomach dropped. "Janie. I want to be with you, but I can't be your farmhand or photographer. I've inherited a business. There's so much inventory, these treasures my father's buried in there... He's a hoarder and not very organized. And I know there's so much potential. I can't walk away from it."

I couldn't walk away from my chance of having something to my name. Something tangible, measurable. I couldn't come to her empty-handed. She deserved so much more.

"I understand." She wouldn't look me in the eye anymore.

"But it doesn't mean we won't see each other ever again. It doesn't mean I'm giving up on us."

"Emir. I can't do long distance. I can't do this."

"You don't have to. I'll take my chances." As much as I hated the idea of her meeting someone else, I couldn't ask her to wait. I could only hope.

Her eyes burned with fire and hands trembled. "What do you mean? You can't keep up a one-sided, long-distance relationship. You need to go home and move on. We both have to move on."

"No. It's my choice. I'll be yours, even if you can't be mine. I'll turn that shop around, make it profitable and sell it. I'll make sure my parents are okay. Cem will help. He'll be there over this summer, maybe even longer. And then I'll come back. I'll set up business here and—"

"Emir. You're talking about something that can take years. Is it even in your hands? I've been reading more about the economy in Turkey, and it sounds dire. Be honest with me. Be honest with yourself."

I had to meet her gaze. Those bottomless, blue-grey eyes I couldn't hide from. "It won't be easy, but no one's more committed than I am. If I set my mind to it, I'll make it happen. In two years, I took my brother from a B-list soap actor to an international star. He had a shot at something big. He blew it, but I made it happen. When my father was still in charge, I couldn't change the course of the antique shop. But now, it's mine and I can turn things around. I can make something of myself, build something that's mine. And then I'll come back, I promise."

Her sigh was so deep it shook her whole body. "Do what you must do, Emir. I understand. I never thought I could keep you."

"But—"

She raised a finger onto my lips. "No. There's nothing more we can say. You need to take that flight and when you do, it's over. The only question is, what do we do with the little time we have left?"

I saw the blaze in her eyes, blue flames licking dilated pupils. I cupped her face, tracing my thumb along her jawline. She was right. We couldn't let the sadness of our uncertain future steal away these moments. I had to store them like nuts for the winter. I would need every little memory to carry me through the next few months. I refused to think it could take years.

"Where's Josh? Still sleeping?"

"I think he's up. I left some breakfast out for him. But I'll drive him to town this afternoon and he'll stay a couple of nights at his friend's house. He doesn't want to be here for the party."

I could imagine that.

"So, we have the house to ourselves tonight?" My body woke up at the thought.

I grabbed the belt of her open bathrobe and yanked her against me. The short silk pajama felt cool against my chest, until I felt her body heat coming through. I buried my face into her neck, inhaling her scent, my lips caressing her collarbone. The things I would do...

"That's right." I heard the smile in her voice, punctuated by a sniff. "I need everything you can give me."

I kissed her, long and deep. It was instant. That hungry, electric crashing of tongues that triggered an erection I couldn't be seen in public with. The way I craved her was unsettling.

With great effort, I released her. "Well, in that case, I'm going to take a long nap."

She licked her lips, panting, cheeks rosy and hot. "Whatever you need. Be my guest."

And that's what I was. Her guest.

I'd be more than that, one day. I'd make my fortune and come back. I'd be worthy of her. But I had to make sure she didn't forget me. I had to give my future self a chance.

I walked away, letting the soft, peachy bathrobe belt slip between my fingers, leaving the end of it resting against the ground as she stood there, arms hanging by her sides, a startled smile on her face.

CHAPTER 35

Janie

When I stepped out of the car after dropping off Josh, I found Emir at the doorway of my house, waiting for me. He'd changed into another fancy shirt and pants that hugged his tall, perfect form in all the right places. He could have stood at the doorway of a five-star restaurant, waiting to lead me to a table that could only be booked weeks in advance. He would have stood out, though, even if he was surrounded by luxury. In Napier, he glowed like a beacon. I couldn't have a low-key affair with him, but that didn't worry me anymore. I didn't care if everyone and their cousin saw us together and had an opinion on my love life.

But if I truly loved him, I would let him follow his own path.

I'd already done the career thing. I'd exhausted myself; I'd given too much and run myself to the ground, but I'd also achieved something. I had clout. I had a house and a piece of land to my name. I understood what it must have felt to have none of that, to not be able to match even the little I'd been able to gather. I'd come across enough male egos to know how fragile they were. As much as I wanted him, I didn't want to strip him of his pride. If he had to make something of himself first, I had no choice but to let him go.

"*Hoşgeldiniz,*" he said, opening his arms.

I walked straight in, smiling through my tears. I had to stop crying. I couldn't spend our last night like this, producing copious amounts of snot. I'd already cried more with him than during the last ten years of my life. It was probably a sign of a midlife crisis, but I'd worry about that later.

"What is it?" He whispered as I sniffed against his chest.

"I'm so angry at the universe." I drew a shaky breath. "The horrible injustice of it all. The timing of us."

"Do you wish we hadn't met?"

His dark voice made my chest squeeze even harder, and I pulled myself away to meet his eyes.

"I don't regret anything about us. I wouldn't change anything that's happened." I sniffed. "I'm crying for me... how lonely I'll be without you. It hasn't even happened yet, and it already hurts."

"We'll be together one day. We'll be together for so long you'll be entirely sick of me." His smile was sad, yet somehow ebullient.

He pulled me inside the house, locking the door. "Choose the first room."

"First room?"

"I intend to make love to you in every room of the house. You decide on the order."

"Seriously?"

His inky eyes told me exactly how serious he was. "I'll feed you first, though."

I followed him to the dining room and a high-pitched yelp erupted from my mouth. Every inch of the dining table was filled with food—fruit, nuts, chocolates, pastries, and an array of Turkish delicacies I vaguely remembered from my Middle Eastern tour. He must have brought some of them with him.

"We can't possibly eat this much!"

"That's okay. Most of it will keep."

I popped a roasted almond into my mouth and turned to him. "I think I want to start from this room."

I led the excitedly jumping Gru out into the hallway and closed the door. Finally, we were alone. My stomach growled, treats on the table calling my name. But this was not a regular date night. I didn't want to waste time eating and drinking. I couldn't wait for him. I unbuttoned my blouse, letting it drop to my feet. His gaze dipped and darkened, tracing my body. The air felt warm, but I shivered from anticipation. Emir approached me, his movements slow and controlled, yet somehow charged. Like he was holding back something explosive.

I unbuttoned his shirt, untucking it out of his slacks to reveal his chest. My fingers hovered over his thumping heartbeat, then followed the trail of dark hair leading down from his navel, curling underneath the black, leather belt. A visible erection strained the fabric of his slacks. I traced the shape of it, drawing in a sharp breath. I felt him shudder at the same time, but he kept his hands still, gently cupping my elbows.

"How do you want me to touch you, Janie? Tell me what you need."

"I'm kind of curious to see what you'll do." My smile was probably a little wicked.

"You want me to surprise you?" He lifted an eyebrow, lips curling up slightly.

I'd miss that face. Those sharp eyes that softened with contact. Hardness that morphed into vulnerability. I'd never met anyone who'd met me with such openness.

I nodded. My skin pebbled. I felt a breeze under my skirt, making me throb.

He took my hand and raised it, spinning me around like on a dance floor. But he didn't let me go full circle, pulling my back against his chest, his hands locking around my waist. That impressive erection nuzzled between my butt cheeks, and he groaned into my ear. In seconds, he had me pinned against the cool wall, his hot breath tickling my neck. His hands landed on either side of my face and that erection ground into my flesh, nearly lifting my toes off the floor.

His voice was tender. "I can surprise you, but I'll keep asking what you want. I'll keep listening. Because I want to learn every single thing that makes you tick. So that we can have something together that's better than anything I could do if I took a wild guess. Do you understand what I mean?"

"But we already slept together, and it was the best I've ever had," I confessed. "Do you think it was an accident?"

I was feeling cheeky. I wanted to tease him and push him until he lost control. Until he bent me over the couch and punished me.

He spun me around again, keeping my back against the wall. I loved the coolness of it, balancing the heat emanating from my core. He had a smile on his face. "Joke all you want, but I've thought about it. A lot. And I don't know. Maybe it was the danger of that night, everything else that happened. I took a shot at what I thought you'd like, and I got lucky."

My eyebrows sailed up. "Are you saying you're not a mind-reading sex god that delivers black-out orgasms without any instruction? I'm shocked!"

He rolled his eyes. "I'm not my brother. I don't improvise my way through life, thinking I'm God's gift to women. I analyze. I rely on evidence. And with you, I don't have enough evidence. So, tonight is about gathering data. Which means you have to be one hundred percent honest about what you like and don't like."

My breath came out a little shuddery. I curled my hands around his belt and pulled him even closer. "Okay. If you do the same."

He pressed against me, driving the ridge of his hard-on against my throbbing, wet crotch, drawing a deep breath from the crook of my neck. "I'm a simple man. If I can get you off, I will enjoy myself, every time."

"But... surely you have preferences? Color and style of lingerie? Big tits or itty-bitty boobs? Perfume or no perfume?"

He hooked his fingers around my white, lacy bra and released the front clasp. My medium-sized breasts embraced freedom, nipples pinching hard. "I want to see you turned on. That's my preference."

"Seriously?"

He dragged his drunken gaze from my breasts to my eyes, sharpening up. "Janie. You should know by now that I say what I mean, and I mean what I say. I want to know what turns you on."

The way he stood perfectly still, waiting for my next move, was the hottest thing I'd ever witnessed. A man who didn't pretend to know what I enjoyed. I didn't have to play along to protect his ego. I didn't have to convince myself I was having a good time. He was giving me space. He was listening.

A small smile tugged my mouth as a memory surfaced. "You remember that terrible bakery?"

He lifted a brow. "That drunk guy harassing you?"

"I behaved horribly. If I'd been alone, I'd never taken a risk like that. But since you were with me—"

"You felt safe enough to flirt with a drunken idiot," he finished, his tone dry.

"And after that, I had this fantasy of you... punishing me." I blinked, my cheeks instantly heating up.

His eyes glinted. "When you thrust out that ass of yours, I wanted to throw you on my shoulder and carry you out of there." He was so close now I felt his body heat from head to toe, like standing too close to the fire. I couldn't escape his scent, only breathe it in.

"That's exactly what I imagined," I whispered. "I imagined you carrying me all the way to the car and throwing me down on the backseat."

He lifted me in the air like a feather, throwing me over his shoulder. I screamed. His thumbs pressed into the hollows inside my pelvic bones, inducing a powerful tug in the bottom of my belly. "Oh, my God!"

Traipsing over to the living room, Emir tossed me onto the couch. I scrambled up, shrieking from sheer surprise and pleasure, circling the free-standing piece of furniture. With two long strides, he caught me on the other side, trapped me in his strong grip and bent me over the back of the couch, his hands riding up my skirt, vibrating with tension. Anticipation. "Like that?"

"Something like that," I giggled breathlessly.

"And then what? Did I teach you a lesson?"

There was a smile in his voice, thick with arousal. I could hardly trust myself to speak, that fire coursing through me. I just needed him to touch me. Take me.

"I think we had the same fantasy," he said, delivering a sharp slap on one butt cheek.

The powerful jolt travelled all the way to my crotch, rendering me speechless. I felt him pressing into me and bucked my ass against his hard-on. "Really?" I gasped.

I needed him to keep talking.

He pressed himself against my back, slipping his hands around my hips. His voice was a gravelly whisper against my neck. "It took all my willpower to stand back. But since you told me off for acting jealous, I didn't want to repeat the same mistake."

Nervous laughter escaped my mouth. I was glad he couldn't see my hot face. "Is it okay that I hate that behavior but also find it hot?"

"You want me to act civilized in public and spank you in private?"

"Yes, please."

"No problem," he hissed into my ear, hiking up my skirt.

My stomach tightened in anticipation of another slap, slightly harder this time. The sharp sensation tingled through me, all the way to my soaking wet underwear. I gasped.

"Too much?"

"Just what I deserve."

"Well, you were quite naughty," he said darkly, delivering another slap.

"I was."

"God, this ass..."

His fingers found their way to where I needed them, slipping between the soaked fabric and flesh. I moved against his hand, desperate for more. I felt his erection between my butt cheeks, hard and hot under the fabric.

"Take off your pants," I ordered.

"So bossy," he grumbled.

He continued working between my shaking legs, pressing me against the couch, and I had no choice but to go along for the ride. It felt too good, too overwhelming. All thoughts vanished and his fingers picked up speed, circling and moving in perfect sync with the involuntary dance my hips seemed to be doing. I felt the erection nuzzled deeper between my butt cheeks, lifting my heels off the floor as he added more pressure. I couldn't stand it anymore.

With vivid images of his smile, I came apart against his hand, my fingers curling against the smooth velvet of the couch cushions. A wave after wave coursed through me. I felt the joy and the sadness, the searing clarity of how much I'd miss him.

Pushing down the welling in my chest, still pulsating, my legs too weak for standing, I turned around. "Now you take those pants off."

He smiled, and that smile still tugged inside me, just like the first time. I'd never get tired of it, even if we had all the time in the world.

Eyes hooded, lips ajar, he dropped the pants in seconds and produced a condom from somewhere. My poor skirt puckered around my waist, I hopped on the edge of the couch, spreading my legs. I felt the emptiness inside me, muscles contracting moments before he filled me, emptying my lungs.

Locking eyes with me, he subtly raised his brows. I gave a small nod and wrapped my legs around him, pulling him in deeper. The edge of the couch wasn't as soft as I'd hoped, but I settled in, embracing the discomfort. This way, I was tall enough to take him, all of him, standing up. I watched his eyes roll up as his hips moved faster. His hands cupped my ass, keeping me in balance, sinking into my flesh with such force I fully expected bruises. But I didn't want him to stop. I needed him out of control.

I wasn't prepared for the fresh cascade of pleasure from the way he filled me, my body vibrating on a higher frequency.

Yes, I thought. Invade me. I didn't want to be independent. I didn't want to be alone.

I felt his release erupting deep inside of me and that unstoppable sensation reached its crescendo, sending me over the edge.

We held on for a long time, neither of us willing to let go. His forehead rested against mine, hot gusts of breath meeting in the middle. He was still inside me, holding still and hard. "Was that what you had in mind?" he asked.

"That was even better."

"I love you, Janie." It sounded almost like an apology.

"I love you, too." There was nothing else I could say. Nothing different, or original. That was the only thing that felt true.

"Did I hurt you?" He asked, finally pulling out and helping me down on the floor.

"No. You made my legs so weak I can no longer walk."

He brushed my hair away from my face, that deep concern making his eyes even more beautiful. "I wish I could take you with me. I wish I could give you more than this."

I shook from frustration. "I don't care about your earnings or business or what it says on your CV. It's not what I value. This is what I value." I gestured the air between us. "Your honesty. That you can set aside your ego to form that connection. That's a miracle. Why can't you just offer... yourself? That's all I want."

He dropped his chin, averting his eyes. "It's not that simple.

Since my father announced his retirement, I have a responsibility. I can't walk away. And I can't afford to waste the flight ticket. I'm not in that position." He looked up, his eyes filled with pain. "I bet you wish you'd found someone with resources."

Fury swelled in my gut. "Most guys with resources are huge dicks. The richer they get, the worse they act. I don't want another one of those. I want to keep you."

Tears sprung to my eyes as my hands gripped his open shirt, hanging onto him like I was drowning. This was the exact opposite of the beautiful goodbye I'd been imagining. This was me, desperate and clingy.

His eyes met me, so full of regret I had to turn away. He pulled me into his arms and held me tight as I cried, taking deep breaths, trying to stop myself after every sob, only to sob harder. Until I finally gave up the fight, smearing his shirt and bare chest with flakes of my tubing mascara, tears, and snot.

"I don't think I can do it in every room," I managed to say between gasps of air. "I think I need to start pulling away. This hurts too much."

"The last thing I want to do is hurt you." His voice sounded choked and tight like he was fighting tears as well. It made me feel marginally better.

"I swear I'm not this much of a crier." I pulled away to wipe my eyes with tissue I snagged from the table. "I've cried more in the last two weeks than the two years before that."

"Seriously? You went through divorce."

I sighed. "I was mostly angry. But now, I feel like I have

something good, and I have to give it up because of... geography and shit. It's so unfair."

He pulled out chairs for us and I sat down, facing him. "I'm mostly angry with myself. I should have built my own business a long time ago. I shouldn't have wasted years on my brother's career, expecting this big payout that never came. I've had opportunities, and I've worked hard, but my family has lost so much with the hyperinflation... If we'd only invested in Euros and US dollars a bit earlier. Or even the crypto market. I didn't act fast enough and... we've had some setbacks. I should be better than this, but I always followed my father's lead. I never went against him. And I guess that's why I took the job as Cem's manager, because for the first time, I was doing something without Dad. I was calling the shots. And I was good at it. But I wasn't good at reading people. I didn't even notice Cem was head over heels in love. I missed all the signs. I didn't even understand how that could derail our plans."

I gave him a probing look. "Do you understand it now?"

He sighed his agreement.

"Let's eat," I said, browsing the array of colors laid across the table.

We ate in silence. Afterwards, I helped him clean the table, then found my notebook and pen.

"I'm going up to the hunting cabin to do some thinking," I said, slipping my feet into my boots. "Alone."

He stood in the doorway, face stony, and nodded.

It felt strange to sit on those steps, surrounded by the familiar greenery, remembering the moments I'd shared with him. That almost-kiss, and the real ones that followed. Everything he was to me, already, when I couldn't keep any of it. I had to stay away, hide as much as possible, to survive the party and these last hours we had left. I couldn't go any further or I'd end up with irreparable damage. It might already be too late. Everything he said and did dragged me deeper into emotional quicksand.

When I got back, I found him waiting at the doorway. Had he been waiting the whole time?

"Are you okay?" he asked.

I gave him a wobbly nod, stopping a few steps away. A safe distance. But nothing was safe when he was still with me. Still in my house.

"I'll miss you so much." My voice cracked as I hugged the empty notebook to my chest. I hadn't been able to write a single word. Nothing was worthy of this day and these moments. Nothing I said could create the distance I needed.

Also, distance was the last thing I wanted.

"You don't have to miss me yet," he said quietly, opening his arms.

The late evening sun made his palms glow.

I couldn't stop myself from walking into those arms. What had I been thinking? That I could somehow rip the plaster and expedite healing when he was still here? He was my wound. But with his heartbeat against my cheek, I felt no pain. I could postpone it.

"I'm sorry I had to run away for a bit."

"It's okay."

"I thought I could protect myself, but I think it's too late. I think I have to just hold onto you all night."

His arms tightened around me. "That's also okay."

CHAPTER 36

Janie

"The sky is clear!" I yelled, stepping back inside my house.

"Yay!" Aria waved from behind the dining table she was setting up for catering.

It was the day of the party. After a sleepless night, curled up with the man my whole being craved, I was running on caffeine, fake smiles, and affirmations. I couldn't be miserable. Today was about celebration. It was about keeping myself busy and focused on other people.

It'd be the perfect way to part ways, I told myself. A day full of smiles and laughter and flower arrangements. My house had transformed into a buzzing center of romance and happiness. For other people.

The usual number of people in my house had already more than doubled. Kerim and his wife had taken over my kitchen, heating and prepping food items they'd brought. Cem and Emir were setting up tables on the deck while their parents sat in the shade, sipping tea. I was glad Josh was away at his friend's house for another day. He would have struggled with this many strangers.

Aria's mom Lyn appeared from Alex's bedroom that had been recently declared the staging area, holding two odd-looking, pink signs with white arrows painted on them. Bright yellow balloons hung off the side. "These should catch the eye, don't you think? I repurposed these old trays I found in the op shop!"

"Yeah, I think those stand out well."

I saw Aria's face momentarily fall before she pasted on a smile. "Thanks, Mom."

Lyn beamed. "Greg went to find some timber to make the signposts. These will last for years. We can use the same signs for the wedding!"

Aria's eyes widened and I gave her a subtle head shake.

"I'll see where Greg's at," Lyn said, hurrying out the door.

I grabbed one of the napkins Aria was folding to help her out. "Don't worry. The signs will be irreversibly damaged during the festivities, possibly by a runaway horse, and won't be available for your wedding."

Aria sighed. "I'd be eternally grateful! I don't know where she finds these things."

"She's just trying to be helpful."

"How're you feeling?" She asked, leaning in. "Is he really leaving tomorrow?" Her gaze swept to the deck where Emir was scooting under my outdoor table, holding a wrench. There'd be no wobbly legs in the house after his exit, other than mine.

"He says he has to go. And I have to let him go."

Aria's eyes flooded with despair. "Can't you... follow him?"

"Not with Josh moving back home."

"Why does he have to go? It's not like his parents are all alone. Cem and I will be there! And..." Her expression shifted and she glanced around her to see if anyone was listening.

"What?" I whispered, seeing Kerim right behind me.

Aria clamped her lips together. Maybe there were too many people around for whatever she wanted to say.

I'd have a full house tonight. Aria, Cem, Emir and their parents were staying overnight, to make sure nobody had to drive. We'd set up the guest room for Emir's parents, Josh's room for Emir and Alex's room for Aria and Cem. My house was also closer to the airport, which made it handy for Emir's parents. And Emir, I thought with a pang. Their flight was tomorrow, but I couldn't allow myself to dwell on that.

"What time is it? I think I need to get changed!" Aria finished the napkins, looking at the clock on the wall.

"Do you need help?" I followed her into Alex's bedroom, where a questionable inflatable mattress awaited her and Cem.

"Are you sure you're okay with this?" I asked. "It tends to deflate a bit overnight."

"Oh, it's for the best. I think Cem's parents are a bit uncomfortable with us sleeping in the same room. It's best if it looks like camping and not like... you know, enjoyable."

My skin sizzled with discomfort. "But they know you sleep together at your place, right? You travelled together and stayed together for the premiere."

Aria bit her lip. "Yeah. It's a bit weird. I think they just like to pretend we're waiting until we're married. Mostly for the sake of their more conservative family members. And me, of course. It'd ruin my reputation. It's easier since we're here, with no other relatives around." She rolled her eyes.

What would they say if they knew their eldest son was sleeping with the hostess, I wondered. Not that we'd do that again in a very long time, if ever.

"Any chance they sleep very soundly with earplugs?"

"Apparently his father sleepwalks. Usually to the fridge. But I'm not sure where he'll end up in here since he doesn't know the layout of the house. With Mom and Dad, he kept walking to the laundry."

I groaned. It was going to be an interesting night.

I helped Aria change into her shimmery, teal dress with an open back.

"So gorgeous!" I exhaled as she did a spin for me. "It's like a wedding dress, just not white."

Her eyes shone. "I kind of wish this was our wedding. I know Cem keeps asking and I keep telling him no, but how amazing would it be if we just got married? No waiting, no more party planning. Just us together forever. We already have the marriage license."

My chin wobbled and I steadied it with a smile. "Well, just say the word and I'll call Len."

"Who's Len?"

"A lovely local pastor I went out with, until Emir scared him away."

Aria burst into laughter. "Scared him, how?"

I told her the story of my ill-fated date and Emir's behavior.

"Oh my God. He followed you and ruined your date? That's…"

"Insanely jealous? Yeah."

Aria's face softened. "But also… he must be crazy about you."

I shrugged, fiddling with the fabric of Aria's dress. I couldn't let my thoughts go down that route. Not now. I'd made a promise to myself to make it through the party without crying.

"You think that pastor would show up to marry Emir's brother? I mean, no one's that nice."

She had a point, but the optimist in me lifted its stupidly resilient head. "I'm willing to ask."

That was one thing I could do for my friend. Asking hard questions of people who'd rather not talk to me was just another day for a journalist.

"What do you think Cem would say? I should talk to him first." Something about the way her eyes darted around the room, teeth working on a freshly painted fingernail, gave me pause.

"Are you serious? What about his parents?"

Aria's mouth twisted, a look of harried panic rising into her eyes. "Cem's parents would probably be relieved, since I'm pregnant and they'll find out soon enough."

We stared at each other in stunned silence.

"You've told Cem, right?"

She shook her head very slowly, eyes wide. "I just found out and it didn't seem like the best timing. I haven't really processed this. I keep forgetting about it and then it hits me again."

"How do you forget something like that?"

Aria drew a breath, one hand resting on her chest, the other on her stomach. "By actively blocking it out because it's too huge and the timing is so terrible. I mean... if I tell him, he's going to freak out and we'll have to cancel the party or something. It'll be a nightmare."

I frowned. "You're not giving him enough credit. He loves you. He wants to marry you."

"I don't know. He's still a celebrity. He's the baby of his family... the way his mom feeds him. Did you see them out there on the deck? She was popping little cakes straight into his mouth. Can you imagine him a dad? It's crazy!"

"If you don't think he's parent material, why would you marry him in the first place?"

Aria buried her face in her hands and sobbed. "I don't know what I'm saying! I'm freaking out."

"You two need to talk. Stay here, I'll get him."

"No! I can't. I haven't even found the words to explain it to myself. I feel like it's all my fault."

"Why? It takes two."

"But we found these old condoms..."

I grabbed her shoulders, searching for eye contact. "Breathe,

Aria. It'll be fine. I know it's not the plan, but life will throw stuff at you, good and bad, and you just have to keep swimming. That's how it works. And this is good stuff, I promise."

She nodded, her whole body shaking.

"Wait here." My stomach in knots, I snuck out, heading straight to the deck. The outdoor area looked ready for the party. The turquoise and white garlands hung over three long tables, mixing with the green vines. The white tablecloths, secured with clamps, flapped in the gentle breeze. I found Cem and Emir sitting on the edge of the deck, each holding a bottle of beer. Gru slept on Emir's lap, snoring loudly. I wanted to trade places with the dog.

I glanced around. "Where's everyone else?"

"They went to get changed. I'll go after I finish this." Emir lifted his beer bottle.

He wore his usual dress pants and charcoal collar shirt with a subtle sheen.

I raised my brow. "What are you changing into, a tux?"

We'd talked about keeping things casual, but I wondered what exactly qualified as casual for my Turkish guests. I'd been in my pale purple dress since breakfast and was only planning to add some lipstick and hairspray before the guests—a few of Aria's actor friends, her uncle, cousins and Pete arrived.

Emir gave me the briefest of smiles. "Just changing into a fresh shirt. It's quite warm so I'm happy if we don't need jackets."

He gave me a questioning look, one I held for needlessly long before I dumbly repeated, "No jackets."

This is why I'd been avoiding him for hours. Simply looking

into his eyes scattered my thoughts, filling my chest with longing and pain.

And now I was holding onto Aria's news, my mind playing the mental chess game of cause and effect. What did this mean? How would their parents take it? Where would they live? And most importantly, how did this impact my relationship with Emir?

"Cem, can you come inside for minute?" I tried to keep my voice neutral, but both men swiveled around. Emir frowned.

"What is it?" Cem asked.

"Aria needs help with something."

"Something?" They repeated in unison.

"It's a surprise." I tried to smile.

Cem got up, followed by Emir, who trailed us inside. I stopped him in the living room. "We just need Cem for this, sorry." My hand lingered on his chest and he leaned forward, enough to seal the connection.

His eyes burned with unsaid words, but I didn't let myself focus on them.

"I'll tell you later," I whispered, rushing Cem down the hallway.

I considered just shoving the movie star into my son's bedroom, but when I caught Aria's panicked expression, I decided to escort him all the way in.

"Wow," Cem said, looking at Aria's dress. "Am I supposed to see you before—"

"It's not a wedding, Cem."

"Fine. Okay. What's wrong?"

"I... I..." Aria gaped at me, her eyes begging for help.

"She's pregnant," I said. "And if you want to turn this thing into a wedding, I'll contact Len to see if he's free."

I'd never seen Cem's face quite like that. He whipped his head to stare at me, then back at Aria. "*Allah, Allah!* You serious?"

Aria nodded. "I think so. I've been testing all week, and I got a positive this morning."

"You've been testing, and you didn't tell me?"

Aria nibbled at her thumbnail, looking up with a pained expression. "I thought if it's false alarm I'd just freak you out for no reason."

Cem rescued the nail from his fiancée's mouth and secured her hands in his. "You should have told me."

She hung her head. "Yeah, I know. I'm sorry. But the timing is awful."

"It doesn't matter. It's our baby. We'll just have to… get ready."

His voice was soft and tender. I backed through the doorway, still holding my breath but also relieved by his reaction. When I was about to slip away, Cem turned around. "What did you say about the wedding?"

"She can call someone to marry us if we want to turn this into a wedding," Aria said.

I had a big mouth. A big, big mouth.

'Do it!" Cem's voice was bright and decisive. He turned back to Aria. "Please? We can have another wedding back home. I mean, Istanbul. But doing it right here, under the radar, it's so perfect."

Aria's eyes filled with tears. "What about your parents? Are we going to give them heart attacks, for real?"

Cem shrugged. "It might not be that bad. Whatever we do here won't be a proper wedding for my mom. But if she gets to throw another one back home, she'd be happy. And she loves babies!"

"We can't tell her yet, it's too early. Right?" She turned to me for confirmation, eyes wide with terror.

I adopted my most impartial news anchor tone. "Some people wait to share the news since the risk of miscarriage is higher in the beginning. But it's up to you."

"So, if you wouldn't tell them about a miscarriage, don't tell them about the pregnancy?" Aria gestured with her hands while Cem stared at her with gooey-eyed devotion.

"I don't think there's a hard and fast rule."

"What do you think?" Aria asked Cem. "Should we just play it by ear? If they freak out about the wedding plan, we distract them with the baby news? Like having extra lighter fluid in case of a fire." Her smile was a little manic.

"Sounds good to me." Cem smirked.

They turned to me. Two expectant faces. Four glistening eyes.

"I'll... make the call. It may not work out, but I'll try."

My heart hammering somewhere in my throat, I fetched my phone from the busy and scent-filled kitchen, and rushed down the hall to my bedroom.

I heard footsteps behind me. Emir. He glanced over his shoulder at the empty hallway. Satisfied that no one had seen us, he followed me into the bedroom and closed the door, leaning on it. "What's going on?"

I contemplated for a fraction of a second whether to tell him.

He'd hear it sooner or later, I decided. And I had questions.

"Aria is pregnant, and they want to turn this into a wedding."

"What?"

"And… I promised to call Len. Remember the guy I went out with."

"Why?"

"Because I don't know any other ministers within a driving distance. Pastor… minister? I'm not even sure what he is, but anyway."

Emir's expression darkened.

"And I need you to behave," I added. "You can start by apologizing to him."

"The fuck I will."

"Care to rephrase that?" I took a step closer.

My tall, dark and terrifying man. I smiled, despite myself, my heart fluttering at the thought of these final, stolen moments. I'd told myself to let him go. I'd made the decision. But it seemed my body was not going to obey.

I stepped close enough to catch his scent, my fingers curling against the crisp, white shirt he'd changed into. I gently tucked at his black tie and whispered, "I know you'll behave. You'd never ruin your brother's wedding."

A sound rose from his throat, like a heavy exhale that turned into a low growl. "But you have to stop torturing me. Seeing you out there, not being able to touch you or even talk to you… I tried to catch your eye out there and you act like you don't even see me."

I stared down at my purple heels. "If I look at you, I'll lose it and ruin the party for everyone. Your parents will find out about us. I can't hide it."

"What if they do? I want to tell—"

"No, you don't! We're not going to steal their thunder." I lay my head against his shirt, careful to let my hair fall between us so I didn't smear his shirt with my makeup.

We were in hiding. What we had was too flammable to be displayed in public. It felt bittersweet to hide the one thing that mattered most, in my own home.

"This doesn't feel like the end," I whispered. Wayward hairs stuck between my lips, and I peeled them off with my fingers.

Emir wrapped his palm around my wrist. "It's not. I'll come back; you'll see."

I knew he was looking at my bed and my body betrayed me, rushing heat between my thighs, but we couldn't risk it. And I had to make the phone call.

"I have to call Len." I pulled out my phone and took a step back.

"Do you want me to go? I should go." Emir didn't move.

"Stay there," I told him.

This was already incredibly awkward. Having him next to me didn't change that, but at least I could spend a moment longer with him and show him I wasn't interested in dating the pastor. That he'd invaded my life and all my thoughts. He deserved to know it.

Len answered with a tentative "Hi, Janie?" I put him on speaker phone.

"Hi, Len! I'm so sorry I haven't been in touch. Thank you for the lovely dinner the other night. I'm sorry how things ended. I know this is long overdue, but I wanted to call and apologize."

There was a pause, then a soft chuckle. "It's okay. It was an interesting night. How are you?"

"I'm okay, thank you. Listen… Are you busy this afternoon?"

His voice brightened. "No. I mean, I can rearrange my schedule."

I stiffened. Was he hoping for another date?

"That would be amazing, because a friend of mine is pregnant and wants to turn her engagement party into a wedding. All we need is a minister. A pastor. I'm sorry, I'm not sure about the terminology."

"All pastors are ministers. Not all ministers are pastors. What time? I do have a few things lined up…" The excitement vanished from his voice, and I pulled a face, glancing at Emir, whose knowing look carried a hint of smugness.

"We're flexible! It would be amazing."

"And do they have a marriage license? That can take about three days to get and without—"

"Yes, they do!"

The line went quiet, and I exchanged another look with Emir.

"I would normally meet with the couple beforehand, get to know them…"

"We can arrange that! This is a very small, casual affair at my house."

"At your house?"

"Yes, I'm hosting it. So, what do you think?"

After another long pause, Len spoke. "Okay. I can make it there at around four. Would that work?"

"Wonderful! I'll text you the address."

We ended the call with some more thankyous, and I turned to Emir. "I can't believe he said yes!"

His eyes were hard. "He gets to see you and check out your house. And you'll owe him, which he'll use to get a second date."

I hadn't even thought of that. "Oh, my God. You're right. And I can't tell him we're an item since we're trying to hide it from the parents. Unless we tell him in confidence?"

"Tell him what?" He gave me a long, sad look and my lungs deflated.

I looked up at the ceiling, thinking. "What if we don't tell him you're leaving? He doesn't need to know."

"Tell him whatever you feel like, Janie. You know how I feel about this, but don't let that worry you."

Tears welled in my chest again, dangerously close to the surface. "I hate this too, but we must keep quiet. For Cem and Aria."

"For Cem and Aria." He gave me a solemn nod.

We snuck out of the bedroom, one by one, to join the party preparations.

Great. I'd have my awkward first date and current lover under the same roof. All I need was my ex-husband, and I could start selling tickets to a Greek tragedy.

CHAPTER 37

Emir

I'd taken the high road, and I had to stay on it. The last thing I wanted to leave Janie with was the memory of me acting up.

Still, the idea of Len the pastor riding to her rescue made my stomach turn. Spotting his car in the driveway, Janie dragged me outside to meet him. "It's best that he sees you straight away, I think."

"You mean, it's best to keep our meeting outside, away from the party guests?"

She cocked her head, looking a little conflicted. "That, too."

Gru shot through the open door, ready to greet Len with drooling excitement. I couldn't match that, but I'd do my best.

Len wore one of those black shirts with a white collar and

smiled like a poster boy for religion.

"Thank you so much for making time for us!" Janie's smile beamed, full of her sunshiny goodness as she shook his hand.

They locked eyes for a moment like two goofy idiots. I swallowed a dozen things I wanted to say, standing strategically behind Janie. When I stepped into his line of sight, his toothy smile withered.

"I'm sorry, I seem to have forgotten your name." He offered his hand, slowly and cautiously.

"Emir," I bit out.

I couldn't resist a brief death stare. Just a little warning.

Janie nudged closer. "Emir is the best man. His brother is the one getting married to my friend Aria. Let's get you introduced."

She tried to lead Len towards the door, but he dug his heels in, eyes still on me. "So, it's your brother's wedding? Is that why you're working on the farm, to prepare for the party?"

"Yes," I said.

"That's nice of you," Len said rather neutrally.

I nodded.

Janie pointed at Len's collar. "Um… we haven't announced the change of plans to the party guests yet. Until we do, could we hide that… thing," She cast him a pleading smile.

"It's called a clerical collar," Len removed the white strip from around his neck, smiling.

He looked so smitten, his eyes lingering on Janie's face, that I had to take deep breaths. No matter how much this bothered me, I couldn't punch a pastor at my brother's wedding.

I followed a few steps behind as Len entered the house, smiling and shaking hands. Janie introduced him as a friend, discreetly leading the pastor, Cem and Aria down the hallways, presumably to plan their impromptu wedding.

I fetched my camera and took some pictures of the final party preparations. It felt good to hold something in my hands as a buffer.

After a while, Cem and Aria joined the others in the living room. The sound of engines alerted us to more guests arriving and Kerim began pouring champagne into flutes. Len must have been hiding somewhere, which I didn't mind, but Janie had also disappeared. Was she with him? I couldn't stomach the thought, so I focused on taking photos.

I could speak English, yet I felt like they were all communicating in a language I didn't understand—small talk with polite smiles, quick jokes, and compliments. So perfectly pleasant and smooth. Well, until someone asked me something and I brought the cheery conversation to a grinding halt.

Had I embarrassed Janie? I'd held my tongue, but I couldn't do the smiles and platitudes that put people at ease. Not that I particularly wanted to put Len at ease. I only wanted to meet Janie's expectations. And she was in another league.

This was why I'd been single most of my life. I despised dating apps, and meeting someone the old-fashioned way required that smoothness.

Hande had picked me. I'd been standing in the corner, just like this, fiddling with my camera. I always had an excuse— Cem was there and photos were expected. She'd asked to see the photos, and I'd shown her. The way she'd lingered over pictures of my brother should have triggered warning bells. But she'd showered me with interest and eventually dragged me away from the party. Of course, I'd fallen for her. She'd been so determined to be with me, she'd convinced us both that my antisocial behavior was nothing but mysterious and sexy. I'd bought all her lies, desperate to be noticed, for once.

"This way, please!" Aria's mom guided the guests to the deck. "Bring your drinks."

I followed the meandering guests, admiring the beautiful setup through my lens. And that's when I noticed Janie. She stood on the deck, talking to my parents, somehow making them smile as she seated them and others around the tables. Once all the tables were filled, she led Aria and Cem into the doorway, facing the dozen expectant pairs of eyes. "We have an announcement!"

The general hubbub quieted as everyone turned to look. Janie gestured at Cem, who filled his lungs, smiling like his life depended on it. "Surprise! Thanks to our host Janie's wonderful help, we've been able to find a pastor and can turn this engagement party into a wedding!"

Janie glanced back at the house and raised her hand, summoning Len. He smiled and waved, probably hoping for someone to cheer. There was only silence. Eventually, we all turned to face our parents, holding our breaths. I edged closer, ready to translate if they'd missed the message. But judging by the tears in Mom's eyes, she hadn't. She looked at Dad, then Cem and Aria and finally me.

"This is not the only wedding, though, from what I hear," Janie prompted Cem.

"No! We will have a wedding in Istanbul later. A proper one. This is just for our New Zealand family. When I asked Aria to marry me, I meant it. I don't want a long engagement..." he cast a pleading look at Mom. "Particularly as we're having a baby."

The shock that travelled through the small crowd on that deck could have powered a small generator. Mom's hand flew to her mouth as she yelped out loud. She gestured for Aria to come closer. Stiff as a board, Aria crossed the wooden floor and stood in front of her. Mom took her hands and held them for a moment. I couldn't hear what she whispered, but from the look on her face, I could tell everything had changed. She offered her hand and Aria greeted her the Turkish way, tears in her eyes.

I caught Cem's eyes as he blew a breath and wiped a hand across his forehead. He'd made the call to drop the news. He was the gambler of the family, one who could think on his feet and somehow land on them. I loved my brother, but sometimes I envied him, along with the rest of the world. Part of me wanted to be like him, to grab this opportunity with both hands and hang on. But it wasn't me.

As Aria moved over to her own parents, both wearing rather stunned smiles, Janie stepped up to address the rest of us. She explained how the afternoon was going to go—much like they'd planned the engagement party, only with the brief wedding ceremony at the start. She spoke eloquently, taking over the space with humor and heart. I could see the star quality, but I loved that I didn't know her as a New Zealander. I didn't associate her voice with the 6 a.m. news. I only knew her as Janie. My Janie.

She caught me staring at her and a smiled bloomed on her face. Sunlight filtered through the vines, giving her purple dress a wild pattern. My hands rose, as if on autopilot, and I snapped a photo. It was the last one I got.

The rest of the day was a blur of wedding activities, drinks, food, group photos and painful small talk. At some point, I had to put my camera aside and become a full-time translator for my father who wanted to discuss child-rearing, education, and opportunities in New Zealand with Aria's dad. More specifically, he wanted to make it clear the child would never be okay on a remote island like this, with no proud Ottoman history of learning and innovation. I did my best to soften his words, but poor Greg could probably tell the true meaning from his passionate frown.

Cem settled in between our mom and Aria's mother, for what seemed like a friendlier conversation. This was my lot— dealing with Dad and his rants, saving my brother's ass. This time, I could tell he appreciated it, glancing over every time Dad raised his voice, casting me a grateful look.

The sun set and the strange wedding party fizzled out. Sober drives were organized for the vehicles outside and our parents retreated to their guest room.

With the catering packed away and the happy couple hiding somewhere, Janie found me on the deck, stripping tablecloths off the tables. For a moment, there was nobody else around.

She began unfastening another tablecloth, keeping her voice low. "What time are you leaving tomorrow?"

"Dad made me order a taxi for seven a.m. He's worried about making the flight."

Her eyes widened. "That's early."

"I know."

"I'm exhausted. I'll have to set three alarms to wake up before you go. Make breakfast."

"There are plenty of leftovers." I gestured at the doorway leading to the kitchen.

"But I want to see you, for the last time."

"I'll be with my parents. I can't even touch you... Not unless you want to tell them—"

"No. Not today." She bit her lip, eyes watery. "Maybe we should say goodbye now. I don't want your last image of me to be one with puffy morning eyes and no makeup."

I shook my head. "You're always gorgeous. But if this is the last time we can talk in private, maybe we need to say goodbye now."

She huffed. "I hate goodbyes."

"It's not a goodbye forever. Only for a while."

"You don't know. We live worlds apart and life on this side of forty is not that kind."

"It was kind enough to bring us together," I tried.

How was I the optimistic one? I'd been angry at life for so long, and now these thoughts were popping up without warning. Thoughts of hope, spurred by pain-free moments. "This is a good thing, Janie. Love is always a good thing."

She dropped the rolled-up tablecloth on the table and glanced over her shoulder. There was nobody around. Blinking her tears away, she crashed into my chest, wrapping her arms around me. I hugged her tightly, inhaling her scent like a drug. It's just a hug, I told myself. But I knew that if anyone saw us, we'd be exposed.

"We'll see each other again, Janie. We'll find a way."

She cried almost silently. Broke my heart without a sound, and I held her for as long as I could, until a noise from the kitchen gave us both a start. Within seconds, she was gone.

CHAPTER 38

Janie

"Janie? Did you hear what I said?"

Tabitha's booming voice send a shiver down my spine, and I made an effort to sit up. "Yes, I heard you."

I'd been distracted throughout the Art Deco Gala committee meeting, and she knew it.

"Well, it's settled then. Janie will MC on Saturday. My nephew Gus will handle the video production. We don't have a stills photographer, unless that Turkish friend of yours is available?"

I startled at the mention of Emir, the mask I fancied myself wearing in public momentarily slipping. I'd joined the committee to keep my mind off Emir, as if it was possible. I'd also hoped it would be too late to rope me into anything too high profile, yet I could say I'd supported the cause.

"No, he's not," I managed to say, my cheeks blazing like two tiny heaters.

The stuffy conference room with its tiny Art Deco windows felt even stuffier than before. Tabitha cast a meaningful look at Maree, who released the straw she'd held in her mouth the whole time, slowly suckling a giant plastic tub of boba tea.

Tabitha's eyebrows shot up. "Oh. Did he go back to Turkey?"

"Yes."

Sensing a juicy piece of gossip, she wrapped up the meeting and sent everyone else home. I tried to sneak out between two old guys, but she grabbed my sleeve, pulling me aside.

I was so tired, feeling so lost and alone, that I sat down at Tabitha's request, deflating like a balloon. Aria was leaving next week. I had no one left, other than my son and my horse, and neither of them were particularly eager to discuss my heartbreak. Tabitha was.

Her dark eyes, sharp and beautifully lined, observed me with avid interest.

"We're all worried about you, Janie."

"Don't worry," I said, trying to smile brightly. "I'm fine."

"Are you?"

Be yourself and anyone who's worth knowing will stick around.

Emir's words popped up without warning, making my heart squeeze with fresh pain. He would have just laid it out, unapologetically. Why couldn't I have an ounce of his character? As much as I'd rolled my eyes at his frowns and stunted social skills, he was authentic, and I was tired of games. I craved his direct manner. I craved everything about him.

"Okay. I'm not." I lifted my chin, for the first time deliberately making eye contact with Tabitha. "I love Emir. I desperately want to follow him across the world, but my life is here. My son is here. I can't."

Tabitha's mouth opened and she stared at me for many seconds. Maree looked between us, mesmerized.

Finally, Tabitha pulled out a chair and sat next to me. "See if you can make us some tea," she instructed Maree, who nodded and tiptoed towards the back of the conference room.

I had to remind myself to breathe. Did I want them to know my deepest, darkest secrets? I'd been trying to protect myself from gossip, present myself in just the right way, but all that pretense had cut me off from truly connecting with people. I didn't ask for help. I didn't show weakness. The only one I talked to was Aria—mainly because she'd first opened up, crying against my shoulder. But suddenly, protecting my image didn't feel that important anymore. If I couldn't have Emir, I didn't want the status. I didn't want to win the divorce. I didn't even care what strangers thought of me.

Well, no. I cared a little. But I felt a strange elation as I watched Tabitha's eyes soften and her face relax.

"Oh, Janie," she finally said. "We've all been there. Falling in love is awful. I mean, it's great, but also awful when you're not young anymore and things are complicated. I fell for my personal trainer. A gorgeous man. Obviously, I had to let him go. We both agreed it was a terrible idea. It was so hard to end it." She shook her head, whipping the glossy black bob from side to side. "But you and this Turkish man... who is delicious I must say... you're both single, right? Why do you let any obstacle stand in the way?"

She placed her hand on mine and to my surprise, I didn't feel like breaking the contact. Her beautifully made-up eyes studied me with compassion I'd never seen before.

"It's not that simple. He has his business to attend to. He's not that wealthy and I... I have one son during the school term and two during the holidays. It's impossible."

Maree returned with three steaming cups of tea. "I couldn't find any milk."

"That's okay." I took a sip of the strong, dark brew, immediately thinking of Emir. Had I even stopped thinking about him? Would I ever stop?

"We can help!" Tabitha exclaimed, her bright red nails dancing in the air as she gestured. "We'll find something for your sons... a holiday program?"

Maree nodded. "There are lots! The aquarium runs one. They might still have places."

"Alex is eighteen. Even Josh might be a bit too old for that, but I can't leave them home alone. They can't drive. I mean, I wouldn't let Alex..."

"We can keep an eye on them. Drop off groceries. Take them out to town."

Tabitha's eyes sparkled. I'd never seen her so happy. Was this all she'd been hoping for? An opportunity to step up and make herself useful?

"That's a lovely thought, thank you. But I couldn't just leave the boys here. My agreement with Shaun is that I get them for the holidays. It makes no sense for them to be here if I'm not."

I gathered my handbag, standing up. "Thank you, but I have to get home to Josh."

Tabitha followed me to the door. "But Josh lives here now. And Alex is technically an adult. Why wait for the holidays? I can move in for a week and drive Josh to school. My kids don't need me anymore. Adrian can cook for himself for a few days. Or Uber Eat as much as he likes without my supervision." She pulled a face.

I allowed myself a tiny little nod, feeling like the worst human. How could I even entertain this idea? But I couldn't stop staring at Tabitha. She looked so much more real. Polished and pruned, but less intimidating. Was this what Emir had been talking about? I'd judged her as fake, but maybe I'd been the fake one and she'd just reflected that. You attract what you are.

"Are you serious?" I asked. "You'd do that for me?"

"If it means you have a chance at happiness," she said firmly, clasping her hands, red nails slotting in neat rows.

My chest contracted. Did I? Even if I made it to Istanbul, I couldn't stay there. I couldn't drag Emir to New Zealand against his will. I couldn't manufacture a happy ending.

"I don't know if I do," I whispered. "I can't see a way we can make this work. I just miss him. I have to stop thinking about him. I'm sure it'll fade over time."

She gave a slow, considerate nod. "Maybe you don't see the

way because you're here and he's there. Maybe you need to go over there, and the answer will emerge. Trust emergence. I have a poster on my wall saying that."

Her mouth twitched, giving me permission to laugh. Together, we cracked up and it only took a few seconds for tears to emerge in my eyes.

CHAPTER 39

Emir

I drew a lungful of hot, dusty air and squeezed myself inside the antique shop. It felt more like a poorly organized storage room than any sort of retail facility, with only narrow paths left between fully stocked shelves that seemed to lean in, threatening to crush the poor soul who attempted to venture into the depths of its belly. Decades of cigarette smoke hung in the air, permeated in every piece of war time memorabilia, cups, saucers, jewelry, weapons, clothing, art, and anything else old you could think of. What had once been categorized seemed to have blended, forming an impenetrable wall of clutter.

'People love to treasure hunt,' Dad used to say. He believed hiding things behind other things encouraged digging and as people spent time uncovering forgotten items, they felt more invested in the things they found. I'd never fully accepted his theory, unless it was based on the lack of oxygen making the customers delirious and therefore more prone to bad decisions.

The deep breath I always took before entering the shop was designed to last me all the way through to the back door, which led to a small back room. The back room was surprisingly bare, as if my father had decided to use the shop as the storage and the back room as his quiet retreat. Cousin Burak, who smoked like a chimney and wasn't bothered by the smell of the shop, had taken over standing behind the counter—or mostly sitting at the small outdoor table, smoking, and gossiping with the next-door shop owners. I'd prohibited smoking indoors, making me one of their favorite conversation subjects. What was wrong with Emir? Why was Emir such an uptight jerk? He thought I couldn't hear him from behind the broken window.

I didn't care if he thought I was possessed by an evil spirit. I had much bigger problems to worry about. Like how to catalogue and sell the infinite number of items around me. Tourism was going through a dip that was either seasonal or permanent. I had no space to do proper inventory. I'd talked to the other shop owners along our steep, cobblestoned street, trying to get them onboard with having a shipping container blocking half the street for several weeks, but was met with resistance. Ali next door had agreed to one week, but it had to be the week he was on holiday. And when I hinted that I'd later need to bring the container back, to restock the shop after renovations, he gave me a murderous look. I was lying anyway. It would take me far more than a week to get to the bottom of the inventory. But I had to start somewhere.

Janie would know what to do, I thought. She'd approach this with that sunshiny attitude of pure belief, and she'd get them all onboard. She'd make it happen. Except she wasn't here, and she didn't speak Turkish, and I had to get her off my mind, at least for now. Thinking of her every day hurt too much. I'd emailed her once to let her know I'd arrived safely, and she'd replied with a short update at her end. Everyone was fine. Josh was back to his old school. Janie was helping to organize the Art Deco Gala. Another movie production was considering Napier. She'd cut together a short video pitch for the documentary. Keeping busy, she said. Trying to move on. I didn't like it, but I couldn't tell her not to.

Flying back to Istanbul had ripped me in half. I felt lost and lonely in my own city, like I was living in a parallel reality. Only half alive. Half awake, waiting to open my eyes and be back on the farm, staring out into the impossibly green hills. Seeing Janie in her muddy boots, swinging a bucket in her hand. Smelling the grass and earth and chicken poop.

I tried not to feel anything. If I could reduce my time in this city to a series of tasks, only engaging my analytical brain, I'd survive. That's why I found it so hard to write to her. If I began telling her how I felt, how much I missed her... No, I couldn't go there. I needed to function. I needed to problem solve. And time needed to get on my side and somehow fast forward to the next bit, because I couldn't stand this one.

The bell over the door jingled. I recognized my father's signature cough before I even turned around.

"No customers?" he grumbled.

He'd taken it on himself to check in every day, even if he insisted that I was in charge, and he had no energy to help.

"Not right now. It's hard for them to see the entrance through Burak's cigarette smoke." I cast a disgusted look at the doorway, behind which my useless cousin was currently wasting the day away.

"You can say that again."

Since his diagnosis and treatment, Dad had become a vocal anti-smoking campaigner, one who did it with a raspy smoker's voice. It felt good to agree with him on something for a change.

"I was thinking of getting a shipping container to help sort out the items," I said, on a whim. Maybe he'd understand. "But the neighbors are not onboard."

Dad looked around, confused. "Sort out what?"

I sighed. "The excessive number of... things that make it impossible to walk around the shop."

"This is not a gallery! People don't want to walk around an antique shop. They want to dig and find treasures. We have the best selection of—"

"No, we don't! And even if we did, nobody would know. There are things in here you don't even know."

"*Safsata!* I know this shop like the palm of my hand!"

I squeezed my hands into fists, trying to stop myself from getting sucked into yet another argument. But the temptation was too great. "If you did, you'd noticed that I've already taken away a vanload of stuff."

Dad's head whipped around as he tried to determine if I was bluffing. "No! I mean... I did notice you moved the hat rack, and the pipes..." He kept turning around, clearly struggling to take in everything.

This is what happened. When old things sat in the room for too long, they became part of the environment. Everything blended and nothing caught your eye. Nothing called out to you.

"Anyway," he grumbled on. "A shipping container is like an invitation for the thieves. You carry things in and out of the shop, out in the open like that... things will start disappearing."

"Are you sure? Most of the stuff is so worthless people might mistake the container for a recycling bin and new things will start appearing instead of disappearing."

Dad harrumphed, unimpressed by my exaggeration. But something about my own words niggled at the back of my mind. Something I'd overlooked. It took another ten minutes of mindless arguing with my father to bring it to the surface, but when it did, blood seized in my veins.

Someone had put something in Janie's house.

Nothing was taken because there wasn't anything in the house they wanted. Not when she wasn't home. Because they wanted her. Someone had installed a hidden camera. I had no evidence, yet I knew it with inexplicable certainty.

I didn't believe in psychic powers, but I believed in intuition— your subconscious mind examining shreds of evidence, fleeting images, and memories, working faster than your conscious mind.

"I have to go," I told Dad, mid-sentence.

I gathered my things and left the shop, wading through Burak's cloud of smoke, telling him I was meeting with someone. I wasn't. I was heading straight back to Cem's house, which was my permanent address since I'd given up my rental apartment to save every penny. I had to call Janie. I needed to hear her voice. I needed to know she was okay.

Coming back here had been a mistake.

I strolled down the hill towards the nearest tram stop. With Cem not around, I didn't want to use our driver. I knew he didn't mind, but I had my pride. I could feel the first pangs of the old headache radiating across my forehead and winced. It was coming back. The incredible gift Janie had given me would be taken away by this polluted city and dusty pile of antiques. And the frown on my face that made stray cats and startled tourists scurry out of my way. I stopped for a moment, trying to relax my face and shoulders, rolling them back. I rubbed my thumb between my eyes, imagining her fingers on my skin, closing my eyes for a moment.

When I opened them, I saw Janie. She was at the other end of the sloping street, a tiny human shape walking up the hill with a green backpack on her shoulders.

I blinked and rubbed my eyes, convinced that I was hallucinating. I'd pictured her so many times, it must have messed with my brain. But I'd never imagined her like this—like a tourist in my town, chin raised in the air as she browsed the shops along the street, slowly approaching me.

CHAPTER 40

Janie

I felt like I'd time travelled to my twenties, but with my 41-year-old joints. Wandering Istanbul's endless cobblestone streets, occasionally so steep they turned into stairs, with a heavy backpack on my shoulders, I was starting to lose hope.

I'd thought knowing the name of the neighborhood would make it reasonably easy to find Emir's antique shop. But of course, I was zigzagging the part of town that was famous for its antiquing, its streets lined with small, crowded boutiques. Their contents seemed to be spilling onto the streets, insides bursting with chaos.

It didn't help that most people spoke little English. I'd asked for directions twice, but nobody seemed to know Emir Erkam. Or, I was pronouncing his name so poorly they had no idea who

I was talking about.

I was just about to cross the road, again, to investigate a shop on the other side, when I saw him.

Emir. In grey slacks and a dark navy dress shirt, just like I remembered him. Except, here he belonged. He looked like an extension of the narrow, historical street flanked by brightly colored buildings and decorative shop signage, multi-colored prayer bunting hanging out of the windows. He was dark and foreign. A man from a different world I had no claim to.

For a split second, I contemplated running away, pretending I hadn't stalked the poor guy all the way to his hometown. I was sweaty and tired, hair sticking to my temples and the backpack digging into my shoulders. I couldn't have looked more like a budget tourist if I'd tried.

But I couldn't run. I couldn't move. His eyes had pinned me on the pavement. For a moment, we both stood within shouting distance of each other and simply stared.

Finally, he charged towards me, eating up the distance with his long legs. I took a quick sniff at myself and winced, but I had no time to do anything about me. I didn't even have time to organize my thoughts.

"Janie! It is you." He grabbed me by the elbows, looking a little startled. Blinking. "I…"

As if remembering his manners, he leaned in to kiss my cheeks. There it was. The Turkish greeting I'd never had. I caught a whiff of his scent, and it flooded my mind with such potent memories I nearly lost my footing.

"I don't know why I'm here," I uttered. "I'm sorry."

Tears threatened to spill, and I forced myself to smile. He helped the backpack off my shoulders, setting it on the ground next to us, then pulled me into his arms. I heard the faint thud as the backpack fell over but didn't look. I could only wrap my arms around him and breathe. I'd never done anything this brave. Or this stupid. But all my arms cared about was locking themselves around his waist and hanging on.

He muttered something in Turkish and squeezed me tighter. "Janie."

We hugged for a long time, both unwilling to move. Finally, I pulled back and placed my hands on his chest, my own heart thumping like it wanted to escape. There was so much I wanted to say all at once. So many questions I wanted to ask, that I couldn't get hold of any thoughts. I only wanted to hold onto the miracle of touching him.

"I'm so relieved." His voice rumbled through me. "Are you okay? Did you find the hidden camera?"

"What hidden camera?"

"I... never mind. Just something I thought. Something I should have thought of earlier."

"Wait, what?" I stared at him in confusion. "Did you hide a camera in my house?"

"No, Janie." He gave me a brief smile that was quickly chased away by a frown. "But I think that burglar did. I was just going to call you and get you to check your bedroom."

A full-body shiver rushed through me. "Seriously? How could

they do that? Why?"

"I don't know why, but I should have thought of that. I mean, they took nothing—"

"That's not true," I blurted, mortified. "They took my yellow panties. I never found them. I should have told you."

"What?"

"It's not important."

His eyes flashed with fury. "It fits! Panties, a hidden camera… It's been bothering me this whole time. Your dressing mirror has that decorative frame. It'd be the perfect place to hide—"

"You were thinking of me?" I cut in, desperate to push away the creepy feeling. I had to focus on that one ray of sunshine warming my heart.

"Of course I am."

"You didn't know if you'd ever see me again."

"I knew."

"You're rather sure of yourself." I cocked my head.

"I didn't think I'd see you here," he said softly. "I only knew my own plans."

"What if we made plans together? I don't know how, but I had to come here and ask you, because I'll regret it for the rest of my life if I don't even try. I thought about it… and I know I'm supposed to be an adult, but I also want to love like I'm losing my mind and like nothing else matters. And if anything stands in the way, we fight. Together."

I stared at him, fearing that my heart would pound right out of my chest.

He smiled. Fully, with eyes lighting up. "Let's." He lifted the rim of my sunhat and brushed my hair behind my ears. When his lips found mine, my heart soared. I couldn't feel the cobblestones under my feet. Nothing connected me to the ground, or the reality. Those strong hands held me, serving as my only connection to life on Earth. Emir. His heart was still open. He was still mine.

He kissed me deeper, lighting up desire that raced all the way down my thighs. Finally, I pulled away and I found my balance, cheeks blazing, every cell alight with new purpose.

"How are your sons? Who's looking after them?"

"Alex is in Auckland and Josh is home with Tabitha, believe it or not. She offered, and it turns out she gets along well with him. She won't shovel shit, though, so Josh is looking after the animals." I pulled a face.

"I'm sure Josh can handle it."

"I have to go back, obviously. But I'm hoping, like an idiot, that I can somehow bring you back with me. Whatever it is, we can handle it. Together." My voice trembled and I had to summon all my courage to look him in the eye. I'd placed my bet and was now waiting for the roulette wheel to stop spinning.

His dark eyes peered straight into my soul. The corner of his mouth lifted. "My Janie." He took my elbow, pivoting us up the hill. "Let me show you what we'll be handling together." His voice held a warning, but I only felt warmth. Overwhelming, indescribable warmth enveloped my heart as I trailed alongside him up the steep footpath, to a small doorway leading to a dimly lit shop.

A curly-haired man with a goatee sat at an outdoor table. He nodded at Emir, giving me a dubious side-eye. I stepped into the shop, noting the stuffy smell of storage and old cigarette smoke. As my eyes adjusted to the low light, I saw the floor-to-ceiling shelves, racks and random items hanging off large hooks in the ceiling. How was it physically possible to fit this much in one room? Although I couldn't make out the back wall, so I wasn't entirely sure about the edges of the space. I could only tell it was full.

"Has this featured on TV?" I asked, my voice a little hoarse. "Hoarders?"

Emir bumped his head on a hanging oil lamp and adjusted his position to stand between two different lamps, his expression mortified. "No. Maybe I should try that. It'd be hard to move around and find camera angles, though."

"You're right. It's just… unreal."

He sighed. "It is. My father has officially signed it over to me, so I have to sort it out somehow. There's no storage space, so I was thinking of ordering a shipping container. See if I can dig up anything that's worth anything to list online."

I trudged deeper into the shop, taking a closer look at the items. Crystals, ceramics, mosaic lamps, vases, war memorabilia, tin cans, old hats. Some of it was likely worthless, but I could easily imagine the decorative and colorful household items in expensive antique and homeware shops in New Zealand.

"Well, if you're getting a shipping container, why don't you ship it? Take it to New Zealand and I'll help you set up a shop. You'll get a better price that way. It's all exotic and special over there."

For a moment, he said nothing, gently leaning his temple against that oil lamp. Then his shoulders dropped, and he let out a long sigh. "God, I missed you so much!"

I hopped over a fallen coat rack to get to him.

We hugged there, surrounded by Turkey's discarded, forgotten treasures, breathing in each other to drown out the smell of dust, decay, and cigarettes, feeling so deliriously happy it made no sense.

"Me, too," I said.

We were so much better together.

Emir

I dismounted Neil, a mild-mannered Arabian, giving him a pat as I settled at our favorite breakfast picnic spot overlooking the coast. Janie arrived a few seconds behind me, riding Molly. The early spring morning was still a little chilly with a shiny layer of dew coating every leaf and blade of grass around us. There were no people around, for miles. It was perfect.

I helped Janie off Molly, knowing she didn't require my help. Molly had relaxed enough for Janie to ride her on her own. Ever since we'd introduced her to Neil, she seemed happier. We each needed a partner in life and Molly had been lonely, just like me.

I threw down the tattered blanket we always sat on and unpacked our simple egg sandwiches and a thermos of coffee.

I'd thought of love as a mystical, overwhelming, dizzying ride I never again wanted to get on. I'd never thought it could feel like this—being part of something bigger and better than myself. Being a team.

In the last months, we'd worked hard, establishing a new business in Napier as we waited for the shipping container to arrive. When it finally did, we'd be ready, even if we were a little overwhelmed by the task at hand. The last week had been a flurry of action—painting and wallpapering the showrooms we'd leased in central Napier. The space was looking great now. Ready for action. The online shop was also ready to go, but listing the items would take a while.

With Josh still asleep, I'd enticed Janie away by packing us a breakfast she could only enjoy if she rode with me up the hill to our favorite lookout.

"I'm here. Where's the breakfast?" She sat on the blanket, smiling excitedly. "And where's the coffee?"

"Patience, woman."

I set everything down on the blanket, deliberately slowly, until she grabbed the sandwich from my hand. I laughed. Hangry Janie was not to be teased.

After a few bites, she settled, and gave me a big smile. "Thank you! This is exactly what I needed."

Turned out, it was exactly what I needed, too. Seeing her happy and relaxed. That's all I ever needed. And I had something up my sleeve that could possibly make her even more relaxed.

"Janie," I said, waiting for her to look at me. "About that spy cam—"

"Please!" She held up her hand, wincing. "You promised. No more theories. No more suspecting everyone we know. We have no evidence, and I don't want to think about those videos being out there, circulating—"

"They're not."

"They're not?" She blinked, the sandwich resting against her lower lip, eyes lit with hope.

"I've got them on a hard drive you can personally destroy."

"What? How?" She was yelling now, sandwich forgotten.

"I had a hunch about that guy, Gus. I had a chat with him, and he confessed. But he insisted he hasn't uploaded anything. I told him that if he can prove it, we might not take him to court."

"But I can't afford to take anyone to court!"

"He doesn't know that, so he sang like a bird."

Janie shook her head, processing the information. "Gus? Really? But, why?"

"He's... infatuated with you. I think it was his twisted idea of intimacy. He's a movie buff. Things on screen are more real to him than people. The more I talked to him, the more I thought he's a bit insane. But the good news is, he handed over all the footage. I had it checked against what's circulating online and they found no hits."

"Wait... how do you do that?"

"I have a good cyber security firm who handles that. I hired them to deal with Cem's dick pics. The results were quite different with him, trust me. You have nothing to worry about."

Janie narrowed her eyes. "But... why would he confess? What did you do?"

I took a breath, my chest glowing. I could never fool her. "I... played him a little." I couldn't help smiling. The plan had taken months and herculean effort to keep to myself.

I wanted to share everything with Janie, but I didn't want to risk anything. She was working with the guy. The documentary had received some funding, and Gus was contracted to do more drone shots.

"Played him, how?" she asked.

"First, I took one of his filters."

Gus had turned up at our door with a flimsy excuse of delivering drone footage he'd somehow misplaced. Janie had invited him in for a coffee, but when he noticed me, he'd changed his mind about coffee and left. But he'd hung around long enough for me to notice him fiddling with a gum wrapper. My mind connected those dots so fast I struggled to keep my face neutral. In that moment, I knew it was him. But I needed more than a gum wrapper. I needed incriminating evidence. And those camera filters sticking out of his camera bag's side pocket seemed like the perfect fit. Specific enough, yet he probably wouldn't notice one missing. He collected gear. He didn't necessarily use or even understand it.

"So, you told him you found it in my bedroom or something? And he believed you?" Janie was still frowning, her head tilted.

"Well, I made it irresistible for him. I steered the conversation to small cameras and started an argument. I don't know if you've noticed, but Gus can't resist correcting you. I made sure what I said was a bit incorrect and he jumped in and practically bragged about how invisible and easy to use those spy cams are, how they connect to your wi-fi and keep running for days. And when I showed him the filter and told him we found the camera, he went all white. I said he has two choices. We take it all to the police or he hands everything to me. We can still take it to the police, but I wanted to give you the choice. He admitted to taking a pair of your underwear, so I guess we need to disclose that if we report the crime."

"If it goes to the police, it'll be in the news," she said quietly. "And I don't want to deal with the media."

There'd been a couple of news stories about us since we'd returned to New Zealand, with grainy photos and speculation. Tabitha told us a reporter had approached her for a comment. She'd been proud to tell us she'd sent them away with nothing.

Janie didn't want to hide anymore. She wasn't bothered by anyone seeing us together, although she was still worried about my parents. They knew about us now and were planning another trip to New Zealand after Cem and Aria arrived. My brother had finished filming in Istanbul, and they'd decided to move back to New Zealand before the baby arrived. Mom's phone calls and texts had gradually become a bit less dramatic and more practical. Now that she had flight tickets, her tone had settled down. I could only hope she accepted my union with Janie.

Because I was going to marry her. I'd made my intentions clear, even if I hadn't asked her yet. Back in Istanbul, I'd scoured the antique shop for rings and brought back the potential contenders in my luggage. I'd carried the bag of rings in my pocket for months like a security blanket, waiting for the right moment. Truth be told, I was terrified she'd turn me down. Our financial situation was tricky. The family situation was even trickier. We'd managed to keep our relationship mostly out of the media, but a wedding would attract unwanted attention.

"No police then," I confirmed. "It's all taken care of, and I don't think Gus will try anything like this again any time soon. We can always tell Tabitha."

Janie chuckled. "She'll keep him in line."

To everyone's surprise, Tabitha had won her place in Janie's inner circle. I still found the freakishly manicured woman rather taxing, but I could tell she genuinely cared about Janie, so I let it go. I'd never had a lot of friends, or the luxury of choosing them, so I understood.

I felt like the shipping container of Turkish antiques. Mostly worthless, with something valuable maybe hiding inside. But, as Janie liked to remind me, special and exotic in New Zealand. It didn't bother me to be called the 'Turkish guy', not anymore, and I'd found a confidante in Kerim, who had decades of expat experience and was teaching me to cook the fancier Turkish recipes. I couldn't wait to surprise Janie with my next one. She'd been doing a lot of baking and cooking lately as I'd focused on the shop renovations.

At times, I missed Istanbul. I even missed my brother. The future was uncertain, and my actions probably made no sense to anyone back home. Mom had told me I looked happy, though, and I could only hope that weighed more than the other issues combined.

"Janie," I said, pulling the small hard drive I'd taken from Gus out of my pocket. "Will you... destroy this naughty hard drive?"

She drew a quick breath. "Oh, my God. I thought..."

"You thought I was proposing," My mouth curved. It did that effortlessly these days.

"Well, you warned me that you would. But then you haven't said anything." She sounded almost hurt.

"Do you want me to propose?"

She fell silent and stayed silent for a long time. Too long.

"Janie?"

"Emir. For a long time, I couldn't even think about it. I felt like I'd be robbing you of a chance to have a family."

"But you are my family."

She weaved her fingers with mine, staring at them. "That's good. I'm starting to believe it. And I'm not too old, yet. I mean it's possible for me to have a baby. Maybe."

"Do you want a baby?" I asked.

"I don't know. How do you feel about it now?"

I'd never felt it was my calling. To be honest, the idea scared me, but if Janie wanted to try for a baby with me, I didn't want to give in to fear. I didn't want to be ruled by that thinking anymore, protecting myself and missing out on life.

"Maybe we can leave the door open?" I suggested. "If it's meant to be, it'll happen."

Her cheeks looked rosy and eyes glowed. "I like that."

"I'm ready to try anytime. But first…"

"What?"

"Will you marry me, Janie?"

I took out the bag of rings and poured the contents on her palm. One rolled off and dropped on the blanket. I'd polished them to the best of my ability, but you could tell their age. The stones glinted in the sun in red, amber, green and blue. They were no Crown Jewels, but unique and beautiful.

She stared at the rings, shaking. "Oh, my God. What is this? Emir, you're supposed to have just one ring. You know that, right?"

"I wanted you to have the choice."

Her eyes glistened. "I can't choose! These are all perfect."

"Have them all. Wear a different one every day. Wear them all. Nobody will think you're engaged, so you can hide it from the rest of the world. But I'll know."

She laughed, tears running down her cheeks. "I don't want to hide it. I love this, Emir. I love you."

"I don't have much but it's all yours."

"Same! I want to share everything." She jumped into my arms, rings scattering across the blanket. "Yes," she whispered into my ear, "I'll marry you, Emir Erkam. And I'll never let you go."

I kissed her lips, salty and wet. In that moment, sitting on that blanket, holding the woman I loved, the green hills glowing in morning light, I didn't worry about the future. I had everything I needed right here, and we'd face tomorrow together. Janie and I.

Bitirildi (The End)

Thank you!

After writing *My Lucky Star*, I couldn't shelf Emir. He had a backstory I chose not to include in the first book (he was the villan, after all) and I felt like I needed to do him justice. So, I eventually edited and published this book to give Emir a voice.

I wrote this book at a low point in my life. My marketing efforts for *My Lucky Star* had fallen flat. There was no market for romcoms with Turkish heroes. But, being wildly unsuccessful gives you the freedom to follow your heart. I mean, if I knew how to follow the money, I probably would. Alas, I don't, so I wrote this sequel.

This book is dedicated to my seven readers, since that's how many pre-orders got when I first listed the book on Amazon. I'd like to thank those seven readers for believing in me. I'd also like to thank my husband for allowing me to publish another wildly unsuccessful book, even though it takes away time with the family. I'm also grateful for my business partner Beks and her understanding when I delayed other work to 'get my book out there'.

Lastly, thank *you* for reading! You have no idea what it means. It's like being part of a tiny, extremely exclusive club. If you could tell about this book to your friend (just one friend), I'd be happy for them to join. I wouldn't even mind if there were twenty of us, although that is a bit of a crowd.

About the author

Enni Amanda is a graphic designer moonlighting as a rom-com author, or maybe it's the other way around. In 2006, she and her husband moved from Finland to New Zealand and fell in love with the gorgeous islands and their laid-back people. They spent eight years traveling between the two rather inconveniently located countries, studying filmmaking and running a film festival. Through all the filmmaking, Enni discovered a passion for screenwriting, which eventually led to writing books (a slippery slope). Her heart-warming, funny stories explore real-life issues like identity, found family, and the housing crisis. These days, she lives in the Waikato, close to the rolling hills of the Shire, raising two cute, rambunctious boys while writing away and ignoring housework.

Menemen

2 tablespoons olive oil

1 medium yellow onion, chopped

1 green bell pepper, cored, seeded and chopped

Salt

2 tomatoes, chopped

3 tablespoons tomato paste

Black pepper

½ teaspoon dried oregano

1 teaspoon pepper

4 large eggs, beaten

Crushed red pepper flakes

In a 10-inch skillet, heat olive oil over medium heat. Add the onions and bell peppers and season with salt. Cook for 4 to 5 minutes, stirring regularly until softened.

Add the tomatoes and tomato paste. Season with a little more salt, black pepper, oregano, and pepper. Cook for a few minutes over medium heat, stirring occasionally, until the tomatoes soften.

Push the tomato and pepper mixture to one side of the pan. Lower the heat to medium-low. Add the beaten egg, and cook briefly, stirring gently as needed, until the eggs are just set. Fold the tomato mixture into the eggs.

Serve immediately with thick slices of bread.

Thank you for reading!

If you enjoyed this book, please tell your friends
and leave a review on your favorite retailer website!
Referrals and reviews help unknown indie authors like
me get discovered.

To find out about my upcoming books,
sign up for my newsletter at
enniamanda.com